BY THE AUTHORS OF THE AW

THE TOWER

CHRIS SKATES
DAN TANKERSLEY

THE TOWER

By Chris Skates and Dan Tankersley

Cover design and interior layout by www.PearCreative.ca

Artwork, "Rage Over Babylon" by Ziv Qual

Printed and bound in the U.S.A.

ISBN 978-0-9891486-1-0

AUTHOR'S NOTE

This is a work of fiction. While it is based on the Biblical account, and the authors have strived to never conflict with scripture, poetic license has been taken. The authors acknowledge the use of modern languages in the text that would not have existed at the time of the actual events. These are used so that the modern reader may better relate to the characters and the unique struggles that the sudden introduction of different languages would have elicited.

The Authors likewise acknowledge that license was taken as to when the city was actually called Babel. For the sake of clarity in the storytelling, the city has been called Babel throughout this account.

ACKOWLEDGEMENTS

Writing fiction based on the sacred text of the Bible can be a slippery slope. The author of such a work has a grave responsibility. James 3:1 says, "Not many of you should become teachers, my brothers, for you know that we who teach will be judged with greater strictness." Surely this cannot be any less true for those who would broadcast their version of Biblical events to the world. Therefore writing a story such as this one must be done with the Bible ever ready alongside pen, paper, and keyboard. Even as we did this, we continue to be concerned about our own human frailty in this endeavor. It is our prayer that we have not allowed too much influence from our own fleshly preconceptions about the events, and that the core truths of this story…which is God's story, not ours…will come shining through.

We incorporate beta-readers to give us feedback on early versions of the manuscript, and their contributions have been invaluable to the development of this novel. So thank you to Sabrina White, Brother Charles Blair, Dorine Sisco, Judy Tankersley,

Ashley Seely Ward, Anne Pafford, Jack Marshall, Denton Wood, Liz Lewis, Jim Mitchell, and especially Steven Wright who went above and beyond the call of duty. We extend special thanks to Chris' wife, Tracy Skates, who actually did a full copy edit of the manuscript TWICE. Her first effort was lost due to a computer glitch and she had to start all over. Thank you, Tracy, for your patience and willingness to help.

We have enjoyed working with Yvonne Parks at PearCreative.ca who designed and formatted the book for us. Writing a novel is a marathon that could never be completed unless others come alongside. This work is no exception. Finally, thanks to our families for their patience, our pastor for his guidance, and most of all to our Lord for giving us a yearning to share His true story with the world.

CHAPTER 1

I have learned to hate grapes. My life these days seems to be lived for grapes or grapevines or one of our other crops. We are constantly working in the vineyard, the orchard or in the fields. Dressing vines, pruning trees, planting, harvesting...the chores never seem to stop. In the old world my father Noah dabbled in some carpentry, we tended a few sheep for wool, and of course he preached. Then once my Dad convinced us to begin, we spent several years working feverishly on the ark. At least in the old world there had been more variety to our labors. And with the ark there had been a goal to attain.

Ever since the ark landed here however and God made His covenant with us, all our father has wanted to do was farm. He wants to till the soil, plant, tend and harvest. I understand how he feels. Farming gives him a sense of peace. He has grown to love working the soil in his hands. And the soil of our new home is rich and fertile. But I do not share his passion for tilling the earth.

In fairness I must acknowledge that God has blessed our farming efforts with what seems like perfect conditions and our harvests have been abundant. In addition to grapes, we grow and press olives and have also established an orchard and a large vegetable garden. The pairs of animals we brought on the ark apparently heard God's command to be fruitful and multiply. Our herds have grown to the point where we allow them to roam freely in the valley. So far they have not ventured far.

Our productivity also expanded greatly, along with the growth of our families. Shem and Prisca have four strapping sons and three daughters in their teens. They have a set of twins: a boy and girl ten years old. Three years ago, Prisca gave birth to a second set of twins, two sisters. Ham and Adina have been the most prolific of all having a child every other year since we have arrived. Since one year they were blessed with twins, they now have four sons and six daughters. Tamara and I had difficulty having children for a few years but then the Lord seemed to bless us in bunches. We had two sets of triplets and one set of twins. All together we have seven sons and four daughters of our own.

Yes, we have been blessed and well provided for in the eighteen years since we stepped outside the ark for the first time. We have been so busy since then. All of us (except our Dad, Noah) have built houses to replace our tents. We have also established this farm and our orchards. In fact, we have been so busy that the day we walked out of the ark now seems a lifetime ago. Still, after having spent over a year on board and with all that we went through, the experience has forever changed each one of us.

Despite the fact that God has blessed our farming efforts, farming isn't my calling. I feel I have been obedient and dutiful and essentially put my life on hold in order to serve on the ark. I have been very grateful to God and I praise him literally every day for saving us through that divinely inspired vessel. But I am ready to move on. In fact, I am ready to move period.

The valley we settled in at the base of the mountain on which the ark now rested was beautiful and filled with plants and flowers we had never seen before. Yet, I wanted to know what was beyond this valley, to spend at least a year, perhaps two, simply seeing this new world God had brought us to. I wanted to explore, but my dad always encouraged me to stay nearby. So far I had taken his advice. But as I looked off in the distance, I could faintly see the glistening water of a gigantic lake. Early on my brothers and I had climbed to the top of the mountain. We could see from that vantage point that the section of shoreline which entered our valley was only a small fraction of a much larger body of water. I yearned to see what was on the other side of that lake. I wanted to take my family and establish a new community in an area all our own.

With the thought of family, and the sudden giggling of my daughter, I was quickly reminded of another reason I had not ventured far. My twins were too small to take on such an adventure.

"Mareyea, what have you done?" I asked in frustration, barely concealing my amusement.

"Me hab gwapes too daadee," came her sticky reply.

I was harvesting late grapes for our tables. These would be used for food as opposed to juice. I had wrongly assumed that the basket I was laying the clusters in was too tall for my little girl to get into. As I often did, I underestimated the ingenuity of a determined two-year old. Mareyea had drug the nearly empty basket over to a cypress log, climbed on the log and landed in the basket with the grapes. She now had mashed grapes in her hair, all over her face, and especially in her mouth. I untied the kerchief from around my neck as I approached her.

"What am I going to tell Mommy when you wind up with the tummy ache?" I asked, not expecting an answer.

"Look at all this sticky in your hair," I went on, smiling despite myself. "Oh boy," I sighed. "I am gonna be in big trouble with Mommy."

"Why Dadee?" She asked as she tilted the palms of her chubby hands skyward and shrugged her shoulders dramatically.

"Because you have made a mess. How many grapes did you eat while I wasn't paying attention?"

"Dis many," she said, struggling to hold up three fingers.

"I have a feeling you need to work on your counting skills," I said as I wrinkled my nose and held her little face up to mine so I could kiss away some of the grape juice. "I'll tell you what. Here is a small cluster for you. You seem to be having fun in that basket so you just sit right there with your grapes. I'll lay the rest nearby while I harvest, then you can help me put them in the basket when we get ready to go."

"Ooohkayy Dadee." She wrinkled up her little nose and smiled mischievously back at me. I had a feeling that she already knew how to diffuse any potential punishment from her Daddy.

I wedged the basket safely against a cypress log. There were hundreds of these logs lying around the valley. They were apparently left from trees blown over in the flood. The time they spent in the flood waters almost seemed to preserve and temper them. They provided ideal timber, and all our homes, out buildings, and furnishings had been built from them. Only my Dad, Noah, still lived in a tent. Since we landed, he had refused to build anything from wood. Maybe this was because he was weary of woodwork after years of constructing the ark. I sometimes wondered if there was a deeper reason.

After I secured the basket with Mareyea inside, I heard a distinct grunting sound, like the sound of a very lazy old man. I looked over toward the grape vine and saw the paws of my dog, Rowdy, sticking out from underneath.

"Some watchdog you are," I said, smiling. "You should have barked or something when you saw her eating all those grapes." Rowdy opened one eye briefly and thumped his thick furry tail on the ground. He had been my constant companion since before the flood and had survived a year long journey on the ark. Now he was too old and lazy to get excited about anything.

I returned to my work. As I continued to harvest, I saw my nephew, Canaan, approaching. I felt the usual sense of dread and my jaw began to clench. Canaan was the youngest boy of Ham's children, and was by far the worst brat of any young person I had ever known. Ham had always been a bit of a bully and malcontent when we were boys, but compared to Canaan, he had been the perfect son.

Now Canaan walked slowly up the hillside towards me, the usual scowl of disapproval on his face. His normal facial expression was to look at you as if you had just said something really stupid and that you deserved of the utmost scorn. His gait was always slow and shuffling, as if he really didn't want to get to wherever he was going. He stepped up to face me on the opposite side of the vine I was working on.

"Aren't you done yet?" he challenged. "You've been up here all morning. How long does it take to pick a few grapes?"

Canaan was the only person I had ever known whose hair was completely white. This included the hair on his head, eyelashes and what little body hair he had on his reddish skin. He sneered at me with disdain.

I put up with way too much from this boy and I knew it, but I did it to avoid conflict within the family. Almost everyone in the family, except my father, had scolded or even spanked Canaan at one time or another. No one, except Ham, had a problem with the discipline of the children being done by extended family if that is who was present when the bad behavior took place. So I stood here, a grown man, and let this twelve year old disrespect me.

"Tell ya what," I shot back. "If you think you can do it that much faster, maybe you can come up here and help next time instead of lying around your house, or whatever it is you do all day."

Canaan merely went on as if I had not spoken.

"You need to help my Dad down at the olive press," he said.

"I need to help? Where are your brothers? Why can't Cush and Phut help him?"

"I don't know," Canaan answered abruptly. "I guess they are out riding or messing around or something."

"Oh, I have no doubt they are messing around, wherever they are. I can assure you they aren't doing anything constructive," I replied.

Actually, Cush and the other boys weren't bad kids. They were nothing like their baby brother, Canaan--they were just a little slow to volunteer for work.

"All I am telling you is, whenever you do get finished here, my Dad says you need to get your butt down the hill and help him finish the olive press."

"You need to"…as pushy as Ham often was I knew he didn't tell Canaan to say it that way. The gall of this boy, this…child, made me grind my teeth in anger. Suddenly, I decided I had tolerated all I could stand. I stepped quickly through the grape arbor, grabbed Canaan by the arm, and spun him around to face me.

"Listen here, you disrespectful little boy. I am tired of your tone and even more tired of your attitude. Now, here is what you are going to do," I went on as I poked a finger in the boy's skinny chest. "You turn right around, go back down that hill and tell your Dad that I am still finishing up, so you are going to help him. Hopefully his heart won't stop from the shock."

Canaan glared at me. Though I certainly had no fear of him, the look in his eyes was unsettling to say the least. Sometimes I wondered what went on inside that head of his. His eyes locked with mine for a long moment.

"GO!" I pointed down the hill, my voice rising. It was all I could do to keep myself from giving him a swift kick to help him along.

Finally, he crossed the grape arbor and began to head in the general direction of the olive press. Along the way he took a detour to walk along the cypress log. I knew he was procrastinating to get a reaction from me, and that made me even angrier. Unwilling to give him the satisfaction, I turned my back to him and went back to my work. A few moments went by as I became lost in thoughts of how differently I would have raised Canaan. Suddenly, I heard Mareyea cry out.

I could tell by the sound of her cry that she was hurt. I ducked quickly beneath the grape arbor. She sat crying with her hands covering her forehead. She looked frightened. The basket lay on its side next to her.

"I was sure I had it wedged. How could it have..." I didn't finish my thought. Out of the corner of my eye I saw Canaan strolling more quickly than usual back down the hill, acting as if he didn't hear my little girl.

"CANAAN." I shouted. "What did you do?"

He stopped and looked at the ground for a moment before turning part way around.

"What did I do with what?" He asked, wearing his usual "how stupid you are" expression.

"You know what I mean. What did you do to Mareyea?" I picked her up and gently pulled her hands away from her forehead. She had a nasty looking knot starting to pop up above her eye.

I wanted to run him down and pummel him. I knew he had done something to make that basket tip over.

"You had better believe we will talk about this some more!" I shouted at his back.

Canaan merely waved a hand back at me dismissively as he continued to walk away. I must confess, at that moment I wanted to run my nephew down and beat him, badly. But I didn't have time to deal with him right now. I turned back toward my little girl and kissed her as gently as possible where the knot was beginning to form. I kissed her chubby little checks and felt the wetness of her tears. As I did so, her crying began to subside. Her tiny bottom lip curled out pitifully as she tried to regain her composure.

"Was Canaan mean to you?" I asked. "Did he push you?" Mareyea only shook her head "no" as she hooked the index finger of her right hand into the corner of her mouth. Then she buried her face into my shoulder and tucked her arms underneath her chest as she leaned against me.

I walked with her in my arms toward the top of the hill where the grape arbor was planted. It was a short walk to one of my favorite spots. I supposed the entire valley had been wooded before the flood, but some violent waters had surged through this area and leveled the forest. The result for us had been a ready- made clearing where succulent grasses had sprang up. The livestock kept it from becoming over grown, resulting in a breathtaking valley of rolling green hills.

I sat down on the hilltop with Mareyea across my lap. I came here often because it was the highest point in the valley. From here you could look to the South and see the rooftops of our houses off in the distance. Curls of smoke rose from all the chimneys as evening meals were being prepared. I could see some of the children playing in the swept dirt yard surrounding the houses. "Our little community," I said aloud. Mareyea stopped pouting for a moment and started to smile, but then thought better of it and went back to pouting and basking in her Daddy's comfort.

I hugged her close to me again as I looked Northeast. In that direction, I could see the shoreline of the lake. Mareyea's downy brown hair tickled my chin as the warm breeze blew it against my face. At the far end of that shoreline my mistress would be hiding. I would go to her soon. If I had to stay here and dig in the dirt and put up with Ham's sarcasm and his son's lousy attitude…well, at least I could look forward to my time alone with her. I hadn't seen her in over a week now. As I began to lose myself in thoughts about her, my fantasy was shattered by my daughter's voice.

"Daddy?" she asked quietly with her head resting on my shoulder.

"What is it, honey?" I answered, tucking my chin tightly to my chest so I could look down at her.

"Daddy, why did Canaan kick da bas kit?"

CHAPTER 2

Ham struggled with the large wooden wheel of the olive press. The press was yet another one of his inventions. Shem had always been an outstanding carpenter and Japheth was an idea man, navigator and traveler. Ever since the family had left the ark, however, Ham had shown a great gift for inventing. He had completely changed the ox cart they used in the old world and made it smoother, stronger and easier to pull. Two oxen could now pull what it had taken four to accomplish.

He had instructed his family to dig a canal off to the side of one of the creeks. Inside the canal he mounted a giant wheel. Half of the wheel was beneath the water. When water from the creek was let into the canal, the current turned the wheel and provided energy to grind corn and wheat. Soon the olive press would be up and running, and Ham assured everyone it would be much easier to extract the precious oil the family needed. Ham was anxious to finish the assembly of the press and demonstrate its effectiveness. For now, the giant round stones were much too heavy for one man to lift into place.

Adina walked up from where she had been working in the garden, with her youngest daughter, Ruth, following closely behind as usual.

"Can I lift up a little on one side while you put it in place?" she asked.

"No, Adina. Can't you see how I am struggling? Can't you see how heavy this is, even for me? It's a two man job. That's all there is to it. I cannot imagine where Japheth is. I sent Canaan after him an hour ago because I knew this part of the job was coming up."

"I just hope he made it to Japheth." Adina murmured under her breath.

"Of course he made it, Adina," Ham said impatiently.

"I am not so certain, Ham. You know how easily he gets sidetracked."

"He wouldn't have done that," Ham said defensively. "He knew how hard a time I was having and that I needed help."

"Why can't the other boys help you?" she asked.

"Because they have gone fishing and hunting with Shem," Ham answered impatiently as usual. "Have you forgotten that already?"

"Of course, that's right. What was I thinking? Well, I'm going to find Canaan or Japheth or someone. You don't need to hurt yourself trying to do this alone."

Ham didn't answer, but instead watched his wife walk off towards their house. He had to admit she was still the most beautiful woman in the family. He could honestly say that she was the best looking woman on earth. That was a pretty amazing attribute for a woman that had given birth to ten children.

Adina had also turned out to be an excellent mother. In their home, she was the one who tried to instill discipline. Ham knew he let the kids get away with way too much, and he didn't back Adina up as he should. But kids should have some time to be kids. One thing was certain in Ham's mind--he had been cheated out of his youth because of his father's obsession with that stupid ark. Oh sure, Ham now believed that the ark had been ordained by God to save them. And he was grateful. But it still did not seem fair to him that the flood had come when he was still enjoying his youth. Ham felt as though he had been robbed. He wasn't going to let that happen to his children.

***

Canaan came sauntering up the path toward the houses, dragging the tip of a large stick in the dust. His countenance gave every indication that he had not a care in the world. He certainly didn't look like someone who felt guilty for injuring his baby cousin. His cavalier attitude was about to change. As he came around a bend in the trail, he could see his father, Ham, working on the press under the shelter, but what really caught his attention was the look on his mother's face as their eyes met. She abruptly sat Ruth down on a bench and marched angrily towards her son.

"Canaan," she said firmly as she approached, "Where have you been all this time?"

"I went to get Japheth like Daddy said," Canaan replied, looking very hurt that Adina would even dare to ask such a thing.

"That's Uncle Japheth. How many times do I have to tell you about calling your elders by their first names alone? But you went looking for him over two hours ago. Your father has been here all this time working alone."

"Well, get mad at Japh...I mean *Uncle* Japheth, not me. I told him to get his butt down here."

Adina firmly grabbed Canaan's wrist. She was attractive but also a very large woman. Her biological father had been from the race of giants. She was much stronger than this skinny preteen boy. She certainly would have been more help to Ham if he would only have let her do so. Canaan futilely tried to pull his arm away.

"Don't you dare be so disrespectful," Adina said. "And I am not asking you what Japheth did; I am asking you what you failed to do. You knew the bind your Daddy was in. You should have hurried back here. Now get in there and help him finish."

As she let go of the boy's arm, she noticed from the corner of her eye Ham walking toward them both.

"Why are you squeezing him like that?" Ham asked as he began to pull Adina's hand away.

Adina crossed her arms over her chest, let out a sigh of frustration and rolled her eyes skyward. She knew what was coming.

"Listen, Canaan," Ham said. "I heard what both of you were saying, and you are right. Japheth should have been here a long time ago and you shouldn't have had to rush back when I know you would rather be exploring or playing. But since you are here, maybe you and Mom together could help."

"Okay, okay", came Canaan's impatient reply.

For her part, Adina just shook her head in frustration all the way to the press. She could not fathom what had come over her formerly terse husband. From the time they had married till they boarded the ark, and throughout the year long voyage, Ham had been the picture of impatience and surliness. But ever since the boys were very small, Ham refused to discipline them. He treated his boys like peers rather than his own children. With their daughters, he was much less patient, but still left all the discipline to Adina. Adina resented having to always be the stern parent, but more than that, she worried about the impact on her children.

As the three of them lifted one of the large stones into place, Japheth arrived carrying Mareyea. At almost the same moment, Noah and his wife, Sapphira, walked up. Noah's face was still mostly hidden by the full white beard he had let grow to nearly the center of his chest, though the top of his head was now bald. His eyes were just as piercing as ever, yet he was a very different man now.

He had been so intense and such a strong leader when he was pushing the family to complete the ark. Then, while on the voyage, it was as if he had broken down. He had recovered in time to lead the family in leaving the ark and establishing their new farms and homes. Yet, he had never again demonstrated his previous intensity. After all those years of pushing and cajoling his family, and pleading with his friends and neighbors to repent and join them on the ark, he now just wanted to live in peace and enjoy his grandchildren.

"Japheth," Noah said. "You should have come to help Ham with this. This stone is too heavy for Adina and Canaan to be lifting." Japheth sighed as he rolled his eyes.

"Dad, I was working in the vineyard…ALONE I might add." Japheth shot a look toward Canaan. "Canaan was more than capable of helping Ham. He should have gone and fetched one of the other boys. The two of them could have lifted this with Ham. Besides, we can settle who should have helped who later," Japheth said. "Right now, there is a matter we must settle. Look at this knot on Mareyea's forehead."

Adina immediately stepped over to her niece. "Oh, you poor thing!" she said in her mothering tone. But as she tried to look closely, Mareyea, still a bit pouty, buried her face in Japheth's neck.

"Japheth, what happened to her?" Adina asked.

"Why don't we ask Canaan?" Japheth replied, staring intently at the boy.

Canaan looked genuinely hurt by this "accusation" and merely stood silent. He then looked toward Noah as if asking for help.

Noah, sensing his grandson's plea, said, "Japheth, whatever happened, I'm sure it was an accident."

"It better have been," said Adina, her hands on her hips.

"It was no accident," Japheth answered.

Everyone looked expectantly toward Canaan, waiting for his response.

"I don't even know what he's talking about," Canaan said finally. "I didn't see Mareyea and I certainly didn't know anything about her falling out of the basket."

Noah ran up and grasped Japheth's shoulders lovingly, pleading with him, "No…no, everyone, Canaan is a good boy. He loves Mareyea. Japheth, this is crazy talk. Canaan, come, we will go to my tent and get you something to eat. Japheth, you stay here and finish helping Ham. When you get busy you will realize what a silly notion this is that Canaan would ever do something to hurt little Mareyea."

With that, Noah whisked the boy away toward his own tent and away from the disapproving glares of his family members. Japheth, still holding Mareyea, looked skyward.

"Unbelievable!" he exclaimed to no one in particular.

"Good, this is settled then," Ham sighed deeply. "Let's get back to work." He turned and went back inside the shed which housed the winepress.

Japheth, Adina and Sapphira stood staring at one another.

"Why can't he see it?" Japheth asked Sapphira.

His mother, still as spry and robust as she had been the day they boarded the ark, appeared not to have heard Japheth's question. She was too deep in thought. Even in her old age, her watery brown eyes contained the fire that Japheth had seen many times in his life when Sapphira's fighting spirit was up.

"I wonder," Sapphira whispered.

"What did you say mother?" Adina asked.

"I said…I was just wondering. If he never saw Mareyea, how did Canaan know she fell from a basket?"

CHAPTER 3

Noah made his fifth trip back to the hearth of the stone fireplace built in the center of his tent. The chimney rose through the center and provided many anchor points for the pointed roof. He fetched a second loaf of flat bread for Canaan, who had finished the first while he watched his elderly grandfather struggle with putting a meal together for the two of them. The old man had yet to eat a bite; his food was growing cold on one of the well-crafted wooden plates from the ark. At no time did the thought of helping Noah occur to Canaan.

"Grandpa, why does Japheth hate me so much?" the boy asked disingenuously.

"Oh no, no…no my boy, your uncle doesn't hate you at all. He just gets frustrated sometimes."

Noah didn't look Canaan in the eyes as he answered, but stared just to the left of them. His formerly blue eyes were very cloudy now and his vision had become quite poor. For him, Canaan's face was a blur, so he guessed at where his grandson's eyes should be and looked there.

He poured Canaan a second cup of grape juice, still not having taken a bite of his own food.

Canaan drank the juice in large gulps, letting some spill down his cheeks and wiping them with the back of his hand.

"Grandpa, did you ever try to ferment any of this?" Canaan asked as he stared into the bottom of his cup.

Noah, having finally taken his first bite of cold food, jerked his head up at the question.

"Oh no, Canaan. You mustn't even think of such a thing. Strong drink was present in the old world. It contributed terribly to the sins of man."

Noah shuddered as he thought of the brutal attack Tamara suffered at the hands of drunken thugs prior to the flood.

"We never want that type of thing here" he continued quietly.

Canaan laughed. He tried to come across as charming but to a listener other than Noah the laugh would have sent chills down the spine.

"Don't be stup...I mean, don't be silly, Grandpa. I don't mean ferment it strong enough to make you drunk. Just ferment it enough to keep it from spoiling. We could store it much longer that way. I have been experimenting with it on my own."

"It *has* bothered me that we often have to throw the juice away in the spring because it spoils," Noah replied. "We never have enough to last through to the next harvest."

"I can show you how to do it some time," Canaan said excitedly. It wasn't the enthusiasm he was faking--it was his motivation that Noah misunderstood.

The old man placed a wrinkled hand on top of his grandson's head just as he had with his father, Ham, when he was a boy.

"Alright...alright...," he said. "You are like your father, always with an idea, always with an invention to try and help the family. Certainly, that would be good for you to contribute. You have convinced me. I will let you show me someday soon."

With that Noah mussed Canaan's hair gently, and then struggled to his feet, carrying his plate in one hand.

"This food isn't any good cold. I will heat it on the hearth and have it later. You go ahead and eat," he said to Canaan as he eased over to the hearth.

With Noah's back turned, Canaan wiped the top of his head off vigorously with his hand as though a spider had just crawled through his hair. He didn't know himself why he did it. There was just something about the old fool touching him that he couldn't stand. He really didn't like anyone touching him. In a moment, he gathered himself and said over his shoulder, "I am going to hold you to that grandpa. I really want to show you what I have discovered."

Canaan then pushed away his plate and stared menacingly into space.

CHAPTER 4

Shem approached from the west. The setting sun silhouetted his form as he crested the hill. He could see the tents and buildings in the distance. His pace quickened. He had been hunting and fishing for three days now, and he was anxious to see Prisca. These days he didn't handle their separations well. Losing their former home and all those they knew and loved outside their immediate family had made Shem cherish Prisca all the more.

As he topped a hill to the east of the families' homes, Shem decided to pull up momentarily and wait for the boys to catch up, as he had repeatedly during their trip. He would delegate to them the task of hanging the game in the smokehouse. Then, he would finally be free to set the pace for home.

"Come along now lads, surely you can motivate yourselves enough to keep up with your old Uncle. Why I am walking off and leaving the lot of you?"

Shem couldn't help but smile to himself as he watched Elam and Gomer roll their eyes at his comment.

"Uncle Shem," Cush complained. "I am not certain that you realize how many times you have said that on this trip. Okay, you can still walk a lot faster than us. We get it."

"I just thought you might want to push yourself a little harder, that's all. Anything to salvage what little dignity you have left after I caught more fish and harvested more game than all of you put together," said Shem with a wink.

He wouldn't have normally given his sons and nephews quite this hard a time except for the fact that they had all made such a point to tease him over and over when they left on their trip. It had only been three days ago that they were all full of the bluster and vigor of young men. That day they had readily teased him by promising to share their game with him since a man of his age would probably need lots of rest breaks and would not be able to hunt for long periods.

"How much farther to home?" Elam, Shem's oldest son asked. He and his cousin Gomer, Japheth's oldest, stood behind the yoke of the two wheel cart they were pulling.

Shem noted their lack of a comeback to his last comment and, deciding they now had an adequate dose of humility, he went on.

"If you will look just over that next little hill you will see the tops of the chimneys."

"Great!" they said in unison.

"I can't wait to get something to eat," Cush, the oldest brother of Canaan, said as he walked behind the cart carrying the leftover gear.

"Not so fast," Shem cautioned. "Before you boys take a break, this game needs to be hung in the smokehouse. Just put the fish on the shelves. We will flip them in a few days. I'll be waiting for you at the house."

The boys clearly did not like this idea but they didn't protest aloud. Instead, they started in the direction of the smokehouse about 100 yards from the family homes. Shem couldn't resist one last gig.

"Don't worry," he called out to them as they faded out of sight. "I'll make sure there is at least a little supper left over for you after I finish eating."

Shem's weathered face crinkled into a broad smile as he saw the boys stop, then start walking again as they laughed softly amongst themselves, only their heads and shoulders now visible beyond the horizon.

Shem rapidly walked on and soon closed to within a quarter mile of his own house. Soon he heard the sounds of his and his brothers' children. Shem laughed despite himself when he heard the giggling of Aram playing chase with Meshech and Mareyea, Japheth's two-year-old baby twins. At times, the life they had built in this valley seemed like heaven on Earth. Shem never wanted to be apart from his family, even to hunt. But the game they had harvested would be a welcome supplement to their winter meat supply.

In addition to the meat, the cart was also loaded with pelts. The furs would be sewn together to provide covers and cloaks for the coming winter.

Finally, Shem stepped around the corner of his house and saw the source of all the noise. Tiras and Aram were chasing one another from one building to the next, while the other children, boys and girls alike, followed in a huge flock. Shem covered his mouth to keep from laughing at them as their feet tangled, and one after another fell and hopped up immediately to continue the game.

Evening was a favorite time of day. In the late afternoon Prisca, Adina and Tamara sat the children in semi-circles and taught them about God and his creation. All the children had heard many stories about the ark and the voyage, and the way God had cared for their parents. But more than that, the lessons focused on God's covenant with Noah and how each of them had a role to play in keeping the covenant. Before bed they prayed with the children.

After the lessons were over, the children were free to run and play, burning off any last burst of energy before suppertime. After a good meal, the children would be more than willing to head for bed.

As Shem watched the children run off towards Japheth's tent, he saw her. Prisca stood by the doorway of the family home, her body turned away from Shem as she adoringly watched the children play. Shem was not due back for another full day so she was not expecting him. He let out a satisfied sigh of relief upon seeing her, as he dropped his goatskin water bag to the ground and leaned his spear he against the wall of the house. He took a step toward her and then stopped. How could it be that after all these years he could still feel this way about her? Their love for each other had only grown stronger since they were children in "puppy love."

Shem stared at his wife for a moment, as if she were his new bride. Her hair was still chestnut brown without any touches of gray. He saw her face in profile now and thought of how the lines only seemed to add to her beauty. Shem removed the knife belt that he wore outside his cloak and let it drop quietly to the ground. He crept closer to Prisca as if he was stalking his prey. As he drew closer, he allowed his eyes to take in every part of the woman he loved.

Finally, as he reached out for her, his eyes settled on the soft white skin of her neck. He startled her for a moment as he wrapped one strong arm around her waist and lifted her hair with the other hand. As he pulled her firmly to him, he kissed her neck.

Prisca spun suddenly and wrapped her arms around Shem's neck as he hugged her tightly, lifting her off the ground with ease.

"How did you get home so…" was all Prisca managed to say before Shem covered her mouth with his.

"Can't you two act your age?"

The question came from Asshur, their 16 year old son, who was still a bit testy since he had been too ill to go on the hunting trip and was forced to stay behind with his mother.

Shem and Prisca did not even bother to look over at him, but they did interrupt their kiss long enough to laugh as they looked lovingly at one another.

"You'll understand how we feel someday soon," Prisca finally answered as she took Shem's hand and led him toward the outdoor fireplace.

"I certainly hope not," their second born son answered over his shoulder as he headed for the house.

"You're home a full day early. What a wonderful surprise!" Prisca continued, smiling up at Shem.

"God was good to us on this trip. I have some fine pelts, the meat of two deer, and several large fowl. We can eat some of the meat fresh and preserve the rest for winter."

"How did the boys do?"

"I've been teasing them, but they actually did very well. They are rapidly becoming men and were a great help to me. We have enough meat now to make it through winter, but with game so plentiful, I plan to make another trip soon just to be sure."

"You wouldn't have to make another trip if one of your brothers would lead the boys out."

"Prisca, darling, we have been over this many times. Japheth couldn't possibly hunt because Tamara would never forgive him for harming animals. Ham…"

Prisca interrupted, "But Tamara certainly finds it in her heart to eat the meat once it is prepared and cooked."

Shem ignored this comment, knowing that Prisca had a valid point.

"Ham stays pretty busy around here, and the boys enjoy going with me. Besides, even though I miss you terribly, I enjoy the trips as much as they do."

"Well, I am sorry to disappoint you, my husband, but not one of the boys, who stayed behind this time, including your own, overworked themselves in the fields while you were gone. In fact, there was a little family spat over Canaan refusing to help

Japheth in the grape arbor. And it seems that Canaan may have pushed little Mareyea and hurt her head. But not too badly."

"That's not surprising, I'm afraid," Shem shook his head in disappointment.

"Shem, what are we going to do with Canaan?"

"I don't know. And Dad seems determined to gloss over his behavior. He is in denial, I suppose."

With that, Shem looked up at the quarter of the orange sun still showing as it set over the horizon. It was a magnificent sunset, as so many in this valley were. Prisca looked up at him after a moment and noticed his eyes were squinted and his lips pursed, as they always were when he was in deep thought.

"What is it?" she asked.

"I wonder why he did it," Shem replied.

"You mean why Canaan pushed Mareyea?"

"No. I know exactly why Canaan did that." Shem shook his head now, trying to change his thought process to something else. He wrapped an arm tightly around Prisca and pulled her closely to his side. He then looked into her eyes and gave her a small comforting smile.

Prisca started to smile back but then placed her hands on his forearms and pushed herself back, as if to read Shem's expression better.

"What then? What is it that is puzzling you about Canaan?" she persisted.

"Nothing. No really, nothing about Canaan. No, my question was about God. Look, let's just not talk about it. I was just thinking aloud anyway."

"Shem! Don't you dare leave me wondering like this. Tell me what is worrying you."

Suddenly Shem couldn't hold back anymore and he blurted it out. "I can't understand why God brought the flood and destroyed the evil in the old world, and then…"

Shem paused.

"And then what?" Prisca asked.

Shem took both her hands in his and looked her with grave concern. Prisca hadn't seen such a look since they were onboard the ark. Shem looked up from her eyes to the last rays of sun now showing in the distance.

"And then he still let it follow us here."

CHAPTER 5

The following morning was perfectly clear, although a little cold for this time of year. There had been very little in the way of seasons prior to the great flood. Since that time however, the seasons had become quite pronounced. The spring and the summer growing seasons were long and fruitful with what seemed to be a perfect amount of rainfall each year since the family had landed. The most pronounced differences were that the harvest season seemed to come with more crisp, cold mornings and the winter months had stretches that were brutally cold. This particular morning was too early to be even the first stages of autumn, but the early morning chill was a reminder of what was to come.

Adina and Tamara had all the children lined up, including the teens. They were about to go on an "explore" as the children called them. This was something they tried to do at least twice a month when the weather and work schedule would allow them some leisure time.

"Alright, everyone grab a hand," Adina ordered firmly. "Older children help the younger."

Cassandra, Adina's eldest daughter, rolled her eyes. "We know all this by now, Mom," she said with a exasperation. "We have done this a million times."

"Well, everybody may not be quite the expert you are, Cassandra," Prisca corrected her mildly.

Cassandra only rolled her eyes again. Smiling down at her favorite cousin, she reached for the hand of Mareyea. Adina and Prisca smiled discreetly to one another, knowing that in spite of their protests, the older children enjoyed this just as much as the younger.

With Rowdy in front, the line of children created quite a site. There were thirty two children in all, two lines of sixteen. The three mothers, Tamara, Prisca and Adina, beamed with pride as they looked them over. They were all lined up in a very uneven row with a younger child in between two older children. Only the eldest boys would not be taking the trip, and deep down they missed it. Unfortunately, there was always work to be done and they were now at an age where their help was needed. Also, the three eldest of Noah's grandsons had been gone for three days on a hunt. Work had piled up. Still, even they gathered here to start each day in prayer together. These times, and the evening meal time, were when important family bonds were formed.

As the elder boys departed to start their day, all the children took turns exchanging goodbye hugs and engaged in some light hearted teasing. Then, with each one taking up a knapsack lovingly prepared in advance, they headed off as a procession.

Adina led the way as usual while Tamara walked between the columns of two. Prisca brought up the rear and kept a close eye out for stragglers. Some of the children, particularly some of the boys, tended to stray away at times on misadventures of their own. The pace remained slow enough so that the older children could keep up safely while carrying their younger siblings part of the way.

Tamara was the most knowledgeable about animals and would frequently assume the lead if one was encountered. Prisca was the most nurturing. Adina, however, was the teacher. She seemed to strike just the right balance between firm discipline and the capability to hold the children's interest. She paused frequently to teach the children everything from the names of plants and trees, to the uses of roots and herbs, to types of rocks and minerals.

On exploration days, the emphasis was not so much on practical learning as it was on the wonder of God's creation, and the magnificent way in which He had provided for them all. In all cases and with every example, the women taught the children how the creation was a demonstration of His glory and a way that God revealed Himself to them.

On this particular day as the warm sun rose in the blue cloudless sky, the chill of the morning was rapidly driven away. After spending some time looking for snails and salamanders in an area of moss covered rocks, the group came upon a gurgling stream. Adina, with her hands on her hips, stopped and looked across to the other side, gauging the depth and difficulty of the crossing.

"Everyone pull off your sandals," she called out.

Prisca, with one of her sandals already in hand, hurried to the front and pulled Adina by the elbow to one side.

"We've never gone this way before with the children," she said. "In fact, I don't recall ever having been across this stream. I assume you have checked this ahead of time."

"No. As a matter of fact I have done no such thing." By now Tamara had joined the other two sisters-in-law. Adina continued.

"Say, we do call these little outings explores, don't we? So let's explore!" Adina said as she shrugged her shoulders. She again received worried stares. "Oh come on! It's not as if I'm going to let the little one just plunge out into the water. I'll go first and let some of the more adventurous ones come with me. I am certain Javan and Aram would jump at the chance."

Tamara rolled her eyes but couldn't help but smile.

"Oh, I am sure those two would," she said thinking of the mischievous streak in her own young son, Javan. "You three go right ahead. We will wait here and watch. And rest assured, if you fall in, we promise not to laugh with you... we will just laugh at you."

"You're very funny," Adina said, cocking one eyebrow.

The crossing was disappointingly uneventful. The water was indeed shallow and the bottom smooth and sandy all the way across. Even the little twins, Mareyea and Meshech, were able to wade part of the way with their mother Tamara holding both their hands.

Once on the other side, however, things rapidly began to look different. Whereas the forest canopy on the other side of the stream was open and relatively bright, on this side it closed in around them. As they pressed along further, the woods became as dark as the dusk of evening. Adina refused to admit it, but even she was beginning to feel the hair on her arm stand straight up.

As the group pressed cautiously forward they came upon an area strewn with huge granite boulders thickly encased by large cedars. The ladies felt as if they were surrounded.

"In some ways this reminds me of the city," Adina said, referring to the city they had left behind that was destroyed in the flood.

Prisca and Tamara nodded in agreement. There *was* something about this naturally occurring collection of granite and cedar that brought to mind the towering structures of the city.

"I am the king of Nod!" yelled Javan, Tamara's eleven year old. He had already climbed high atop one of the larger boulders, thrusting a makeshift sword overhead. Just like all of the other children he had never seen a weapon or a king, but he had heard stories, particularly from his Uncle Ham. Ham liked to aggrandize the world they had left. As he told the boys tales of that place and time, he always seemed to conveniently forget the violence and hatred that was such a part of the pre- flood world.

"Javan, get down from there before you fall," Tamara called to her middle son.

"I won't fall, Mother," Javan answered as he leapt from the top of the boulder to one of the lower rocks.

Tamara grabbed Adina's arm and hid her face in her sister-in-laws shoulder.

"I can't watch him," Tamara said. "He takes such risks. I know he has to learn his limitations, but I just wish he would be more careful."

"He's a young boy," Prisca commented. "You know they have to flex their muscles at that age."

"I know, but my other boys weren't that…"

"Hey, look!" Javan pointed his imaginary sword to the far horizon. By now many of the other children had made it, some with considerable help, up onto the rocks. They all stopped their play to look out past the tip of the cedar limb to see what had caught Javan's eye.

At first the women could not see where the children were looking. Then, one at a time they climbed onto one of the lower boulders. From that vantage point they were able to look far over the treetops to the distant mountain peaks.

"It's the ark!" Tamara exclaimed.

"I haven't seen it in at least ten years!" said Prisca, excitement apparent in her voice.

In the first years after the family landed, a significant portion of the hull of the ark was stripped of planks that were invaluable in building the families initial homes and furniture. Ultimately, however, transporting the lumber down the mountain proved too treacherous, so the framework and outer timbers were left intact. Because of that, the shape of the ark remained readily apparent.

Within three years, as winters became colder, snowfall high on the mountain covered the ark from view. Then, for a few summers the snow would melt enough that the ark was once again visible. In later years, the snowfall grew heavier until the ark became covered so deeply that it remained hidden year round. It was as if God was placing this sacred monument under a shroud only to be revealed on special occasions. This was one of those times.

Only the older children had ever had a glimpse of the ark. None of them had ever made the treacherous climb up to it. Now, from this angle, the entire outline of the ark was visible.

"I haven't seen it this clearly since the third year after our landing," Adina commented.

"Wow! It seems tiny," Aram said. "You mean all you guys and the animals lived on that thing for over a year?"

"It does look small from here," Adina answered. "But you must remember we are several thousand feet below the mountain's peak."

"And many miles away from the base of the mountain," Tamara added. "If you were closer to it you would be amazed at how big it really is."

"Yes, Grandpa Noah always tells us the ark was much larger of da houses and barns added togever," Mareyea said, throwing her arms out as she tried to describe the ark's size.

"That's right, sweetheart," said Tamara. Then with her arm around her little girl and their faces cuddled cheek to cheek, she pointed at the ark and said, "If you could climb up there, you could run as fast as you can and it would still take you a long time to run all the way around the ark."

"Can we take an explore up there some time and climb around inside it?" Javan asked.

"That would be a question for your father and your Uncle Shem," Tamara answered.

"Weren't you scared when you were in there and all you could see was water all around?" Arphaxad, Shem and Prisca's twelve-year old, spoke now for the first time. He was the most quiet and pensive of all the children, but when he spoke he usually had put much thought into what he said. This would likely be one of his last outings as he was now of age to work with the men. The three sisters-in-law smiled at one another at his question and looked back to the ark.

Prisca said, "Yes, son, there were many times when we were frightened. In fact sometimes we were even terrified. Other times we were very heartbroken and sad at all those who we had lost. But there were also days when we laughed and played games. We were happy that God had saved us. I suppose you could say that the entire voyage was both trying and bittersweet."

The questions went on and on for a long time. The children had all been told vivid stories of the great flood and life on the ark, but they never tired of them. Now the stories seemed to come to life all the more with the actual ark as a backdrop. After a long time of questions and stories, Adina stood up.

She noticed that young Ruth, now only seven years old, had climbed down and walked off a ways on her own. She was squatting down in the midst of a bed of tiny violet flowers that had sprung up on the forest floor. They thrived in a spot where a patch of sunshine peeked through the treetops. Adina walked quietly up to her daughter.

As the pair sat there together, it would have been obvious to any observer that they were mother and daughter. Ruth was the very image of her mother when she was a little girl, only more petite.

"Those are very pretty flowers you found, darling," Adina said.

"Yes, they are beautiful, aren't they?" Ruth answered as Adina wrapped an arm around her shoulders. "You know, Mother," she continued. "I was just here thinking of these tiny flowers. Look at all the tall trees and giant boulders all around them. I'll bet sometimes they get scared here in their little patch all alone."

Adina sensed that this would be a good time for the parent to just quietly listen to see what her child would come up with. So she squeezed Ruth's shoulders a little tighter and leaned in closer to listen.

"But you know what, Mommy, I mean, Mother?" Ruth had recently wanted to sound more grown up and had started calling Adina by the name she heard her siblings use.

"No, what?" Adina encouraged.

"They are here and they seem to be getting along just fine. The sun comes in through the trees and warms them, and the earth is moist enough for them to grow. And the boulders might intimidate them, but they also protect them from heavy winds. I think God has placed these little flowers just where He wants them to be; just where they need to be. And that's the way with us too, Mother," the little girl with big brown eyes looked into the eyes of her mother now for the first time. Adina smiled back enraptured.

"God placed you in the ark. He placed us in the valley and no matter what happens He will be with us. He will take care of us."

"Honey, that is so beautiful and so true. I am very glad you shared that with me," Adina said. "Now, let me tell you something," Ruth looked up into her mother's eyes once again with both adoration and attentiveness.

"Ruth, I have watched you since you were a tiny little baby. I have watched as you have grown and as you play with the other children, and I sense something special about you. I am going to tell you something extraordinary about yourself that a little kind old lady once told me about myself. You, my dearest, have a heart for God." Ruth blushed and smiled as she looked back toward the flowers. Adina continued.

"That means that you hear Him very clearly when He speaks. You hear His voice in your heart and you hear Him when He speaks through His creation. Cling tightly to that gift, Ruth. Nurture it by spending time in prayer and in God's presence and I promise that He will use you in a mighty way someday."

At this, Ruth turned, threw her arms around her mother and hugged her tightly. Adina kissed both her daughter's cheeks and returned the hug.

"We had best start heading for home," she said. "As it is, we will be past suppertime getting home." Adina stood up and started brushing pine needles off her clothes as she walked back towards the others. After a few steps she realized Ruth was not beside her so she turned and reached out her hand in order to take Ruth's. Ruth had not moved from her spot near the flowers. As Adina looked back she saw Ruth standing and staring down at them.

"Come along dear," she called back.

Ruth lingered a moment more, still fixated on the flowers. "I'll be okay, Mommy," she finally said. "Even when you are not beside me, I'll be just like the flowers. God is going to take care of me." She looked up. "He promised."

Adina frowned for a moment. What did Ruth mean "when she was not beside her?" Before she could contemplate further, Ruth ran to catch up. The two held hands and walked back to the others.

One by one everyone was helped down to ground level. While they were waiting around for everyone to climb down, Javan and Aram ventured off on their own. In just a few steps they came to the mouth of a cave formed between two boulders. Soft powdery sand covered the area in front of the cave. Looking from side to side Aram rapidly set about making large footprint shapes in the sands with Javan's stick/sword.

"Quickly, Javan, go and get the others and tell them you have found the home of some great monster."

Javan smiled broadly at the thought of what they were about to do and ran to fetch the others. With very little planning, the two boys did a seamless job of playing off one another.

Before the group rounded the boulder at a steady jog, Aram could hear their voices.

"I am sure it's just an animal's den," came Tamara's voice. "Perhaps a bear lives here. If so, we had better be careful."

The women and children formed a semi-circle in front of the cave. Many of them still had a look of skepticism.

"See," Javan pointed excitedly at the tracks setting things up perfectly for Aram.

"I am not so sure, Javan," Aram began. "Surely this is not a monster's den." He inched closer and closer to the cave, building the suspense as he waited for the perfect moment to scare the others.

"You see," he said now as he was just a half step inside the cave. There is nothing to worry about…I see his eyes…oh my gosh…I see his red eyes glowing…run for your lives!" With that both he and Javan let out their very best screams and ran full speed for the stream.

Realizing they were being left behind, everyone else, including the women, began to scream despite themselves. The three mothers scooped a small child under each arm paying no mind to who had whose child and they rapidly began to catch up to the already fleeing kids. Just as Prisca was beginning to hike her skirts to gain more speed, she looked up at Javan and Aram, who were already by the stream bank. Both were laughing hysterically. Aram had gone so far as to collapse upon the ground holding his sides.

Soon everyone realized they had been frightened nearly to death for the amusement of the two boys. Tamara crossed her arms and pursed her lips, but before she could get mad, she began to laugh. The laughter soon spread until one by one they each ended up sitting and laughing till their sides hurt.

CHAPTER 6

We were just beginning to get worried when we heard our little band of troops coming up the trail. It was easy to tell they had enjoyed a lovely outing because, though they looked tired, there was much laughter. Javan led the way, marching with his knees up high, and a cedar limb sword thrust over his head. He was barking out some type of cadence, but it was hard to hear over the multiple conversations of the others who seemed to be all talking at once.

Bringing up the rear, as was usually the case after these long outings, were our lovely wives. They were carrying little ones while leading others by the hand. They were a little disheveled and slightly haggard but were a beautiful site nonetheless. Rowdy, well-worn himself, was about a minute behind the others.

The day had warmed but now that the sun was setting, it had cooled just as rapidly. Shem and I had a good fire going in our outdoor fireplace. The fireplace, built from large stones hauled up from a nearby creek, had been the first permanent structure we built after settling in this valley. We had all pitched in to build it and the surrounding circle of benches.

In our old homes we had enjoyed a much smaller version and it had always been a popular and important gathering place for evenings of family fellowship. Now, with a larger family, we continued the tradition almost every evening if the weather allowed. By this fireplace we told stories, shared songs and music, and worshipped God. It was the best way to spend time with our extended family.

We also continued the tradition of everyone eating together for the evening meal. This was a practice we started while on the ark. We tended to have breakfast in our homes with our immediate families. Lunch was whatever we could easily carry in a daypack as we worked the orchards or in the fields, but dinner was a special time.

Shem had long ago built a grand outdoor table that would accommodate all of us. On one end sat my father and mother, the patriarch and matron of our family. On the opposite end of the table there was a lower section where every child sat from the time they could feed themselves until they were big enough to sit at the full sized table.

I was helping my mother, Sapphira, by moving loaves of freshly baked bread from the hearth to the table as Tamara approached. Shem rotated a spit slowly over the fire which contained the fresh fowl he had harvested during his hunt. The succulent smells of the golden brown meat filled the air.

This meal would be a welcome change from our normal diet of mutton. Mother stood over a smaller cook fire stirring a kettle of boiled potatoes, carrots, and onions. These simmered in the same kettle where she had prepared batch after batch of vegetable stew while we were on the ark.

"I was just starting to get worried," I smiled, as I slid my arm around Tamara's waist.

"Sorry, we didn't mean to stay that long. We have had quite an adventurous and entertaining outing."

"Guess what everyone!" Javan spoke up. "We saw the ark today."

"It was feet feet feet tall up on a high mountain," Mareyea added enthusiastically as she jumped up into the air.

Prisca, who was now standing by the fire with one hand on Shem's shoulder, said, "Yes, honey. From where we were we had perhaps the clearest view of the ark we have had in years."

"We should all go there tomorrow and see it again," I added.

"I would love to see her again as well," Noah said. "Who knows? It may be my last opportunity. I am getting awfully long in the tooth."

"Not to worry, my dear," Sapphira said. "You will outlive us all."

Soon we were all gathered around the table. Tonight it was Dad's turn to give thanks to God for the wonderful meal He had provided for us. As we joined hands and listened to my father's beautiful prayer, I couldn't help but open one eye for a peek.

I looked at the joined hands. Wrinkled ones held smooth, rough and powerful held delicate and soft, mother's fingers were held in babies' fists. I looked across the table at what had become a routine meal, but which was finer than anything we ever dreamed of in our pre – flood homes. The crackling fire radiated its warmth upon my arm and cheek, and suddenly tears formed in my eyes. Who were we? Why was the most high and merciful God so good to our little family? Despite all we had lost from the old world, God had restored us a hundred- fold.

As Father said "amen" he must have sensed my emotion as our eyes locked for a long moment. He smiled, and I smiled back at him. He had read my mind, for he squinted his blue eyes and crinkled his nose in acknowledgement. We were both feeling the same thing—an overwhelming feeling of joy.

I smiled back and then we both looked at our wives. Without realizing it, or meaning to, I reached up and placed a palm gently on Tamara's cheek. Tamara looked up at me with pleasant surprise in her eyes. She then went back to busily preparing Mareyea's plate. I looked back at my Dad just in time to see Mother take his hand from her face and kiss it. Then she released it to hold her own plate up to him for a serving of stew.

I sat there a moment longer just soaking it in, looking from one smiling face to the other. I had no idea that in a few short days everything would change. In less than a week we would reel from one blow after another. We would experience devastating pain the likes of which we hadn't experienced since the night we sat inside the ark and heard the screams of the damned.

CHAPTER 7

"Grampa....Grampa," Canaan called, purposefully sounding like he had when he was a small child. He was walking up the narrow trail that led out from behind Noah's tent and down to the stream. Just the night before, he had sat with the rest of his family around the large table and enjoyed a meal. The very next afternoon he chose to forget all about that pleasant time of fellowship. Now, he was looking for his suddenly missing grandfather.

The trail was lined with roses that Sapphira had transplanted here soon after they left the ark. It was from one of these rose hedges that Noah reached out an arm and grabbed the back of Canaan's tunic, startling him so much that he actually felt his chest muscles tighten.

Canaan had to laugh despite being slightly annoyed with the old man. He certainly hadn't expected this kind of reaction. He had watched Noah drinking wine for two hours and the old curmudgeon was actually starting to be a little fun. Canaan hadn't thought he would ever get Noah to take that first sip of the wine he had fermented.

He had lied to his grandfather, assuring him once again that the wine was far too weak to cause drunkenness and that instead it was just barely strong enough to preserve the juice of the grape a little longer than normal. After some initial protests and slow sips, the sweet wine had been most satisfying. The taste was so pleasing in fact, Noah had failed to realize the alcohol was having any effect on him. Now, Canaan couldn't believe he had pulled it off. Noah, the great patriarch, the powerful man of God, was drunk.

The old man nearly fell as he grasped Canaan around the shoulders and leaned on him for support. "My dear grandson, you should have seen…" Noah interrupted himself temporarily with a wheezing laugh. "You should have seen your face," he tried to go on, but he was laughing more now. He had left his staff back in the tent so he leaned heavily now on Canaan to support his arthritic legs and maintain his balance.

"I know. I know," Canaan guffawed and feigned an imbalance of his own. His childish pet names for Noah and his stumbling gate were merely illusions created for Noah's benefit. Canaan hadn't had a drop of wine. As he had watched his grandfather drink cup after cup, he in turn had only sipped water or grape juice. He wanted to make Noah feel as comfortable and secure as possible in matching him drink for drink.

Now Noah held his belly as the laughter subsided momentarily. "Oh Canaan, this has been fun but it has gotten so warm out here."

It was at that moment that another idea occurred to Canaan. "You know what we should do?" Canaan asked excitedly. "We should go down and bathe in the stream like we used to when I was little. That would cool us off."

"Yes…yes, it has been years since I have done that. Your grandma always draws water for me in a tub. She is afraid this old man will slip on the rocks, but I have a feeling that today I just might surprise her with how agile I still am."

With that, Noah did a rather pathetic little hop as if he were jumping from one rock to another. Canaan smiled with derision at the clumsy old fool.

"Now, do you intend to stand there gawking, or are we going swimming?" Noah asked as he winked at Canaan.

With that Noah ducked back into his tent. Once inside he began to strip off his clothes. Canaan supposed he intended to streak down the path to the stream wearing nothing but his sandals. Canaan, now inside the tent as well, made a half-hearted effort to pull off his own tunic but then stopped. He watched Noah as the old man clumsily pulled his tunic over his head. For a brief moment Canaan was embarrassed to see the pale whiteness of Noah's wrinkled skin. That embarrassment was quickly replaced with utter contempt. So this was the great and righteous Noah? He certainly didn't look like anything special now, standing there pale, white, and naked. This was what Canaan had wanted, only he wasn't sure why he wanted it.

For some reason, people like Noah, Shem, Prisca, and even his own mother Adina, just irritated Canaan by their very presence. Noah had never shown Canaan anything but kindness and love, but there was just something about the way he was always trying to teach everyone about goodness and righteousness. Canaan didn't want to hear all that. And he didn't like the way it made him and his father Ham feel.

Ham had commented many times how he believed that Noah, Shem and Japheth all felt that they were better than he was. Even though Canaan could not put his finger on a single example of where that had actually occurred, he still resented them. It was all so boring. How many times did he have to hear about that stupid flood and the stupid ark and what all God had supposedly done for them?

From what Canaan had observed, there was not much need for God in this valley. He had everything he needed here without God. Everything, that was, except a little fun and excitement now and then. And he could think of nothing more fun than bringing the high and mighty Noah back down to earth. As he watched the elderly man swaying back and forth he knew he was about to get that opportunity.

"Canaan, I may have to wait a few moments before I go swimming with you," Noah said. "I'm not feeling very good all of a sudden."

"Oh, Grampa," Canaan answered impatiently. "You'll be fine in a moment. Just sit down and steady yourself."

Canaan walked over to Noah and placed his hand very lightly on his grandfather's elbow. It was as if he was touching something repulsive.

"Yes, help me sit…"

Before Noah could complete that sentence, his eyes rolled back in his head. He slumped heavily toward Canaan, who quickly let go of the elbow and stepped to the side, allowing Noah to hit the ground with a thud.

Noah grunted in pain as his shoulder hit the ground, and then the old man passed out. All those stories from Ham about the "good old days" of drinking and wild parties had paid off. The repeated practice brews to come up with just the right flavor had now become worth it. Canaan's brew had worked more effectively than he had hoped. He looked down at Noah now, lying stark naked on the floor of his tent. He shook his head from side to side and laughed. At first it was a chuckle, but as he walked toward his own house to find his father, Ham, his giggling grew to a full belly laugh.

Canaan was so caught up in his laughter that he didn't notice that the old family dog Rowdy had walked up gingerly and placed a protective paw on Noah's foot. He then turned his head and pricked up his ears as he watched the boy depart. For a moment, Rowdy didn't feel old anymore. His protective instincts had been awakened. He looked toward Canaan once again, then out into the distant rocks. He sensed it there, the same thing that he sensed in Canaan. Rowdy bared his teeth and growled deeply in his chest.

CHAPTER 8

"Japheth! Shem! Come quickly," Ham called out, his eyes wild with excitement. "You are not going to believe this!"

"Ham, what's going on?" Shem asked irritated. He and Japheth had been busy working in the vineyard when Ham had come practically screaming for them to follow him to Noah's tent. It was obvious that no one was hurt and there was no emergency, because Ham's calls were frequently interrupted by hysterical laughter. Both of Ham's brothers had left the vineyard and were now walking with a sense of purpose up the path towards Noah's tent.

"What could possibly be so funny?" Japheth asked, starting to smile despite himself.

"Just come on and see," Ham answered over his shoulder as he led the other two.

As they topped the little rise upon which Noah's tent was staked, Shem suddenly caught a glimpse of a bare leg from the knee down just inside the tent. At the sight of that he stopped walking abruptly.

"Ham," Shem asked with a suspicious scowl. "What is going on here?" The look in Shem's eyes had rapidly gone from one of intrigued curiosity to serious concern.

"Come on and look and you'll see for yourselves." Ham continued walking up to the tent door.

Japheth took two cautious steps toward the tent before Shem grasped him by the arm and stopped him.

"We aren't taking another step until you tell us what is going on, Ham. Something is not right here."

With that Ham trotted back to them, a look of glee still upon his face. It was as he approached closer that Shem smelled alcohol on Ham's breath for the first time. At this same moment, Canaan stumbled out of Noah's tent with a cup in his hand.

Ham took Shem by the forearms and then looked back towards Canaan. He giggled again at Canaan's stumbling, and then looked back at Shem. At this point both Shem and Japheth saw something in Ham's eyes that they hadn't seen since the flood. And the sight hit them like a punch to the stomach. Shem realized in an instant that the post- flood lives they had built and enjoyed would never be the same. It wasn't the alcohol alone; all that drink had done was unleash what was in the hearts of the partakers. And it was the content of these two hearts that worried Shem.

"Ham," Shem said and then paused. "Are you and Canaan drunk?"

"That's it," Ham began to speak rapidly now. "We may be a little drunk. Canaan figured out how to make wine. I never knew how they made it back home. Anyway, he actually got the old man to drink some and he is right in there passed out and as naked as the day he was born. We might be tipsy, but Dad is passed out drunk." Shem pulled away and watched as Ham doubled over with laughter. He looked down at his intoxicated brother with shock and disgust.

"Ham, what have you done?" Japheth asked, I horror.

"What do you mean, what have I done? Canaan did it. Then he came and got me. I just think it is hilarious, that's all."

Canaan was now leaning against a small table outside of Noah's tent. Though he hadn't drunk any wine while encouraging Noah to drink, he had partaken since then. His eyes were cloudy and he swayed back and forth when not holding onto the table.

"Go on in and take a look." Ham walked around to shove Japheth and Shem in the back toward Noah's tent.

Shem wheeled toward his brother, "Ham, don't you even realize the magnitude of what Canaan has done, and that you have participated in? Do you know how demeaning and demoralizing it will be for our father when he wakes up and realizes what has happened to him? It wasn't enough that you tricked him into getting drunk somehow. Now you have shamed him further by gawking at his naked body. Ham, this is the man whom Almighty God chose to speak to. This is the man whose obedience saved you and our whole family from drowning. Canaan, you wouldn't even have been born if it wasn't for your grandfather's obedience. You have committed an abomination against God's elect."

Ham looked stunned by the passion of Shem's words, yet they seemed to make no impression on Canaan. The boy just waved a hand towards his uncle dismissively and sat down heavily upon the ground with his back to the leg of the table. Canaan tried to say something about a little fun but his attempt at speech resulted in mostly nonsensical gibberish.

"This is going to be bad. We have to do something," Shem spoke to Japheth now. As he turned to face his brother he saw that all the commotion had drawn attention. Adina was helping Sapphira walk faster than normal up the trail toward them. Just behind them followed Prisca and Tamara. The children followed the women in single file.

"Don't come up here," Shem called to them authoritatively. The women, sensing urgency in Shem's voice, stopped. They turned to the children behind them and told them to stop as well.

"Before we go any further we have to cover Dad up. Do you think we can dress him?" Japheth asked.

"That would mean we would see him too. That would shame Dad even worse. No, we have to cover him somehow without seeing him," Shem replied.

"There," Japheth pointed toward some bedcovers hanging out on the line to air dry. "We can take one of those, lay it on our shoulders and walk backward toward Dad, letting it cover him as we go."

"I suppose that is the safest thing to do for now," Shem said as he walked toward the cover. Then with Shem on one corner and Japheth on the other they walked toward the tent. Suddenly, feeling a twinge of contrition, Ham clumsily grasped the center of the cover as if to help.

"Stand aside, Ham," Shem insisted. "You and Canaan have done enough."

Ham stared back at them blankly for a long moment. Then he looked over at Canaan. Embarrassment and regret swept over him, but he realized that it was far too late for those emotions now. Ham took a step backwards, and then took two more without speaking. He started to run down the path towards his house but then saw the women and children blocking the trail. Unwilling to face Adina, he walked, and then ran in the opposite direction, towards the stream.

"We can talk to him later," Shem said. "Let's first take care of our father."

With that the two men walked into the tent backwards. They gently lowered the blanket until it covered their elderly father up to his neck. Only when they were certain that the cover was in place did they turn to face him. Noah stirred briefly and tried to speak but was still in a semi-conscious state.

"Oh, dear father," Shem said with tears welling in his eyes. "After all you have accomplished, after all your talks with God, how could you have been so naive?"

"He's going to be deeply hurt, Shem," Japheth added. He placed a hand on Noah's forehead and lovingly brushed the long grey hair from his face.

Shem eased back into a sitting position with his forearms wrapped around his knees. He didn't want to leave the tent and have to tell Sapphira and the others what had occurred. No matter. They might be able to keep it from the children for a time. But all the adults would have to be told. There would be repercussions, but Shem didn't know what they would be. The head of the family had been disgraced in a vile manner.

"Eighteen years," Shem said absent mindedly.

"What?" Japheth asked.

"Eighteen years of wonderful peace and tranquility in this valley. Certainly we have had our quarrels and struggles but we have had a good life here since the flood." Shem went on. "You say that as if that life is about to be over," Japheth replied, a joyless and nervous smile on his face.

"I am stricken by the magnitude of sin's consequences and how if we do not always remain vigilant, it can enter into lives and wreak havoc," Shem continued.

Japheth pursed his lips tightly together and looked at the ground. He didn't want to believe what he was hearing, but he did. He had seen it before. They all had. They had all endured it and didn't want to do so again. Shem went on.

"Don't underestimate this, Japheth. I have a feeling this is something far beyond a prank gone wrong. I feel the same way I felt when Dad and I looked out the window of the ark and saw the sin playing out in the lives of those who were mocking us just prior to the rain. I just cannot help but feel that nothing in our lives will ever be the same. I fear the peace we have known in this valley will never come to us again."

CHAPTER 9

I had had enough. I reached this point from time to time and it seemed to occur more frequently than ever lately. I sometimes just reached a point where I had had all I could stand of belligerent nephews, raucous children and those wretched grape vines. I could not fathom why Canaan had done what he had to my father. But for now, we had made Dad as comfortable as possible and left him in Mother's care. There was nothing more I could do back home, and I was fed up with being there.

When I reached that point I knew what I needed. I needed to see her. And that is where I was headed now. I had walked the approximately three miles from our valley, careful that I wasn't being followed or observed. I had made it this long. I didn't intend to have to explain myself now, not yet anyway.

I looked back over my shoulder frequently as I topped the final hill and headed down to the hidden area near the lakeshore where she would be waiting. It was the same spot I had come to just a week before, and where I had gone every week for the last five years. I paused briefly as I approached the shoreline. I often paused here and just stared out across the vast expanse of water. What was the land like on the far side of this lake? What might I find there? There was a yearning in me to discover the answers to those questions that I couldn't explain.

I walked along the shore for 200 yards or so. I was beginning to relax and lose some of my paranoia. If no one had seen me yet, they weren't likely to be following me now. When I came to the mouth of a dry stream bed, I turned to walk into it.

This was a perfect place for me to hide her because the sides were steep enough to mostly shield her from view. From where she would be sitting, no one could see her from the shoreline. They would have to walk right up to the mouth of the stream and see past the brush wall I had built. My breathing became a little more labored as I struggled around that leftward bend. Then, just as the ground flattened and the ditch widened, I saw her there.

I always worried that a heavy rain would come some day and top the wooden gate in the levy, destroying the launching berth I had built for her. But she was safe and as beautiful as ever. She was twenty-five feet from bow to stern and made of some of the most choice cypress lumber from the ark. I had painstakingly smoothed each board to remove the black pitch and reveal the beautiful wood grain. It had taken me months to plane and match the boards to a fit that was even tighter than we had achieved on the ark. The result was a keel that was as slick and smooth as a table top.

Someday, perhaps this year when the heavy rains came, she would be ready to launch. That was the most significant reason I had built her here. I had let Shem in on my secret project early on so that he would help me to build two wooden gates to hold back water. One held back the normal flow of this creek. The second was installed in a smaller version of the canal we used at our corn mill. For now the canal gate was opened and water flowed freely around the boat and into the lake. When I had her ready to sail, I would close the canal gate to seal it off. Then, when the water in the stream backed up high against that gate, I would lift it to send a rush of water toward my little boat and float her out into the lake.

For now the boat rested on scaffolding similar to what we had used when building the ark. The scaffold for the ark had been designed to collapse when the waters rose and caused the ark to float. The weight of the ark made that scaffold stronger. When the weight was removed, the scaffold fell. This scaffold for my boat was more self- supporting. When the time came to launch, I would have to cut away two key joints with an axe. I anticipated that the ride down the stream bed would be both thrilling and critical.

When the day for the launch came, I would bring Shem back here with me. He had helped me gather some of the lumber and assisted with some of the initial construction. He agreed to keep my secret until I was ready to share it, but he had no idea how far along she had come and how close she was to being ready. I really don't think he believed I would ever finish.

But finish her I would. And when I did, I would sail far away from here and make a life for my own family that wouldn't include farming or nephews. I wanted to know what it would be like to have a home with just me, Tamara, and our children. I wanted to discover with them. I wanted God to show us a little valley or perhaps a mountaintop meadow that would be our very own. God had told us to replenish the earth. There was a very big earth out there that we had yet to see. I intended to see more of it before I died. It wasn't that I didn't love my extended family. We had endured so much together and I loved them all very much. It was just that in some ways, I felt we were still cooped up on the ark. After all these years I wanted to be free from that. My Dad, brothers and sisters-in-law seemed to be keeping me tied to that most difficult time of my life. It was as if I wasn't just married to Tamara anymore. I felt married to my whole family. For over 20 years now, from the building of the ark to serving my Dad in his farming, my life had been consumed with what was best for our entire group. I felt I had done my share. I was ready to make a life of my own choosing for me and my household, with God as my guide.

Despite my desires, I knew I was at least months away from trusting my little ship with my family. I had wanted to build a boat like this since we first saw the mountain peaks emerging from the receding floodwaters while on board the ark. After many months on land I had wanted to sail from the ark to the mountains to see what they were like and to perhaps gather food. But whenever I would talk about it, my father and Shem would just shake their heads and laugh.

"Just another silly scheme from little brother," I suppose they thought.

I had known then I could build my own boat. Still, it was best that I hadn't attempted it at that time because I didn't know enough. Once I had the idea I began to be more mindful of the ark and how it behaved in the water. I learned from my observations that I would need to do many things differently in order to have the type of craft that I wanted.

I wanted something much faster and more agile. The ark, with its box-like dimensions, was incredibly stable, but after the water receded and I was able to get perspective from the distant mountain peaks, I realized that it was lumbering and slow. Unlike the ark, my boat came to a point at the bow. I had modeled her shape after the dolphins I had watched jumping and playing alongside the ark. Like them, she would glide through the water, or at least I hoped she would.

Since we had lived in the valley I had experimented with all sorts of toy boats floating in whatever puddle or stream I could find. I started with nothing more than leaves or pieces of bark. But before I ever found this building site, I had graduated to hand carved boats. I experimented with different shapes and designs. I splashed them, lay on my belly and blew on them, and even threw rocks at them to see how they would behave. I had finally settled on the boat I had now. She would be steered by a tiller and propelled by the wind. I felt confident that she would move us rapidly, smoothly and safely across the huge lake and that we would be able to sail her back here for visits when the wind was right.

As I let myself daydream, I realized I was doing it again. I had unconsciously climbed the steps, stepped over the bulkhead and sat at the pilot's seat with the tiller grasped in my left hand. Sitting and daydreaming like this, I had already sailed her about a million miles in all sorts of waters. I got frustrated with myself sometimes because of the productive time I had wasted in these fantasies. Then again, it was fun that a part of me was content to just let her provide that escape. As long as I was pretending to sail she would never be damaged, or capsize, or perhaps result in my death. After all, I really didn't know how a boat of these dimensions and this weight would behave. This was no toy.

I looked around and realized I had better get to work if I was going to accomplish anything today.

I stopped once more and thought of my father. I didn't want to think about how hurt he would be or how he would react when he awoke and was told what had happened. And he would have to be told. If some stranger were to meet my father today they might make the mistake of assuming he was a fragile old man. While he certainly was in the twilight of life, he was most emphatically not fragile.

My Dad had strength of character and willpower which I was not sure any of us sons possessed. He had single handedly willed the ark into completion when all the rest of us wanted to give up. It was his belief in God and his faithfulness in teaching all of us that had resulted in our being saved. There was no telling how he would react to this level of disrespect and humiliation from his own flesh and blood. I determined that I wouldn't worry about it now. I wished I could go back and undo what Canaan had done, but I couldn't. It was better to keep myself busy.

I reached down and grasped a wooden mallet from the tool box. I had a little more reinforcing to install. Soon I would need Shem's help as it would be time to climb the mast and attach the sail. I didn't yet know what this would be, but for now, I envisioned many hides sewn together into a solid, rectangular sheet.

I looked up the length of the mast and imagined that the fluffy white clouds were obscured by a sail. With my head back, I closed my eyes and for a moment was back on the ark. I swayed as I recalled the gentle movements of that massive vessel in the waters. There had been so many times where I couldn't wait to be off that ark and back on dry land. But the good days-- the clear days with favorable winds-- had done something to me. Now I couldn't wait to be on the water again.

I looked back at the mallet and turned it in my hand a few times. I began to whistle and went to work.

CHAPTER 10

Ham and Adina sat on either side of Canaan. The boy had his arms folded in defiance across his chest. Ham had his head lying on their kitchen table. Adina, her back turned to them both, covered her eyes with her hand. No one had spoken for over half an hour. She had asked every question that she could think of. All of them began with the word "why". No matter what she asked, not a single sufficient answer had been given. There could be no good explanation for an act so senseless.

They sat there for a long while in silence, when suddenly their eldest son Cush, now eighteen, burst into the door. He was out of breath and red faced as he barged into the room.

"What is it now?" Ham asked. He was clearly very irritated, and Adina wondered for a moment if his irritation was with Cush, Canaan, or with himself.

"Grandfather is coming down here," Cush said with a slight twinge of fear in his voice.

"Grandma tried to calm him down but he won't listen to her. I have never seen him like this. He left in such a hurry he…"

"CANAAN!"

Hearing the strong, booming voice from his father, Ham was instantly taken back to a time when he had stood in the large crowds in the city and listened to his father preach powerfully, warning the people of God's coming wrath. Ham had not heard this power in his father's voice since then. Though Noah was hundreds of years older than Ham, the tone in the old man's voice frightened him.

"Canaan, where are you hiding?" Noah shouted again.

Ham looked up at Adina. Neither of them knew what to expect.

"He has to face him," Adina said. "Maybe if he apologizes and begs for forgiveness…."

"I'm not sorry," Canaan spat indignantly.

At that Adina pulled the boy up by one arm and dragged him from his chair. Ham hung his head as he followed behind meekly.

Noah wheeled around to face the trio as they emerged from their door, his eyes shooting fire. A good distance to his left stood Sapphira, a look of anger and fear upon her face. Prisca and Tamara stood behind her. In the distance Shem ran toward them.

"Dear Father, all respect is due you," Adina began.

Noah appeared not to hear or see her but instead stretched his right hand toward Canaan. His open hand shook, but not because of his age. There was a power emanating from him that all around could sense. Without realizing it, Adina pulled her collar tight around her throat and looked at the ground. All the color drained from Ham's face, and he yearned to just simply disappear.

Adina tried again, but she couldn't look Noah in the eye. "Father please, the boy…"

"Cursed be Canaan," Noah's voice stopped Adina's words in her throat. "A servant of servants he shall be to his brothers."

Canaan's eyes rolled back into his head and he fainted. By the time Adina and Ham kneeled beside him he was already starting to awaken.

At that moment Shem arrived and stood next to Sapphira. He had heard his father's words and was as stunned as the rest of them. Shem realized more than anyone else that his father was now speaking under the authority of God. Noah heard Shem approach and now turned to face him. His hand was still outstretched.

"Blessed be the Lord, the God of Shem. Let Canaan be his servant. May God enlarge Japheth. And let him dwell in the tents of Shem. And let Canaan be his servant." As soon as he finished these words, Noah's hands dropped to his side. His eyes still ablaze, he turned and walked up the trail that led out into the wilderness.

Everyone stared in his direction. They were all dumbstruck. No one dared speak or even make any movement. Any prior concerns about Noah's ongoing capability and authority to lead had just been dispelled in an instant. Much of the family had gathered now and each member watched Noah fade into the distance.

The older generation had been reminded; the younger generation had just been educated. This elderly man was more than just Dad, more than just Grandpa. This man who had laughed with them, played with them, worked alongside them, supped with them, and for the first time failed in front of them, was one of the most powerful men of God who had ever walked the earth.

CHAPTER 11

Shem, Japheth and their elder sons, along with Cush and Mizraim, the two eldest sons of Ham, had packed a cold supper and headed out away from the farm. There was to be no large family meal tonight. Each family had retired to their homes very early. Sapphira had followed Noah away from the farm at a distance. No one knew where they had gone or when they would return, but no one was concerned for their safety either. None yet realized the everlasting consequences of Canaan's curse.

"I fear for the wolf that would try to attack those two with the mood they're in," Shem commented as they walked.

"Even if they were attacked," Japheth added, "the poor beast would break its teeth trying to bite either one of them."

It wasn't intended as an insult but rather a point of honor. All in the group accepted it as such and would have otherwise laughed, but there was an uncertainty in the air on this night that none of the young men had ever experienced. Shem and Japheth were another story. Both were concerned, but their faith had been tested before.

"Don't worry, lads. No matter how this turns out, God will see us through," Shem said to his sons Elam and Arphaxad. He had noticed the look on their faces as they walked along and came up beside him. They were fine strong boys, and becoming fine men. Shem knew they would do some growing in the coming days. At the time he could never have known just how much.

"Dad," said Elam, Shem's firstborn. "I never particularly got along with Canaan." He gave an apologetic glance to Canaan's older brother, Cush. "And it hurts me to know what he did to Grandpa. But the thought of him being cursed hurts even more."

"Your kind to say that," Cush replied. "But as his brother I can tell you there is a side to Canaan that you have yet to see. He disturbs me, and at times he nearly makes my skin crawl."

"In some ways I almost feel this was inevitable," Gomer spoke now. "I hate to say it but it almost seems he was destined for this."

Japheth spoke up. "Well, I know it is difficult not to think about such a thing. Yet, there is nothing any of us can do tonight to undo what has happened. In fact, only your Grandfather, with God's guidance, has the authority to ever undo the curse. For now let's just try to enjoy some fellowship. You boys are going to lead this family very soon. We wanted to bring you out away from everything that has been going on and have a chance to just fellowship as men."

Shem forced himself to smile. "Yes, we can call it the first meeting of the family leadership council." At this, he put one arm around Elam and the other around Arphaxad, and the two brothers smiled back weakly.

Originally this outing had been planned for fathers and their eldest sons, but as it turned out, Ham was in no mind to do much of anything, so he didn't come. Shem and Japheth made sure to encourage their nephews, Cush and Mizraim, to come along anyway. They needed a break from their house. Likewise, Shem made sure that his middle son, Arphaxad, came along. The opportunity to go out and spend time with these men and older boys was a great thrill for him.

"This is the spot," Japheth said as he tossed his knapsack to the ground. "This is my favorite thinking spot."

It was the same hilltop where he had sat and comforted Mareyea just a week prior. Only now the view was quite a bit different. The night sky was as clear as crystal, revealing a countless number of stars. The surface of the lake was like a grand mirror with not a ripple across the surface to break up the reflection of the heavens.

Japheth lay on his back using his knapsack for a crude pillow. One by one the others joined him. They lay there for a long while, each lost in their own thoughts.

"Do you see that star there?" Japheth sat up and pointed to the northern horizon. "If you watch long enough you will notice that star never moves. All the other stars around it gradually move throughout the night in sort of a circle. Not that one--it always stays in that one position."

"How in the world did you know that?" Shem asked.

"Lots of observation," Japheth answered. "Many a night when we were on the ark and I couldn't sleep, I would sit at the window and watch the stars. By lying on my back like this, and using the window sill as a straight edge against that one star, I could get some idea of how much we had traveled."

"Interesting, Dad," Gomer said. "But I'm not sure you will ever use that knowledge again."

"Oh, you can rest assured I will use it," Japheth answered. "Someday that star is going to guide me across that great lake. I am going to see a new land that no one else has ever seen or set foot on, at least not since before the flood."

"Ah, my brother is plotting another one of his great voyages," Shem said with a touch of sarcasm. "Are you ever going to give up the dream of having your own boat? You have been talking about that since we first saw land in the distance when we were still on the ark."

Japheth lay back down and smiled up at the sky, knowing his brother Shem had no idea how close he truly was to sailing his boat. "No, you can rest assured that I'm not quite ready to give up on that dream yet."

"Are you going to take us with you, Dad?" Gomer asked.

"You had better believe it. That is, assuming you and your brothers want to go. In fact, I plan on taking your sisters and your mother as well."

"I am sure everyone will want to go," Gomer answered.

"Not that anybody has invited me," Cush interjected. "But I think I would just as soon stick around here and keep both feet on dry land.

Everyone laughed at this, relieved to hear a bit of humor from the boy whose family had been through such a difficult couple of days. As the laughter died down, everyone sat quietly for a time.

Finally, Shem spoke again.

"Men, your Uncle Japheth has given us a wonderful lesson tonight."

Japheth leaned up on one elbow and looked at his brother with surprised. "Thank you, Shem," he said. He was clearly gratified by the recognition.

"You're welcome. And no, I am not kidding you. I really mean it. But I don't mean just in finding our way in your dream boat. Guys, the way your Uncle Japheth is going to keep his eye on that star is the same way that we all must keep our eyes on Almighty God."

Everyone looked to Shem. Some sat up; others just turned their heads to face him.

"That's right. God in our lives is just like that star. He is always there. He is always the same. He never changes. Japheth, no matter how rough the waters become, as long as you can find that star and focus on it, you can find your way. Isn't that what you are saying?"

"Yes," Japheth answered, "I think you could. In fact I am almost certain of it."

"You see," Shem continued. "God is like that for our family. God brought us through the flood and to this bountiful, beautiful valley. And it is my sense that we are about to enter very rough waters once again. I don't mean literal waters, but rough times in all of our lives. I just have a strong sense that what Canaan has done is just the start of an all-out attack on our family by the same evil forces that consumed the world before the flood."

Shem stood up now and looked around at the group. Japheth sat fully upright. Now that he saw where Shem was going with his analogy, he felt a lump in his throat.

"But men, it doesn't matter. Remember this, no matter what happens, if we keep our eyes and our focus upon Him, we will make it through. This family was spared from the flood and God will not allow any forces of darkness to destroy us now. It *is* going to get dark. It is going to get difficult. Just remember what Grandpa has taught us about Him," Shem pointed towards the heavens. "Be obedient to Him, focus on Him, and we will lead this family through."

No one spoke. Then suddenly Arphaxad got up, went to his Dad, and hugged him tightly. Soon everyone was on their feet and hugging one another. They stood and looked back toward the faint lights of their homes. They placed their arms around each other's shoulders, forming a long line of the descendants of Noah.

CHAPTER 12

Noah sat down heavily on a smooth stone. He had been so lost in his own thoughts, he had not even noticed his wife, his dearest confidant, following him. She hadn't wanted to be noticed. Instead she had remained quiet and followed at a respectful distance, sensing that her husband first needed time to calm himself, and then he would need her. When she saw him plop down on the boulder, she knew her time had arrived.

Noah heard the sound of sandals upon pebbles and knew without looking up that it would be his wife coming. It was fully dark but the moon was bright, making the path visible.

"You shouldn't be way out here this late. The woods are no place for a woman at night," Noah said without looking up.

"The woods are no place for an old man anytime when he has to walk up these hills." Sapphira puffed out her cheeks and sat down as heavily as Noah had, only with more flair and drama. As she did so she kept watch upon Noah out of the corner of her eye. She and Noah had been married for hundreds of years.

No one knew him any better. Yet, Sapphira could not ever recall seeing her husband as she had when he cursed Canaan just hours before. At this time, even she was unsure if she could get away with her little joke. Finally she saw Noah's shoulders rise as he breathed out a chuckle. At that, Sapphira relaxed just a bit.

"You seem pretty winded yourself, old woman," Noah said with a chuckle of his own. He was barely speaking above a whisper.

Sapphira was indeed winded. It had taken a great deal of her remaining strength and stamina to keep up with Noah as he walked down the trail. Suddenly, she decided to speak seriously.

"Noah, I know how upset you must…"

Noah stopped her cold by holding up his hand. His brow furrowed and he looked at her, a hint of the former intensity coming back to his eyes.

"Not yet. I am not ready to speak about this. Not even with you."

Sapphira started to say more but then decided against it and sighed deeply. She wasn't planning on asking for mercy toward Canaan; she wasn't so sure that her grandson deserved that. She only wanted to reiterate her love and support for her husband. Now instead of telling him, she decided to just show him.

She ran an arm through his and laid her head on his shoulder. In that moment, neither of them felt any differently than they had as a young couple. For a long while Noah didn't respond, then, suddenly, he turned on the boulder where he was sitting and threw his arms around his wife.

With his chin resting on top of her head he said, "Sapphira, I am so very tired. I am not sure I want to go back. I am not sure that I can."

Sapphira didn't have to ask what he meant. She had been feeling the same way. She was experiencing a level of fatigue that she had never experienced before. She was beyond tired.

"Noah?" she asked. "Has God shown you how many years we have left?"

"No, my dear, he hasn't," Noah answered. "But we both know we are in the twilight of our lives."

Noah looked up with a start. He cupped his wife's chin in his hand and turned her face toward his. He had known this fact for a long time but it was startling just the same to say it aloud to the woman he had loved his entire life.

"I cannot believe you have sensed it too," he said "I didn't want to say anything…I…I have felt it for some time, this feeling of just wanting to stop and rest. I started sensing it for weeks before everything happened with Canaan. Ever since I went walking tonight, after I began to calm down some, I actually prayed that God would take me home soon."

"It hurts to hear you say it," Sapphira replied. "Yet at the same time I understand why you would feel this way. It isn't just the physical fatigue. The Lord knows we have had a hard life, but after a lifetime of striving and struggling, you are almost too weary to continue. I know because I have had many days like this myself."

With this she placed her hands on Noah's cheeks. She felt the familiar scratchiness of his snow white beard on her palms.

"It should never have happened to one who has tried so hard to serve God and to always be obedient. You didn't deserve such a thing from your own grandson. The entire family feels the same way."

"It isn't just that," Noah began. "I just don't feel that I can bear up under the weight of leading this family much longer."

The patriarch fell silent for a time, then stood and looked into the night sky. He didn't know it but he was watching the same star that Japheth and the others were as they lay on a distant hill.

"Do you know what I would like to do just once more?" Noah suddenly asked.

"No. What?"

"I would like to see the ark again."

Sapphira raised her head from Noah's shoulder and turned to face him.

"Neither of us has been back to the ark since we moved the tents into the valley. It was just a few weeks after we landed."

"Yes, I know," Noah replied. "That is precisely the reason I want to go there. And I want to go there now."

"Oh you do? Well, husband, do you also remember why we haven't returned to that site? It happens to be very near the top of a large mountain. Shem and Japheth would not want us to attempt that climb at our ages."

Noah looked around and swept his hand in an arc indicating the surrounding area. "I don't see Shem or Japheth anywhere nearby. There is a reason I walked in this direction. Just up that way," Noah pointed toward a faint trail uphill from where they now sat that passed between two large boulders, "is the route that would take us to the ark. Remember, it is not a particularly treacherous climb. It is just…well… a little uphill. Our daughters and the grandchildren showed us that the entire ark is now exposed from melted snow. It is the first time that most of it has been uncovered in years. Who knows if we will ever have this kind of opportunity again in our lifetimes? "

Sapphira smacked Noah on the shoulder, "A little uphill? Why, it is likely both our hearts will stop from the effort before we get halfway!"

"And so what if they do?" The fire blazed briefly in Noah's eyes. "I would rather die climbing the mountain to get back to a place where I regularly talked with Almighty God than to wither away down here being tended to by my children like an old toothless dog. They mean no harm by it but I don't like the patronizing way they look at me, as if they feel sorry for me. And that will only get worse now…now that all this has happened with Canaan."

"No, I don't think it will get worse. In fact, after the impression you made tonight, I think it will get significantly better."

Sapphira had many other valid arguments to make but as she looked into Noah's eyes she knew that any arguments to the contrary were futile. This was the man who defied the whole world in his determination and dedication to follow and obey God. This was the man who mounted timbers on the ark all alone at a time when his own sons doubted his sanity. This was the man who preached righteousness to an unhearing populace, even after they repeatedly rejected him even to the point of physically beating him. His mind was now made up to attempt this thing, and he would do it - or he would die trying.

Again Sapphira took Noah's face in both her hands. "Noah, look into my eyes. I will answer you the way I have always answered you. If you are going, I will go with you."

Noah covered her hands with his and leaned forward until their foreheads were touching. The night was clear and pleasant without the touch of chill that had been present on prior nights.

Noah stood, "Come, we shall make a bed here among the pine boughs. I will cover us with my cloak, and we can snuggle together for warmth," he winked. He was clearly exuberant about her choice. He continued.

"In the morning we will enjoy a breakfast of berries and spring water and then begin our climb. We can take all the breaks we need. We will be at the door of the ark well before nightfall."

Later, as they snuggled together, Sapphira had a moment of genuine fear. It was only a moment. For as fear began to grip her, so too did the hands of the man who had led her and her children to safety against all odds. Noah had led her into a relationship with Holy God that she had never dreamed possible when she was a young woman. Through that relationship she had enjoyed a rich and full life that truly began on the ark, and had continued until just the day before. Canaan's sin had once again brought her face to face with an old familiar darkness around her.

CHAPTER 13

None of us was concerned when we returned home from watching the stars and discovered that our parents were still not home. Earlier that day Canaan had been cursed by my father. Now he was missing and so were my mother and father. Canaan was young and could easily survive as tonight was the warmest we had experienced in some time. And quite frankly, none of us were too concerned about him right now anyway. We were still too angry with him. My parents were another matter. Staying out late together in prayer or deep thought didn't cause us too much concern. But when the next morning arrived and they still were not in their beds, we became genuinely worried.

I was returning from checking on their tent when I met Shem at the outdoor fireplace.

"I know they haven't been home, I just checked there myself a few minutes ago," Shem said, anticipating what I was about to share.

"We had better begin searching for them," I replied. "We should have everyone join us."

"Everyone, perhaps, except Ham and Adina. They have enough to deal with in their own family," Shem said.

I only nodded in agreement, and we separated to gather everyone together.

***

Noah drove his staff into a crack in the rocks and used it to gain a better foothold as he took another difficult step. He reached a flat spot where his footing was secure. He then turned and held the staff out for Sapphira to use as a handhold as he pulled her up alongside him. Both of them were out of breath.

"Time for another break," he said as he offered her a drink of spring water from a bag strapped across his shoulder.

"How much further," Sapphira asked for what seemed like the hundredth time.

"Darling, I have told you I am not certain. My recollection is that it is just…"

As Noah turned to point up the mountain he caught a glimpse of something. He was unsure at first and then he realized that he wasn't imagining things. He was now looking at the dark, pitch covered gopher wood that made up the roof atop the ark.

"Sapphira, we have made it," was all he said. Then Sapphira's eyes followed his until she too could see the roof still far above them in the distance. The site caused both of them to forget all about taking another break. Without another word, they simultaneously began to scramble further upward. It was almost as if it were a race as they each felt the rush of adrenaline in their blood. Then, after what seemed like just a few moments, they were standing at the end of the ramp, chests heaving. They looked up into semi-darkness, into the confines of the divinely inspired vessel that had been the whole world to them for an entire year. Once again they were on the verge of entering the ark.

CHAPTER 14

"I know I saw Grandpa heading this way yesterday," Arphaxad said.

"And I saw Mother following him," Tamara called from behind me.

"Look here," Cush called out as he knelt and smoothed some leaves gently away from the sand. "Look to the right of the trail. Aren't these impressions from the end of a staff? And here in the dust is a footprint. Grandpa did come this way."

"He came this way alright," Gomer called. "Look here on these boulders." He then held up his palm which contained a few berries.

"Do you all realize what this is?" I asked as I continued to look around. "This is the junction in the trail that leads up to the ark. And these footprints are heading right up the mountain."

***

Noah walked up the ramp carefully. The pitch had preserved the wood somewhat but some of the planks felt a bit crumbly underfoot. Once at the top of the ramp, Noah breathed in deeply, and with Sapphira leaning heavily against his back, he stepped inside. They had no torch but some of the shutters were still open and the boards that had been removed from the hull allowed a decent amount of light to come inside. Snow left over from the winter and out of the reach of the sun's rays still filled some corners along the starboard wall.

"Let's go to the ladder," Noah whispered, unsure why he was speaking so quietly. "I want to see the view from our old spot at the upstairs window."

They shuffled their feet along the floor, still unsure of their footing. Suddenly, as they entered the darker passage that would lead to the living quarters and the ladder, they noticed a musky smell. Before either of them could inquire as to the source of the odor, they were paralyzed in their tracks by a roar.

***

"Japheth, surely you don't think they tried to make it up to the ark?" Prisca asked. "Why would they? Why would they take that chance?"

"I cannot answer as to their motives," I replied. "But there is no denying that they went this way." I spotted a fragment of rough woven cloth on a thistle. I held it up for all to see.

"That's a piece of Grandpa's old cloak!" Elam exclaimed.

***

Sapphira screamed and buried her face in Noah's back as she saw the outline of a huge bear rising up on its powerful hind legs.

"No...no," Noah said gently. "We only startled her, she means us no harm." To Sapphira's amazement, Noah stepped forward and reached his hand out toward the bear. Sapphira gasped.

"Not to worry," Noah spoke as if he was talking to a toddler. "She will realize in a moment that it is me. We just frightened her."

Sapphira then realized that the bear had not growled a second time. Still, her eyes were so wide with fear that she felt they would pop out of her head. In the years since they had been on the ark, the non-domestic animals had grown more and more wild. On her own, she would have never dreamed of approaching a predator in this manner.

The bear now settled down on all fours as Noah continued to ease toward it.

"There now, that's a girl," he said as he actually reached out and began to scratch the bear around its ears.

"Dear Lord," Sapphira breathed. "I didn't think any of us could still approach a wild animal like we did in the old days."

"No one else could have but she knows me. They all know me." Noah replied. He was kneeling by the bear's massive head now and smiling. It grunted affectionately while Noah wrapped his arms around her neck and hugged her.

"Have you seen this bear before?" Sapphira asked, still stunned.

"No, never."

"Then how does she know you?"

"It was passed down from her mother I suppose. The animals know God used me as their help. I mostly avoid them. They need their fear of man. But when I choose I can still communicate with them. It is a gift that God has never removed from me. Come around here. She has cubs. She will call them in a moment and you can play with them."

At almost that same instant, the bear growled a deep but gentle growl, and from further down the passageway came the squeals of two cubs.

"Yes, you all have a nice warm den here in the ark don't you?" Noah asked. "Well you are most welcome to it. We won't disturb you for long."

"I didn't realize how much I missed playing with the animals and cuddling them," Sapphira said as she tussled with the front paws of one of the cubs.

"You held their great grandfather," Noah said as he nodded towards the cubs that were now thoroughly enjoying wrestling with Sapphira.

After a few moments of interaction the mother bear growled a little louder and ambled to the ramp. She stopped at the top of the ramp, looked over her shoulder, and called her cubs to her, but the two continued to be engrossed in their play. Sapphira stood so as to encourage them to follow, but it was too late. The mother bear turned back and firmly cuffed the nearest cub with her large front paw. She called the cubs a third time and they fell in line behind her obediently.

"Come, my dear," Noah held out his hand. Let us go and sit by our window."

***

I couldn't run another step. I was pushing myself so hard trying to catch my mother and father that I felt like my lungs were on fire.

"Uncle Japheth," Arphaxad called out. "We have to catch up to them soon before something tragic happens. If we are this out of breath from the climb they must surely be on the verge of collapse."

"They have several hours head start on us, son." Shem had caught up to them now. "They didn't have to push this hard. Don't underestimate them. They just might have already made it to the top.

***

The ladder that led up to what had once served as the families observation platform while the ark was underway had fallen into bad shape. Several rungs were missing so that Sapphira had difficulty making it to the top, even with Noah's help. Once there, Noah realized that the benches were missing. They had long ago been taken to their current homes. In fact, one of them was alongside the table in Noah's tent even now.

"With the planks missing that were removed from the hull for use as building materials, I think we can sit right on the floor here and have a good view," Noah began.

"Oh, Noah," Sapphira explained. "Look, we can see the entire valley and all our homes from here. Look! I can't tell who that is but there are some of the children playing."

"Yes…I can just barely make them out from here," Noah replied, squinting. "Sapphira, you are shaking."

"I think that climb up the ladder may have been the last straw," Sapphira agreed. "I had better sit down for a moment. You don't look well yourself, old man. You had better sit too."

"Nonsense, I feel invigorated by our little adventure. But just to ease *your* mind I will sit with you."

The two sat again, quiet for a long while. Then Sapphira once again leaned her head on Noah's chest. She could hear his heart pounding from the physical exertion.

"I think all this exercise has done something to you, Noah," she said, rising up to look him in the eye. "Your heart seems as strong as ever."

Noah cupped her head and pushed her gently back to his side. "That is the way my heart always races whenever I am near you. You should know that by now."

The two relaxed again for a few moments. Then Sapphira said, "Noah, do you think our great--great grandchildren will ever know all that happened on this ark and by this window?"

"My darling, I think someone will be reading or talking about what happened on this ark for hundreds of years to come, maybe even thousands."

"Truly?" Sapphira replied.

"Yes, I truly do."

Silence broken only by the sound of breathing filled the air for a time, and for a moment Sapphira thought Noah had fallen asleep.

"I didn't know, Noah," Sapphira blurted out. "I didn't know whether I could believe in you or not. I am sorry to admit that, but I looked out this same window before the flood and doubted you. I looked out on dry ground and wondered if it would ever really rain. Then later when I looked out at nothing but water, I doubted yet again.

For months and months and months I saw all that water and wondered if I would ever again see dry ground. I doubted you and at times I doubted God. I'm sorry now, Noah. I just want to give you the pleasure of hearing me say…you were right. You saved my life and the life of our children. You made the lives of our grandchildren possible."

"Now, now," Noah stopped her. "You mustn't give me credit for things done by God. I was merely a messenger, that's all."

"Perhaps," Sapphira acknowledged. "But you were also a builder, a preacher, an encourager and when needed, a taskmaster. Maybe I give you too much credit but you don't give yourself enough. I am just so sorry for the times I doubted you, and the things I thought about you at times."

"That is not important to me at all, my dear. What is much more important and meaningful is that you never let me go. You never gave up on me. You have always been with me. That is what I choose to dwell on. And that is the definition of courage, and faithfulness. That is the epitome of love: to keep on showing love and support even when you don't always feel it. You showed me that kind of love, my darling."

"I love you, Noah. I love you more now than when we were newlyweds." Sapphira wrapped both arms around Noah and hugged him tightly.

"I love you too, Sapphira," Noah replied with a hug of his own.

"We did make it, didn't we?" Sapphira asked, her head again resting on Noah's chest. "We made it to the place God planned for us."

"Almost, we're almost there," was Noah's only answer.

***

By the time we reached the door of the ark it was nearly dusk. With no hesitation we ran up the ramp.

"Watch your footing, everyone," Elam called back over his shoulder. In their youth, Elam, Gomer and Cush had outrun Shem and I by quite a distance. Tamara had stopped with young Arphaxad further down the mountain, unable to keep up with our pace. As Shem and I approached the ramp, we were dripping with sweat and nearly sick at our stomachs from climbing so fast. We could hear the boy's racing throughout the ark calling their grandparents. Then we heard someone Elam call out to the others that he was climbing up the ladder.

A moment later we heard him cry out, "Grandpa, Grandma, no!"

By the time Shem and I made it to the top of the ladder all three boys were in tears. Gomer had his hand on my father's forehead for a second before he jerked his hand back. I didn't need to look closer. I knew they were gone.

This could not be. They were very old to be sure but they had both been in excellent health. I looked over at Shem whose face showed that he was as shocked as I.

"Do you suppose the climb was too much for them?" I asked.

Shem didn't speak for a long time. It appeared that he couldn't. Then he dropped slowly to both knees beside my mother and placed his hand on her forehead.

"The climb may have been part of it, but look at them, Japheth. They died in each other's arms. I think they wanted it this way, in this place. Once again they chose the ark to embark upon the most important journey of all."

Suddenly my father sat bolt upright. When he did, our mother blurted out, "I'll get the children!"

Both of them looked around as if they were unsure of where they were for a moment. After blinking several times they frowned up at us.

"Shem, Japheth, Cush…what on earth are you boys doing up here bothering us. Can't you see I was trying to have a little privacy with your grandmother!"

"Noah," my mother said, her face now flushing crimson. She pulled her cloak up tightly around her neck. She continued, "You boys didn't have to come all the way up here. We were going to come down soon anyway."

For our part, Shem and I were almost angry at being put through all this worry, but instead we found ourselves relieved. The smiles on the faces of the teenagers soon became infectious.

"Well, we didn't exactly want to climb up this mountain again just for the fun of it," Shem said, stifling a chuckle.

"We thought you might be in danger. And judging by how deeply you were sleeping you may have soon been in danger. It will get much colder up here at night than it does in the valley."

Dad was still more than a little miffed that we had spoiled his little getaway. He had managed to get stiffly to his feet now and was clearly using his staff to stand a little more erect than normal, shoulders back, chest thrust forward.

"Well of course I was in a deep sleep, boy! I will thank you to remember that I am over six hundred years old and I just climbed a mountain."

Without another word, he brushed past me and headed for the ladder.

"Grandpa, where are you going in such a hurry?" Gomer asked while covering his smile with one hand.

"Why, I am walking home of course. You all have ruined the whole mood here."

I looked over at my mother who was only shaking her head from side to side and smiling to herself. She thrust her chin in Dad's direction, "Boys, go and help your Grandpa down the ladder. His knees are sure to be stiff."

"I heard that," Dad called, still not having descended past the top rung. "I built this ladder, I cut the logs for the runners and rungs and drug them to the ark and put them together while these boys' daddies played children's games in the fields. I can assure you I do not need their help to climb down. Why, I will climb down it and come back up again three times if I care too."

"We know you could if you wanted to Grandpa." Elam said. "It just makes us feel better if you let us help. Here, let me go down first then Cush and Gomer can help from up here."

"Well, I suppose if it makes you feel better," Dad said.

By the time we all got outside the ark, Tamara, Arphaxad and the others had caught up to us. We were all too tired to make the climb back down the mountain that night so we decided we would camp right here at the ark. As we had departed from home to search for my parents, several of us had hastily placed some food and water in rucksacks in preparation for a long day's walk. We all combined our meager provisions and came up with a passable supper. Scraps of lumber and downed trees provided ample firewood, and we soon had a roaring bonfire going.

Once again we found ourselves gathered around a fire lost in thought. So much had transpired in the past two days that we hadn't had time to get our minds around it. Likewise, none of us was certain what Dad was thinking about Canaan and the curse. We were all uneasy, I was certain of that. It was not just that we felt bad for Ham and Adina. We were afraid for ourselves. All of us who lived in the pre-flood times knew darkness. We were all too well acquainted with evil. Canaan's shameless behavior had contained an element of that darkness. What did that mean for our way of life and our families? We would not have to wonder for long.

CHAPTER 15

"Everyone," Noah said as he stood. His voice was suddenly strong and clear. Though he used his staff to overcome the soreness in his legs, he seemed to stand more upright than at any recent time.

"Please, I have something to say to you all," he continued. "Elam, Cush, Gomer, Arphaxad, all of you young men, have any of you ever wondered why your Grandmother and I continue to live in a tent while all of you have solid homes?"

The boys all stood and stared silently at their grandpa. He spoke with a power and authority that none of them had heard from him in their young lives. They suddenly found themselves too intimidated to give an answer. Noah sensed this.

"No, no...speak up. You may give an honest answer."

"Yes, I have wondered," Cush and Elam said at almost the same time. Then they smiled at one another.

"I have wondered as well, Dad," Shem said. "In fact, I have asked you about it on more than one occasion but you never really answered."

"Yes, yes, I know you have son, and the Lord knows that your mother has wanted a home with walls and shuttered windows, eh Sapphira?" Noah winked at his wife. Sapphira only sat and smiled knowingly as she reclined with an arm around Arphaxad. The adults sensed that she and Noah had had this conversation before.

"Boys, before you were born, your parents, your Grandma and I knelt just over there by that pile of stones. Though it may look like just a pile of stones to you, it is actually an altar to Holy God we made years ago. It was a pleasing altar to Him. And on the day we all knelt before Him, He made a covenant with us. On that day, for the one and only time, not only did I hear his audible voice, but your fathers and mothers heard Him as well."

The teens looked around the fire at their parents, Cush looking at his Uncle Shem. They in turn returned a smile and a nod of assurance.

"Shem," Noah pointed toward his eldest son. "What did God say that day?"

"He said many things Dad, I am not sure which you are asking me about. He gave us authority over the animals, permission to eat meat, He…"

"Yes," Noah interrupted. "He did all those things. But there was only one thing that he said twice."

Noah's face was lit by the orange glow of the flames. Despite his very difficult hike and a poor night's sleep the night before, he was becoming animated and clearly enthused. Everyone gathered there was beginning to feed off his energy, but none was sure of the answer to his question.

"He told us to fill the earth. He told us to populate the earth," Noah said, answering his own question. "Be fruitful and fill the earth."

The elder man was walking around the fire now, making eye contact with each family member. He was in his element once again. Noah was born a consummate story teller, teacher and preacher of righteousness. It had been a long time since any of the family had seen this side of him. It had been too long. They leaned closer to the fire, waiting for whatever came next.

"Children," Noah continued with affection, "the valley is not our permanent home. It was never intended to be that."

Almost everyone around the fire, with the exception of Sapphira, began to shift about uneasily now.

"I know," Noah said. "You love your homes here. We have lived a kind of perfect life here. No one has been sick. Our crops have been abundant, our livestock prolific, and our vineyards and orchards have excelled. With the exception of Canaan, the rest of us have gotten along marvelously and become as close as any family could be. All of that is wonderful. It has been a twenty year reward from God for all that we went through. But I believe...I should say, I feel strongly led, that the time has come for us to fulfill our covenant with God."

Shem crooked an elbow over one knee and pulled himself up until he sat with his back straight.

"Father, you have never talked to me about this," Shem looked toward Japheth who returned his brother's gaze and shook his head in agreement.

"You never told any of us," Shem went on. "Now that we have built so much and established our lives in this valley, are you now telling us we must pack up and move once again? Dad, don't you think our voyage on the ark was adventure enough?"

"What I think is not the issue," Noah answered. "What did God say? That is what matters. And no, I have not mentioned it. I wasn't really sure when the time would come. I am not sure this is the time. But I am certain that God wants us to spread out to populate the earth."

"Oh, no!" Prisca exclaimed. "We mustn't split up!"

Shem put an arm around Prisca as if Noah was telling him he had to leave his wife as well. "Dad, it was hard enough to hear when I thought you were just talking about us all leaving the valley together, I never dreamed you meant for us to go our separate ways."

"I don't know that I am saying that." Noah said. "Maybe God will guide us to only split into two groups and branch out. I don't have a clear direction about all the details just yet. And I am not saying that we should begin packing tomorrow. What I am saying is that this entire episode with Canaan cannot be for nothing. God is sovereign over all of us. I believe that he spoke through me when I pronounced...when I ...when I pronounced what I did upon Canaan." Noah struggled with the difficulty of his action but there was no indication that he doubted the action was just.

Japheth had been silent during almost all of the conversation. But his thoughts had rapidly gone tothe boat and his dreams of exploring the far side of the great lake.

"Dad is right," he said. "I have had a similar sense for a long time now. In fact, I can be ready within the month to take my family across the vast lake."

"Japheth, were you going to tell *me* about this?" Tamara asked incredulously.

"Of course I was, in due time," he answered.

"I think we are all being very rash here" Shem said. "Dad, I heard God's voice that day too. And I have never had the sense that He meant anything other than to raise many fine strong children in the admonition of the Lord. We can do that right here in this valley."

"As I said at the beginning," Noah replied. "We don't need to run home and begin packing. For now we only need to open our hearts to the possibility that God meant exactly what I interpreted from what He said - that we must spread out and populate the earth," Noah looked at Shem who only stared intently at the fire.

As the eldest son, Shem had become the de facto leader of the family at times when Noah could not fill that role. Yet even he was most uncomfortable interpreting anything God had said differently than his father.

"In the morning," Noah continued, "we can take our time making it back down to our homes and we can resume our lives as much as possible in light of the new circumstances with Canaan. But we must watch. We must listen with a renewed vigor for a sign from God. For something tells me that He will make His wishes very clear to us all."

Shem let his hand slide gently down Prisca's back and then rested his hand on the ground. He turned and looked back at the altar. "You know, Dad, it would only take a few minutes for a group this big to get that altar into shape. Perhaps this would be the perfect time for us all to talk to God as a family. We can ask Him for guidance in this."

Everyone immediately thought Shem's idea was inspired. They quickly lit two torches that they had brought with them and went to work on the altar. In a short while, Noah and Sapphira, two of their sons and daughters-in-law, and their eldest grandsons, knelt there. As the family had many years prior, they sought guidance from the Wonderful Counselor. This time, even after much earnest prayer, there was no audible voice, though no one was disappointed. They all believed that in His time, God would show them the way, perhaps in a different way than He had before.

After their prayer time, the torches began to fade and the family moved back over to the fire. The boys added more wood and stoked the fire until all could feel the warmth from the crackling flames hissing over the firewood.

Prisca then began to sing a song of praise. It was a song that Sapphira had taught them all on the ark and one they sang often. Gradually, one by one, everyone joined in. Most sang softly, content to let Prisca's lovely voice be the lead. They continued in that spirit of fellowship and togetherness until the fire began to burn down to glowing coals, and one by one, they drifted off to sleep.

CHAPTER 16

Despite everything, despite all that he had done, he was still her son. Adina was heartbroken by what Canaan had done to Noah. It was more than that really. She was crushed. She knew Canaan had problems. She knew how Canaan rejected all of her teachings about God and the love He had for Canaan. She knew how he had refused to embrace the teachings of Noah and his uncles.

Yet, never in her worst nightmare had she contemplated that he would conduct such premeditated evil as this. And of all the people in the family to do it to, he had chosen Noah. On the rare occasions when even Ham lost patience with Canaan, it was Noah who took up for him, supported him, and held out the most hope for him.

She approached her son as he sat on the side of a steep cliff. After Canaan missed the search for his grandparents, Adina determined she must find him. Ham was too dejected to help her so she had struck out on her own and looked for hours here in the high ground. She knew he would be here somewhere, for this was where he often came and sat in silence. He came to this spot where, unbeknownst to him, the first rainbow had once terminated.

There was a portal here, unseen by both Adina and Canaan. Likewise, neither of them knew this was the spot where Satan had descended for a time back into Hell on the day God established His covenant with Noah. None of the family members were aware that the rainbow, and the truth that it represented, had scalded Satan's back as he fled the voice of God on the day of the covenant.

Canaan had no conscious idea of what attracted him to this spot. Sometimes while sitting here, he could almost hear voices but their words were always too faint to understand. He wanted to hear them. He wanted to understand them. He sat with his feet dangling over the side of a steep drop off. It was at least 30 feet to the craggy rocky bottom below.

Adina watched him for a moment from a distance with tears welling in her eyes. Her youngest son was now cursed. He sat there on a long flat stone staring literally into the abyss. When Noah had awakened and found out what Canaan had done, there was a fire in him the likes of which Adina had never witnessed. Noah had pronounced a curse on Canaan not just because his pride was hurt, but because Canaan had brought the enmity from the old world into the new.

Adina approached Canaan slowly. She didn't know what to say to him. He had run away the day before, right after the curse was pronounced. Soon after Canaan left, Ham had gone back outside to work on the olive press. He worked feverishly as if the sweat that poured off his forehead would purge the regret he was feeling. He had been working there when Adina left.

Adina, for her part, had to force herself out of bed each morning. Despite all her efforts to raise Canaan toward righteousness, she felt she was a failure as his mother. She harbored unmerited guilt because of her bloodline. She was acutely aware that it was her line which contained the blood of the evil giant race that had terrorized people in the pre-flood world. She had overcome the urges that such a genealogy attempted to wield upon her by her strong relationship with God. Canaan had never shown that willingness to resist sinful urges. Adina couldn't help but feel that some of that was her fault.

"Canaan." Adina spoke gently as she came along to sit beside her son. She felt chills run up her spine when the stone she sat upon tilted. She looked over the precipice but stayed there just the same in order to be close to Canaan.

"I…I don't know what to say, but I felt I had to come and find you. There is something you need to know."

"It's not fair!" Canaan's deep throated shout startled his mother.

"Son, I hate so much that this has happened to you. But don't let bitterness consume you. Instead look at it as an opportunity to start anew."

"START ANEW?" Canaan was practically screaming now and Adina closed her eyes and cringed.

"Do you think I want to hear your crap right now? Maybe if you were on my side once in a while things would never have gone this far."

Adina felt tears running down her cheeks and she cringed at the pain of Canaan's words. How could things have gone so wrong with her son when she had tried so hard to always follow God and teach her children His ways?

"Canaan, you have no idea how much I have been on your side since the day you were born. You have no idea how hard it has been at times to be the only one who will take a stand and try to show you the right path. But right now there is something else you must know."

"I think I am through with hearing you," Canaan declared.

"Canaan, please talk to me before you go," Adina reached for her son's arm.

Canaan wheeled around, fury suddenly in his eyes. "Don't you touch me," he said as he flung his arm toward his mother.

Adina dodged to avoid Canaan's flailing arm and felt the boulder she had been sitting on tilt once again. She lost her balance and reached out an arm to catch herself as she fell. Time seemed to freeze, and she actually had a millisecond to ponder that it would hurt her wrist when the heel of her hand struck the rocky ground. But her hand did not strike the ground. Instead, it kept falling through mid-air, until suddenly her feet were above her head. She had gone over the edge of the precipice.

She flailed wildly. She reached her hands out desperately like claws and managed to grab onto a crevice. The strain on her arm sent shooting pain through both shoulders. Her body flipped and she felt her ribs slam into the rock wall. She was hanging now about a foot below where Canaan stood at the edge, watching her with detached interest.

Canaan's first instinct was to reach out to help but then, curiously, he pulled his hand back. He watched with fascination as his mother reached out for him, but still he made no effort to assist her.

"Canaan, son, grab my hand," Adina cried out. She looked backward and realized in that instant that she would not survive a fall. She looked back toward Canaan but he had moved no closer.

"Canaan, what are you doing! I can't hold on much longer! Please son, help me!"

Canaan squatted now, elbows crooked over his knees, and he as he watched his mother's eyes bulge with fear, he felt a smile curl the corners of his mouth. Then a look of realization crossed Adina's face and in place of abject fear, Canaan though he saw disappointment in her eyes. In another moment, her grip gave way and his mother disappeared over the side. Canaan only jerked his head as he heard a sickening thud arise from the depths of the ravine.

He stood there awhile, unblinking, feeling no emotion. Finally, it struck Canaan as odd that she hadn't uttered a sound. He had never seen anyone die, although he had thought about it often. He always assumed there would be screaming or cries of some sort. "Oh well," Canaan said. It occurred to him that he was quite hungry and Adina had brought a satchel with her. He walked over to it, opened the flap and found fig cakes and fresh water. Fig cakes - his mother knew those were his favorite.

For the first time Canaan felt a tear well in his eye. But the feelings of sadness passed quickly because he stopped himself from thinking about the care his mother took and started concentrating on the cakes. He devoured the first one in just two or three large bites and then swilled the water. Holding the jug of water, he finally walked over to the edge of the cliff, sat the jug down and lay on his belly, looking over the side. She didn't even look hurt. She almost looked like she was sleeping, except that her mouth was gaped open. He couldn't be sure but it almost looked as if she were trying to breath.

Canaan reached over and grabbed a handful of pebbles. He made a game out of trying repeatedly to toss the small stones into Adina's open mouth. Instead the pebbles just kept hitting her in the forehead or on the face, or missing completely. He eventually tired of this game, but not before he saw Adina gasp once very deeply, lift her head up, and then stop breathing. Canaan returned to the satchel for another cake.

After a time, Canaan took a few moments to contemplate what had just happened and how it might affect him. Everyone would find some way to blame him for this too. That much was certain. It was so unfair. Was it his fault that his mother had been clumsy? Sure, he hadn't helped her but he hadn't done anything to her either. He didn't plan any of this. It just happened. And it happened in a moment where he didn't feel much like being helpful. Even now he was still a little angry with his mother for not sticking up for him more.

Finally Canaan got an idea. He sat up and began to smear dirt on his face and smack his cheeks with handfuls of pebbles. He had to look as if he had done everything in his power to save her. He would tear his tunic before beginning the long run back to Ham's house. Once there he would cry frantically for the others to come and save his dear mother's life. He didn't look forward to running that far.

He reluctantly went back to work on his disguise, pausing to stare once more at his mother's now lifeless body. As he did so, he cocked an ear. He could hear the voices clearly, only they weren't speaking now. The rocks all around him seemed filled with the sounds of demented laughter.

***

"We could run over this beautiful hill if you would just stop lying there, staring up at the clouds."

Adina woke with a start, though she wasn't really sure she had been asleep. She seemed to remember looking up a steep cliff at Canaan, but now all she saw was blue sky all around. There was no cliff. Just then it occurred to her that she had heard a familiar voice.

"Afraid to race me, aren't you? One as tall as you should easily be faster than one as short as I. Fine then, we could walk I suppose, though I have found running to be a much more enjoyable way to get to and fro. Not only that, it is also quicker, though I suppose that would go without saying, wouldn't it?" the source of the voice laughed at its own joke. "I am wondering," the voice continued "do you plan to lie there all day?"

Adina had been afraid to look around because was unsure of her surroundings. But only one person she had ever known had such an interesting manner of speech. It was Nayna, the woman who had led her to a relationship with God, but had died just prior to the flood.

Adina couldn't believe her ears. She sat up, leaning on one elbow. At that moment, she remembered her fall. She was shocked to feel no pain whatsoever. In fact, she felt wonderful. She realized, as if slowly awakening from a dream, that Nayna had been dead now for over 20 years. Adina looked around at the breathtaking beauty. Gone were the craggy rocks and dull sand of the ravine. After sitting all the way up, she saw her.

Adina was still too surprised to speak, but Nayna smiled broadly when she saw the recognition on Adina's face. Nayna walked over and took Adina by the hand as the taller woman stood. Nayna swept her hand out to her right, as if preparing to make an introduction. "I have come to lead you to the most beautiful city that has ever existed, my child. It is a city that will stand forever and ever. He wants to see you, you know."

Adina came to her feet and realized she had never moved with such ease before. "Who wants to see me?" she asked tentatively, though she knew who Nayna was referring to.

"Him, that is who," came the answer. "He saw us there, on your roof all those years ago, before the flood, when you were inquiring about Him. He saw you in the ark, too, on the night that you lost your parents. He has been waiting ever since to hold you in his arms. Come, you have worked very hard, it is time for you to receive your reward" Nayna said. She reached for Adina's hand and the pair ran like school girls over the horizon.

CHAPTER 17

I shook my head slowly from side to side as I walked. I didn't even realize I was gritting my teeth until my jaw muscles began to ache. I was on my way to my boat, but even that did not seem like an escape on this day. It is impossible for me to put into words the ripple effect that Canaan's actions against our father had on the entire family.

Eighteen years ago, when the ark landed, we had been afraid. We were afraid for many days to leave the vessel that had been our safe haven for the previous year. We were afraid of what might await us outside, afraid of the unknown. When God finally inspired my father Noah that the time was right to step outside, we began to feel secure. Then, we raised tents in the mountaintop meadow outside the ark. Eventually we migrated down to the fertile valley that was now our home.

Although by that time we were no longer hearing the voice of God audibly, as we had on the day the first rainbow appeared, we often felt that we heard Him in many little ways. We knew He was still with us. Despite the difficult conditions and all the work that had to be done to establish crops and herds, we soon began to realize that God was still providing for us. He was still caring for us. Over the years we had thoroughly embraced our new lives and felt we had nothing to fear. There had been difficult days and many more challenges but there had never been fear.

We had all lived in the old world. Each one of us had seen the evil that was ever present in the city and in the community near our homes. Several in our family had been victims of the violence and abuse ourselves. Dad was beaten on more than one occasion while trying to warn people of the coming flood. Ham was drugged and had to fight for his life. Just prior to boarding the ark, Prisca, Adina and my mother Sapphira were attacked by a mob. Adina's parents were murdered and she herself was the offspring of an attack upon her mother. Tamara was nearly raped and killed; I still gritted my teeth in anger at that thought.

Yes, we were intimately familiar with the way things were in the pre-flood world. That knowledge and experience helped transform us over time from abject grief over those left behind, to a sense of relief that we no longer had to live under a pall of darkness or the threat of an attack. We soon came to take great comfort in that and felt secure enough to put down roots, establish a thriving community, and raise children.

That comfort disappeared in an instant with Canaan's actions against Dad. What Canaan did resounded far beyond just getting drunk and passing out. For him to perpetrate that level of disrespect upon the one man who had led us so valiantly and with such love, was to revisit the evil of the old world we had left. It was the admission of darkness into our valley where we had been allowed to live, for the first time in our lives, in peace and light. And now even Dad was considering breaking up the family. For a long time, I had wanted to sail and explore. But I always assumed that the rest of my family would stay together; that they would be here for me to come back to.

I pondered all of this as I rapidly walked with determined steps in the direction of the boat. I continued to shake my head in near disbelief. I knew Canaan's history. Though many in the family refused to see him for what he was, I had always seen him as a malcontent and troublemaker. That was apparent to me even when he was a small child.

Even with all the persecution and beatings my father had to take when trying to warn others about the flood, he had never once reacted in anger. It had taken the disrespect and ill intent of his own flesh and blood to raise that kind of ire. I sensed that the curse wasn't just an act of vengeance on the part of my Dad. I believe that for the first time he saw in Canaan a type of darkness that was a danger to our future and a threat to hinder our walk with God. There was more to all that had happened than I could fully comprehend.

My mind was in turmoil. I was growing concerned for Adina who had gone looking for her son while we were all still at the ark, and who now, a full twenty four hours later, still hadn't come home. I was worried about my brother Ham and his other children. Despite myself, I was even worried for Canaan. We were all frustrated and angry with what Canaan had done, but he was family and we cared about what happened to him. I had spent all of yesterday and most of today comforting my own wife and children and conferring with Shem over what this all would mean. Was this a sign that it was time to leave the valley?

Neither of us knew. All we knew for certain was that our lives had taken yet another turn.

I stopped walking at that thought. I wanted to escape for a few hours but even work on the boat wouldn't provide that for me now. I was running from the one thing, the one person, who could provide any comfort at all. I had not prayed in days. I didn't understand the reason why myself. Perhaps I was angry that, after all God had brought us through, at a time when we should be enjoying our rewards and blessings, he would let all of this happen. I didn't *feel* angry but I had to admit I couldn't explain my reluctance to pray in any other way. I knew what I needed to do.

I looked to my right and saw a cypress log lying next to a rose hedge with brightly colored red flowers on it. It looked like a ready-made altar. I walked over and got on my knees.

"Dear Lord," I began. "I shall never forget how many times I doubted you, and how in each of those situations you came through. You were always there and always provided for us. So many times when I feared you had abandoned us, as I look back on it now, I realize that you had a plan for us. With all that you brought us through, I know I should not doubt you now. But dear Lord, I must confess that once again I cannot for the life of me see how what has happened with Canaan can be good for any of us or for your glory.

I don't understand what good purpose can be served by this. We have tried to obey you both on the ark and in our lives in the valley. Dad made a mistake in trusting Canaan. Perhaps that was a sin. Dad said we should be spreading out and repopulating the world. Did we commit some sin by putting down roots hear and staying too long? Perhaps we are being punished for that."

As soon as the words came out of my mouth I knew better. The God I had known and sensed throughout my life was not a vindictive God. He was just, merciful, gracious and longsuffering, but never vindictive.

"Lord," I continued. "I simply don't understand, none of us do, why you would bring us through so much to escape evil and sin in the world, only to allow the sin in Canaan's heart to follow us here. Why didn't you protect us? Why didn't you create Canaan to be righteous?"

It was at that moment that I sensed a voice in my head asking, "I created Canaan with a free will, just as you have free will. Canaan uses that free will to make choices that bring great pain to others."

"I praise you for that Lord," I continued to pray as if carrying on a conversation with my father. "I praise you for allowing us the privilege to choose. But why does Canaan have to have sin in his heart instead of goodness?" I asked.

"What about the sin in your own heart? Was all that left behind in the old world as well?"

I was startled at the thought. I sensed I was hearing the still small voice of God rather than my own conscience.

"I still don't understand Lord. What does any of this have to do with me?"

"You were delivered from a world that was completely consumed by sin, but you still exist in this world that has been fallen since your forefather Adam. Sin did not suddenly reappear here, nor did it stowaway upon the ark. The darkness that began with Adam never left. The forces of darkness have never ceased to strive. It will always be so until I come, but until then, I am with you…always."

I suddenly raised my head and opened my eyes. I didn't understand "When you come? Are you going to speak to us again audibly?" I asked aloud. What 'forces of darkness'? I still didn't understand what my heart had to do with Canaan's actions. I waited a moment, then two but I didn't hear the voice again. I bowed again hoping for answers to more of my questions. Just as suddenly as the voice had come into my head, it now appeared to be gone. I squinted my eyes tightly and clasped my hands under my chin, trying hard to bring the voice back, but I heard nothing. Before I could try again, I heard Tamara cry out from afar.

"JAPHETH!"

The cry was distant and faint but the urgency in my wife's voice was startling. Something was terribly wrong. My prayers interrupted, I rose to my feet and looked toward the far horizon. I began to walk and then run in that direction. As I jogged up a little rise, I saw Tamara on her bay horse, Shiloh, in the distance with dust kicking up around his feet. She rode Shiloh at breakneck speed.

When she saw me she pulled Shiloh up short and jumped recklessly off his back. She then ran on foot in my direction. I began to run faster as well though my feet felt heavy, my legs reluctant. I wanted to reach her but then again I was already dreading to hear whatever she was about to tell me. Even from this considerable distance, the look on her face brought my heart into my throat. I had only seen that look one other time. That was on the night the ark first floated away from our home and Tamara heard the cries of her own mother as she drowned just on the outside of the hull.

Now, as we drew closer, Tamara's foot must have caught on a root or something because she fell head over heels, making her seem all the more pitiable. She was trying to get up when I reached her. She placed her hands on my shoulders. I lifted her up gently but she didn't wait until she was on her feet before she blurted out the horrible news.

"Adina," she gasped. "She's…."

"What is it," I implored. "What about Adina."

Her eyes were wild and tears began to stream down her dirty cheeks though it was obvious these were not the first she had shed.

"Oh dear God Japheth, Adina is dead."

CHAPTER 18

Tamara had ridden off to find Japheth mere moments after Canaan came tearing into the encampment, his clothes ripped, his knees and elbows skinned. In an almost surreal way he had been crying out as he approached like a small child. Over and over he cried, "My mommy, my mommy!"

It hadn't made sense, particularly to Sapphira. She had never before heard that term of endearment from Canaan. Sapphira hadn't had time to ponder that for long for the next words from Canaan had shocked her to the point of paralysis.

"My mommy came to help me, and…and she fell. I grabbed her hands and tried to save her but I couldn't hold on. I think she is hurt very badly. She looks like she is asleep."

Everyone except Japheth and Tamara was there. Noah and Shem had declared a day of rest following the day they had descended the mountain. When Canaan approached, most of the family was gathered around the main fireplace at the center of the family compound. There was still some murmuring among the family that perhaps Noah would remove the curse from Canaan. Most were still wondering why Canaan ever started this entire episode with wine and drunkenness. That was, until Canaan erased all thoughts about the past from their minds with this news about Adina.

Those who were sitting began to stand slowly. They looked from one to another with frowns. They had absorbed enough bad news for one week. Their brains were not ready to contemplate this. Ham placed his hands on the sides of his head and twisted his long graying hair into his fists. His teeth clenched. His lips drew back from his teeth in a grimace. He walked away a few steps and then began to stumble.

Shem came to his senses first.

"Where is she now?"

"She's in the mountains, near the precipice where I always go to throw rocks and to think. I needed to think about what grandpa had done to me." Canaan continued to speak in a little boy's voice. His expression was one of a confused child who had been wrongly accused of spilling something. To everyone but Ham, Canaan's voice and countenance seemed out of place in this situation somehow, and it cast doubt upon Canaan's story from the outset. Still, exactly what had happened was irrelevant now.

"How can you think about yourself right now? Tell me where exactly your mother is, we have to get to her. You boys fetch some rope," he said to his sons. "Cush, Gomer, go and fetch the cart, she may not be able to walk, Mother you…"

Shem's voice trailed off. As he looked around Sapphira was already coming back from her tent with the bag in which she kept healing herbs, salves and bandages.

"I don't know if I have the strength to run back up there. I am tired," Canaan began.

Before Canaan could finish Shem was on him and had lifted him by his tunic until the two were at eye level.

"You will find the strength or you will die trying to make it up that mountain. You're the only hope your mother has, don't you see that?"

Canaan did see that. He saw it very clearly. That is why he tarried. He had never climbed down to check to see if Adina was breathing. Now he figured the longer he waited the less likely Adina would be able to tell the others anything with her dying breath.

Shem held the boy like that for a long moment. He couldn't help but visualize wrapping his hands around the boy's scrawny neck and squeezing as hard as he could, but that wouldn't help Adina.

"Phut, go with Arphaxad and Asshur. Run quickly and bring the oxen around, you will need to push them or they will want to tarry. We will immediately head for Adina. You will need to catch up. Mother, you ride on the cart. Bring as much of your medicines as you think you might need.

"I will handle the medicines, Shem. Don't you worry about what I am doing, go get to Adina," his mother replied.

"Where is Japheth? Shem continued. "Are he and Tamara still not back? Prisca, go and find them....no ....no on second thought Adina may need you. Come with us instead. Let's go. We don't have a moment to spare."

Prisca, Shem, Elam, Gomer and Cush headed up the trail towards the mountains. Shem looked up to see tears streaming down Cush's cheeks. He reached over and pulled the boy to him."

I know, I know how hard this must be. But you must be strong just a little while. You can help your mother." Shem then abruptly pushed Canaan in front of him up the trail

"Suddenly, Ham gathered himself. He ran over to the group and took one of the heavy bundles of rope from Cush's shoulder. Then he spoke to Canaan more harshly than he ever had.

"Go! Get moving," he ordered the boy.

At this, for the first time, Canaan became genuinely scared. If his father could become angry with him, then he realized how much trouble he could be in. He had to ensure that they didn't reach his mother in time.

Canaan began to jog a few steps, and then walk, slowing his pace a little more every few feet. Every time he did so, first Ham and then Shem would order him to speed up.

After approximately a mile, Canaan who was several yards ahead of the group, stopped and sat on a large boulder and hung his head.

"You have to remember. I ran all the way down to get you all. I cannot make it back up without rest and water."

Shem looked back for the cart. Far down the trail, but making steady progress, he could see the team of oxen. Phut and Asshur were following closely behind cracking whips above the oxen's back with Arphaxad pushing the cart with all his might from the back. Sapphira held on and rode inside.

Canaan leaned on one elbow next to the boulder.

"I…I can't go another step. Let me rest and catch my breath before…"

Ham couldn't stand anymore. He sprang onto Canaan and pinned him in place with his knee on Canaan's chest.

"Don't you understand, boy? Your mother is up there somewhere. She is in pain, probably bleeding, perhaps dying. We have to get there as soon as humanly possible and…"

As Ham practically spat the words into the boy's face he looked intently into his son's eyes. It was the boy's eyes that betrayed him.

"You do understand, don't you?" Ham's tone was lowered now. The awful truth was coming to him in small increments.

"Ham, what are you talking about?" Prisca asked. Now Shem was beginning to look from Ham's face to Canaan's. He too was suddenly focused on waiting for Canaan's answer.

"You…you want us to be delayed." Ham went on. "Are you hoping your mother dies, Canaan?"

Shem searched his nephews face, grasping, unbelieving. Then abruptly, Ham backhanded Canaan across the face stunning him. Prisca grasped her brother in law's arm but Shem made no move to stop Ham. Prisca wasn't nearly strong enough to prevent Ham from striking the boy a second time. Then Shem reached for the hunting knife he wore on his belt.

"Let me say this in a different way, Canaan." Shem began. Prisca had never heard his voice sound as it did now. There was an edge to it, a rage she could not identify with.

For his part, Canaan, for the first time in his life, felt abject fear. His father had never before raised a hand to him. Canaan now came face to face with a fraction of the fear his own mother had experienced just a few hours prior.

"You get on your feet and you run. You run to where you last saw your mother," Ham was only a fraction of an inch from his son's face now. "And if you stop once more to so much as wipe your brow…I will not protect you from Shem. He will take that knife he is holding and gut you like a deer carcass right here on the side of this mountain."

Both Prisca and Canaan stood stunned. Neither had ever seen Noah's sons like this. In fact they had never seen anyone in this state of primal determination. Canaan sensed that this was not an idle threat. He fought to regain his footing. With his hand covering the swelling on his cheekbone, he began to jog. In a few steps Canaan looked behind him to see if the others were following. They were close behind, matching Canaan's gait.

In what seemed like an eternity they finally reached the point where Ham saw Adina's satchel lying on the ground. At that he passed Canaan by and ran towards the cliff. He dove onto his belly and pulled himself just over the edge. What he saw took his breath away.

There at the bottom of the ravine lay Adina, her head surrounded by a halo of dark blood. One arm was draped gently above her forehead as if she had lain down to merely take a nap.

Prisca, running a little behind Shem, was soon by Ham's side kneeling on both knees. As she too saw Adina laying there she gasped and brought both hands to her mouth. She looked over at Shem, expecting him to say something comforting or wise, but there was nothing to say. Shem could not process what he was seeing either. Both of them then looked to Ham who suddenly sprang to his feet.

"We'll find something to tie off to and I can lower you down," Shem began. But before he could say another word, Ham kicked off his sandals and began lowering himself over the side with his powerful arms.

"I have to get her out now so Mother can treat her," was all he said.

A sob escaped from his chest and broke through his lips.

"You can't help her by killing yourself, Ham. Wait and let me tie you off." Shem pleaded.

Ham had no intention of waiting. He found a toe hold here, a handhold there. Suddenly he slipped, sliding down ten then twenty feet on the craggy rock face of the cliff. He managed to catch himself on a protruding boulder but felt searing pain in his ribs. He stopped for only a moment to look at his now skinned chest and legs.

Blood was oozing from points all along his front. As soon as he realized nothing was broken he began climbing down again. He could now hear the ox cart coming steadily up the trail. His descent continued rapidly in that manner, first climbing, then sliding and falling toward- the spot where Adina lay. There was no concern in him for his own safety. "I want to die," he declared under his breath. "I want to see Adina again."

"Mother, come quickly. We've found her," Shem called.

When Shem looked back down he saw that Ham, terribly bruised and bleeding himself, had finally reached Adina. Shem,

Prisca and Sapphira watched intently hoping for a sign of life from Adina that they knew in their heart would not come.

Ham reached out to take Adina into his arms, but as he touched her cheek he recoiled rapidly as he felt the coldness there. Ham reeled back crab crawling backwards as far as the boulders would allow him. He continued to kick his bare feet at the gravel pushing his back firmly against the unyielding rocks. He looked for breathing, the rise and fall of his wife's chest that he had witnessed so many times as they slept, but there was none. His mind began to process the reality that she was gone.

The large man gathered himself again. He refused to accept what was happening and as quickly as he had retreated, he now crawled back to Adina's side.

"Darling," he inquired as if he might wake her from sleep. Then he realized he had never used that term of endearment with her while she was alive. He reached out his hand, very slowly and deliberately this time, and once again touched her cheek. There he felt a coldness that would remain on his fingertips for the rest of his life. Adina was dead.

After all these years, after all the love and tenderness Adina had shown him, it was only now that Ham realized the depth of the blessing she had been to him. "Here lies a princess," he thought. "His princess entrusted to him by God. He would never feel her arms around him again; never feel the warmth of her touch or the thrill of her kiss. For all these years she had always been there for him, right at the tips of his fingers." Now the fingers that had seldom caressed her in life stroked the stiff coldness of her face in death.

Suddenly Ham let out a wailing, blood curdling cry toward the heavens. It was a cry of abject heartbreak and regret. It was born of guttural pain. No one present that day would ever forget it. As he cried out over and over, Ham scooped Adina's limp lifeless body into his arms. He gathered her up as he would a small child. He cradled her and rocked her and felt the cold stickiness of her blood running across his elbow and forearm. Then, thinking of Cush just at the top of the cliff, he scooted Adina back into the rocks out of site and tried futilely to stifle his sobs.

CHAPTER 19

Tamara rode as fast as she safely could to make it to the mountain trail. As she approached the family homes, she pulled the horse up short. Shem, Prisca and the others were already coming down the trail. It was apparent from the site of the cart that Sapphira was riding in back with the stretched out body of her daughter- in- law.

Despite already having the news, Japheth and Tamara both gasped at the sight. Ham looked up at the two of them, his face drawn and haggard. His legs and elbows were scarred from climbing up and down the cliff and he was covered in dirt. His work had been arduous and grizzly. There had been no good way to retrieve Adina's body. Each foot up the cliff had been stress filled. Cush walked behind the cart. He seemed to be fixated on his mother's closed eyes. The other boys followed slowly behind Cush, their faces long, their feet dragging. The entire family was clearly devastated.

Though Japheth had long ago suppressed his former romantic feelings for Adina, he was not ready for this. He wanted to leap from the horse and run to the cart screaming. He wanted to cry out for Adina and hug her one last time. But he knew that such a display of emotion would only make things harder on Adina's children and scar the memory of this day even further. It was so unfair. Just a couple of days prior she had been laughing and joyful with the children.

Japheth threw a leg over the horse and slipped down as gently as possible. He reached up and helped Tamara down, though she had dismounted the horse hundreds of times without any help at all. They held hands as they walked ever so slowly to the cart. They leaned on one another for support. With every step it seemed as if a weight was pressing down harder and harder upon them. As they approached the cart, Japheth began having trouble seeing. A dark circle was closing in on his peripheral vision and he thought he would lose consciousness any moment. Nothing, not even the loss of his former home and so many loved ones in the flood, had hit him this hard.

As the cart stopped, Ham stepped alongside it and looked adoringly at Adina. Then his knees buckled and he sat there on the ground, his back resting against the wheel. Japheth looked at Tamara then he looked up and saw Shem and Prisca wearing a similar expression. All couldn't help but think, "if only he had looked at Adina that way during their marriage." But it was too late.

The entire family was now gathered around the cart. Tamara and Japheth, Shem and Prisca, stood in front of all the others who were now gathered in a semi-circle behind them. They all looked with great sympathy as Cush, Ham and all of Adina's children who sat upon the ground clinging to one another. No one spoke. No one knew what to say.

The ark had been a crucible of common hardship. It had been an existence where Noah's family had been forced to rely heavily upon one another through every form of adversity. Within the hull of the ark a transformation had occurred in every person. They had grown closer to God than they ever thought possible and in so doing had grown closer to one another. Within that hull, within that crucible, bonds were formed that were stronger than any of them had ever before known. Now one of those bonds had been severed. A thread that was central to the tapestry that was their family had been ripped away. The loss came in such an unexpected and abrupt manner that no one knew what to do.

Noah, who had been out in the wilderness praying for Adina's safe return, now quietly approached the cart. Without breaking stride, he climbed inside to sit on the opposite side of Adina's body from Sapphira. Just as Sapphira clutched one hand, Noah took the other and began to cry softly.

"Oh my dear sweet daughter," he said hoarsely. "you must not leave us. It is too soon for her to leave us." Then he cried out, "Lord, please do not allow this to happen." With that he clutched Adina's hand to his chest and slumped forward onto Sapphira's shoulder.

Prisca was the next one to break down. She had been brave as long as she could while they all worked to bring Adina home; now she could hold back no longer. Always one of the most passionate and emotional family members, she now threw herself upon the back of the cart and clung to Adina's feet. Shem went to her a moment later. When he could not pull her away, he gently swept her up into his arms and carried her toward their home.

Tamara covered her mouth and ran toward her own house and Japheth soon followed. One by one the brothers and their families left Ham and his children there with Noah and Sapphira to mourn in private.

CHAPTER 20

The family returned from burying Adina and sat down to a meal. They sat outside at the long table with everyone together. This meal was different in that Shem, not Noah led the entire family in prayer. Noah had said very little since Adina's death and instead had spent a great deal of time alone in the hills with Sapphira. Though they hadn't said anything to their children, both of them suspected that the loss of Adina was the beginning of yet another monumental shift in the families' history. Today they would discover that they were more right than they had imagined.

Noah looked from one face to another, pausing briefly upon each person and ending with Canaan. Noah observed that while every other family member picked at their food and ate slowly, if they ate at all, Canaan gulped food down as if he had not a care in the world. The sight of it annoyed some and infuriated others.

Shem's jaw muscles worked as he eyed the teenaged Canaan. He knew that this boy had had something to do with his mother's death. He knew it in his gut as surely as if he had witnessed it himself. His tension was not just the result of anger, but was more a function of his struggle to withhold his inner thoughts so as not to upset Ham and his other children any further.

Ham sat on the end of one bench, his back to Cush. He cupped his forehead in his hand and stared at the ground. He was devastated. His mind was reeling. All his married life he had known deep in his heart that he was treating Adina unfairly. He had known that he had never shown her the kind of love she deserved. Despite this knowledge, he had been too caught up in his own quest for importance and worth to put forth the effort to change the way he related to his wonderful wife. Now with Adina gone, Ham realized for the first time that he had lived his life largely ignoring the one whom God had given him to make him a better man. It took the loss of his Adina, his helpmate, for Ham to finally realize all he had allowed to slip through his fingers. Ham finally realized that the aspirations for leadership that he had once obsessed over were meaningless without her.

Japheth, like Shem, stared at Canaan. Shem previously had an opportunity to vent some of his frustrations toward Canaan on the way up the mountain to find Adina's body. Japheth, on the other hand, had been forced to bottle up his feelings. He had not been home in time to help with the recovery of the body and there had been no occasion for him to talk to Shem or Canaan. As Noah looked at his son's face he could see that his emotions were about to boil over. Noah tried to prevent the pending explosion.

"Japheth, will you walk with me?" Noah asked.

Japheth did not divert his eyes away from Canaan. The boy, oblivious that he was being watched now by nearly the entire family, lifted a cup to his lips. He drank the juice inside as a person dying of thirst, turning the cup up at such an angle that the liquid ran out both corners of his mouth and down to his chin. As he sat the cup down with a thud against the table, Japheth stood.

"What did you do boy?" was the only sentence Japheth could muster in his anger.

Suddenly Ham looked up, a puzzled frown upon his face. For his part Canaan looked genuinely surprised again.

"What do you mean? I don't know what you are talking about. I haven't done anything."

"What did you do to your mother?"

"Japheth, this is not the time or the place," it was Shem speaking now. His manner made it clear that he shared Japheth's desire to question Canaan, but not right now.

Canaan did not answer. Instead he shook his head and rose from his place at the table. He walked over and placed a hand on Ham's shoulder. Ham covered the boy's hand with his own. His grief had now overpowered the anger he had felt towards Canaan when the boy had delayed the search for Adina.

"Japheth, my children and I have been through enough. We don't need to hear your inquisition," Ham said.

Japheth looked incredulous but stopped his questioning and, with Tamara tugging gently at his arm, sat back down heavily upon his bench.

"Prisca, Tamara, take the children for a walk now. Let them get away from all this. You older boys go along as well." Sapphira spoke now, her voice still hoarse from crying. Like Noah, she had said almost nothing since the discovery of Adina's death so that hearing her speak so firmly surprised everyone. Tamara and Prisca rose and began to gather the children. Most of them were eager to go and be away from thoughts of mourning.

Only Noah, Sapphira, their sons and Canaan remained sitting around the table. After the group was well out of earshot, Japheth spoke up again.

"Ham, I am sorry to have blurted out what I did. Now is not…"

"No, Japheth," Sapphira spoke again as she held up a hand towards Japheth to stop him. "Speaking in front of the children was a bad decision. But speaking up about this was not. We have all catered to Canaan far too long. That has now led to horrible tragedy."

As she said this she looked sternly from Ham to Noah. There was a fire in her eyes as in the old days on the ark. Noah too wanted to know what had gone on near the edge of the ravine. He took over the questioning.

"Canaan," he spoke very firmly now. "Tell us what happened. Tell us what really happened."

For the first time Canaan looked panicked. He wasn't supposed to be asked these questions. He had told his story and everyone should have believed it. He looked desperately at his father.

Ham was about to defend him, just as he always had, but as he looked into Canaan's eyes and saw the panic there, he too knew his son was hiding something. The realization of it gave him a nauseated feeling in his stomach. Ham looked at Noah, then at his brothers, then back to Canaan.

"What are you hiding, son," as he spoke, Ham gripped Canaan's hand tighter in order to keep the boy from pulling away.

"I…I'm not hiding anything. I told you as soon as I got down here that she fell. I told you I couldn't grab her that I…"

"No, that's not what you said at all," Sapphira said. "You said you did grab her but that you couldn't hold on to her. Why are you lying about this now, Canaan?"

"I'm not lying," Canaan tried to pull away from his father but was powerless to break his grip.

Somehow every one of the adults now knew. Even Ham knew. They didn't know how or why but they all had the sickening feeling that Canaan was at least partially responsible for the death of his own mother.

Canaan sensed it too. He sensed that the talent for manipulation that he had relied on all his life was now failing him. His eyes widened and bulged.

"Why are you all looking at me that way? What are you going to do?"

"Look at him," Shem said to no one in particular. "He knows he is caught. Look at his eyes."

"I didn't do anything. You are all scaring that's all. The way you are looking at me is scaring me." Canaan answered them but he could tell that his explanations were falling short. "I am telling you I didn't touch her."

"You didn't touch her to help her?" Japheth asked. "Or do you mean that you didn't touch her to push her? Your mother had hiked all over those mountains leading you and the other children on explores. She never even stumbled much less tripped. Yet, when she was alone with you she falls to her death? Something doesn't make sense here."

"I didn't do it!" Canaan was screaming now and tears began rolling down his face but there seemed to be no remorse in them. "I didn't push her. I…I wanted her hands off me….I was trying to keep her from hitting me and she just fell on her own."

For the first time since their run up the mountain to find Adina, a look of anger now crossed Ham's face. "You tried to keep her from hitting you?"

Canaan nodded "yes." Ham continued.

"So are you saying that this was more than just an accident?" Ham's voice was becoming high pitched now as if he was about to start crying. The others around the table fell silent as they watched the drama now unfolding before them. Their already broken hearts were now hurting even more for Ham.

"Once again I refused to face your awful behavior and now my failure to hold you accountable has cost me everything," Ham said to his son.

Shem and Japheth saw Ham falling into dejection and noticed his hand around Canaan's forearm loosening. They lunged at the boy to seize him before his father let go of him. As they reached out to grab him, Canaan fought like a wild animal to break his father's grip. He punched at Ham's fingers with the heel of his hand. He kicked his father's shins. Japheth, throwing himself prostrate across the table now, flailed for a swatch of Canaan's tunic. As he felt the rough fabric slip out of his hands he saw Canaan's arm pull free. It was in that exact instant that everything went black. No one heard the explosion for the shockwave reached them first. No one had time to prepare. Suddenly a force like a sledgehammer knocked them all from their feet.

CHAPTER 21

A tremendous roar followed as everyone flew through the air. Noah and Sapphira were literally blown off their bench and landed with a thud ten feet away. Shem was dazed but rose to one knee just in time to be hit in the face by a blazing hot wind. As he skittered along the ground, pushed by some invisible force, he turned away and shielded his face with his hand. Dust filled his nose and made its way into his mouth. He heard the sound of wood being ripped and split as he looked up in time to watch shingles and shutters being ripped from the families' houses.

He crashed into a body. It was Japheth who reached out for Shem as he held firmly with his other arm to the stone fireplace. Shem reached for his brother's hand and the two locked arms at the elbow. Japheth looked in the direction of the wind as if he could see its source, but as he did so, everything became black.

A thick, choking dust engulfed them. Both men gagged and gasped, their nostrils filling with a hot thick dust. At this moment they did not even think of their families. Instead, their sole focus was on getting one more breath of air.

Then, just when they thought they would never get another breath, the air began to clear. First there was a wracking cough. Then the air cleared a bit more and they were able to breathe more easily.

"Shem, breathe through the cloth of your cloak," Japheth managed to croak through his dry throat. By doing this, they managed to get enough air to survive. After what seemed an eternity, the brothers stood unsteadily and began to walk in the direction where they had last seen their parents. With each step the ground erupted in puffs of powdery ash.

They found Noah and Sapphira, barely recognizable in a pile of grey. Noah had created a makeshift tent from his own cloak and the two of them were miraculously unhurt, with the exception of bumps and bruises. Shem told them to wait there, and then he and Japheth immediately turned their attention to finding their wives and children. They began walking and shouting out their names.

"Gomer, Tamara, Mareyea, Meshech!" Japheth called first.

"Prisca, Arphaxad," Shem shouted in a different direction.

The two brothers continued in this manner, both now fighting a wracking cough that had overtaken them. Every few seconds they interrupted their calls with prayer.

"Oh dear Lord, please let them be alright," Japheth said.

"Lord, protect them until we can find them," Shem whispered.

After what seemed like hours, but was in fact only minutes of searching, Shem began to hear murmuring cries. He held up a hand to Japheth, but his brother had already heard and was moving slowly, trying to pinpoint the direction of the sound.

"They sound like they are near the stream," he said as he began to run in that direction.

Shem followed, running in a stiff- legged unnatural gate, as he tried to both listen and run. It was only then that he realized that blood was running down his shins from both knees. Within a few yards the cries grew louder and he was able to run full speed. Both men could feel their eyes widen as they strained to see their families through the still thick haze. Shem was the first one to see a child.

"Mareyea!" Shem shouted.

His niece was wandering along the stream bank. It was clear that she was stunned and disoriented. Shem felt a small bit of relief as he first noticed that she was not nearly as covered with ash as the two of them were.

"Mommy is lost," was allthe little girl said, as Japheth swept her up into his arms.

"Be careful Japheth," Shem cautioned. You'll hurt her by hugging her so tight."

Shem stood there for only a second watching the reunion. He had a hand on both their backs, sharing in their joy but within seconds his eyes were scanning the stream bank again.

"Shem," he recognized Prisca's voice calling to him.

"Prisca, I'm here," Shem ran towards the stream as the sound seemed to be coming from the middle of the water.

At first Shem could not see Prisca or anyone else as he stood at the stream's edge, his eyes frantically scanning. Then he heard a cough. As he turned he saw Elam helping his mother, Prisca, from beneath the roots of a felled tree. The tree had been growing along the stream bank. The flow of the stream had eroded the soil away from the roots and formed a small cavern behind them, and the force of the initial explosion had caused the tree to fall. As Prisca, Tamara and the children knelt along the edge of the stream, it provided a perfect fortress, protecting them from the heavy ash fall.

One by one their wives and children worked their way out of the labyrinth of tree roots. As they emerged the men were relieved to see that not only were they unhurt, but they barely had any of the ash on them. Even Rowdy, ever the protector, was with the children and appeared unhurt. As soon as Tamara could free herself she ran and swept Mareyea into her arms as Meshech clung to her leg.

"Sweetheart, what happened?" she asked the still stunned child. "You were right beside me and then I looked around and you were gone."

"When you went behind da tree roots I thought dat a monser had you and I ranned," Mareyea answered, beginning to cry.

Tamara shot a look at Aram and Javan and then immediately felt bad about it. The boys looked at the ground ashamedly. They could not have known that their little joke about a monster in the cave nearly resulted in Mareyea being killed.

Suddenly, Shem and Japheth looked at one another and in the same instant said, "We have to find Ham!"

"Tamara and Prisca, we need to get these children inside one of the houses. They need shelter," Shem said. "Japheth and the boys and I will look for Ham. Once we find him, we can close ourselves up in the big barn. That is probably the strongest building we have," he suggested.

As they started to trot back towards the area of the fireplace, Elam, Shem's eldest son, spoke up, "If none of us knows what just happened then none of us can be sure if it's about to happen again." Everyone realized he was right. Regardless, they would have to seek shelter somewhere as soon as possible.

Shem and Japheth reached the large outdoor table and saw that it had been flipped over with one side resting on one of the benches.

"Have you seen Ham?" Japheth asked.

Noah only pointed toward the mountains.

"What do you mean?" Japheth asked. "That is where all this ash came from. Something is terribly wrong in the mountains and you are telling me Ham went that way?"

"He followed Canaan's footprints," Noah answered. "He didn't seem the least bit concerned about his own safety. He wanted Canaan."

"He was defending him mere moments ago," Japheth said.

"That was before the reality of Canaan's role in Adina's death sank in, I suppose," Shem added. "I am sorry to say they are on their own. We have no time to search for them. We have to get the children to safety."

Shem turned around to see that the entire family now assembled behind him.

"We can take shelter in the barn," he said.

"Yes, but what good will that shelter do us if we cannot breathe for the ash in the air. I nearly choked from it," Japheth said, still coughing.

"We need to move away from this area." Noah said, his head beginning to clear.

"Everyone think," Shem called out. "What shelter is there for us outside this valley?"

"What about the cave?"

It was Javan. The boy had made the suggestion almost apologetically, but he had inadvertently come up with the best possible solution under the circumstances.

"Yes, that makes perfect sense," Tamara said. "The cave that the boys found was barely visible for the boulders all around it. Those large boulders might protect the entrance."

"Well, it is probably the best alternative we have," Shem agreed. "It is not as if we have a large number of choices. How long will it take us to make it there?"

"If we hurry," Prisca said, "we could make it in half an hour."

"The cave it is then," Shem ordered. "You boy's help me get food and supplies and we will be on our way immediately."

Japheth started to speak, "Food won't matter to us if we…"

Before he could finish his thought, the ground began to shake. Rowdy, who was standing in the stream, began to whine in a way that Japheth had never heard. Then he took Japheth's hand gently in his mouth and began to pull him, something he had also never done before

"He senses something is wrong," Japheth said. "We had better get moving."

"Japheth, Tamara knows the way to the cave. You two go in front and lead everyone else. Cush, I know you are worried about your brother and your Dad. I know you are reeling from all that has happened to you but the rest of us need you right now. I need you to help your grandma. Carry her if you must. You are strong enough to do it. We will have to move faster than she can walk."

The younger man nodded back without speaking. His look was one of determination. As Shem had suspected, this mission allowed Cush to focus on something other than grief and fear, which was critical to his own survival now.

Japheth motioned to Tamara to lead the way. He herded the children just behind him and they hurried in the direction of the cave. It was difficult to see the trail as the ash had completely coated everything.

Shem instructed each boy twelve and older to carry one of the smaller children. Arphaxad carried Meshech, while his brother Asshur carried Mareyea. Even as they began to walk rapidly, a distant mountain began to rumble and the ground beneath their feet began to shake. Tamara whistled for the horses, and out of nowhere, three appeared. They too were covered in dust and were clearly frightened but seemed comforted by Tamara. She grasped a handful of mane and sprang effortlessly onto the lead horse.

"Cassandra, Ruth," she called out. "I have been teaching you to ride. Now you will ride for your lives. We will put as many of the small children in front of us as we can. Remember how I showed you to guide the horse with pressure from your legs? Do that now. We don't have the reins, sowrap your arms around the children and grasp the mane with all your might."

Japheth looked up at his wife but did not protest her idea.

"I know you all realize that this is the next generation of the human race. I will ride to save as many as I can," she said looking at the faces of Shem, Japheth and Noah. "Prisca, you know the way to the cave. I will be there with these children waiting for you." Tears began to well in everyone's eyes. They were unsure if they would ever see one another again. They trusted God, but they had also just buried Adina. Noah said what they all hoped.

"You ride ahead, Tamara, but rest assured, we will see you at the cave. God will not allow the destruction of this family. If that were His plan, then there would never have been an ark."

Tamara looked at the young girls with her. Both had tears streaming down their cheeks but their jaws were set. They were ready. Tamara dug her heels into her horse and the others followed. In seconds the group was invisible behind a cloud of dust.

CHAPTER 22

Those left on foot were only a little over half way to the cave when the rumbling from the mountains grew more intense. Instinctively, everyone looked back toward the sound. As they looked on in shock the side of one of the mountains was blown away. Hoards of white steam sent rocks, boulders and trees flying through the air for hundreds of feet. An avalanche of boulders, trees and mud was barreling down the mountain and toward them with lightning speed.

Though the mountain was over three miles away, they would have to move much faster if they were to live. Everyone, even Noah, began to run.

"God give your servant the strength," Noah prayed aloud. It was clear that though he was frightened, he was far from panicked.

They did not look back again. Had they done so, they would have seen the entire mountainside moving like water. There was no way they could outrun it. The only hope for them all was that the volcano was far enough away that the full force of the avalanche would not reach them.

They couldn't move nearly fast enough to suit Javan and Aram. The two boys could run just as fast, if not faster than the adults. Japheth showed Gomer and Elam how to make a seat by lacing their hands together and had them lift Noah up. Then he scooped his mother, Sapphira, away from the now winded Cush. He held her in his arms like a child and ran with her that way until he thought his arms would break and his lungs would burst. Finally, when he thought he could run no further he saw some of the children in front turn and splash across the stream. The cave was very close now.

Shem ignored the burning in his lungs. He needed desperately to stop and catch his breath, but every time his pace began to slow, the sounds of the oncoming avalanche drove him on. The group dared not look back. The tremendous pops of snapping tree trunks grew closer by the second.

"Oh Lord, please let Tamara and the others be there," Japheth prayed silently.

CHAPTER 23

We arrived at the mouth of the cave completely out of breath and with our hearts racing. The horses stood just inside but I didn't see Tamara. Then, just as my heart began to sink, I heard her familiar whistle from inside the cave. She was trying to coax the reluctant horses further inside.

"Tamara," I called out breathlessly. "We are here, we are coming in."

"Oh, thank God," she cried from within. "Try to get the horses to come with you. There is room for them, I think."

"The horses are on their own," I answered as I stepped into the cool blackness.

There was no time to consider a torch or even explore the interior of the cave for dangers. I stepped in first, feeling my way along a wall. I could feel the pull of little hands at me as two of the children clung to me. We moved along like that, forming a human chain as we moved deeper inside.

"Everyone," I called over my shoulder. "I want you to each call out your name loudly and clearly. I want to make sure we have all made it into the cave."

"Meshech," came the first name. "Elam, Asshur, Cassandra, Javan, Mareyea, Tamara…"

As each family member called out their names I breathed a larger sigh of relief. I was also greatly relieved to hear the voice of my mother and father call out strongly. I was concerned about what all this exertion would do to them. Likewise, I was certain we had left someone in our haste. But God was with us. With the exception of Ham and Canaan, we were all together. I wondered for a moment if we would ever see our brother again.

From the faint light coming into the mouth of the cave, I could make out the outline of the horses' heads. They raised their heads and looked backwards. Every instinct they possessed alerted them to pending danger. The lead horse suddenly broke and ran, the others following closely. The Lord had created them to flee from danger, not to hide. Their way was not to seek shelter but to escape with their speed.

Inside the dark cave, simply taking one step was harrowing in its own right. Muffled exclamations where heard repeatedly as one after another we each banged a shin or knee cap on some protrusion. For at least 100 yards, the cave was nothing more than a narrow passage way. Then suddenly, the wall curved away from me.

"We seem to be coming into an open area," I said. It was not necessary to talk loudly now. We were so deep underground that silence filled the air. One by one we entered this "room" and gathered in a cluster. It was indescribably dark.

"I hear water running," Arphaxad said. We all held our breath momentarily to listen. The sound of a rushing waterfall was apparent in the distance. Likewise, we could feel fresh air saturated by a light mist against our skin.

"Perhaps we shouldn't try and go any further without a torch," I cautioned. "Surely we are far enough back to be protected now."

I moved forward a few more feet until I came to a long flat section of rock that felt almost like a bench.

"Here," I called out. "Here is a place where we can sit and rest a while. If you have to, crawl over here towards my voice. Don't try to walk. You might trip and hurt yourselves."

In a few moments we were all sitting side by side on the damp rock. It was actually at just the right height to be comfortable, and it kept us from having to sit on the uneven ground. My back was screaming in pain from carrying my mother all that way. I ran a hand backwards and felt the flat wall of the cave. It would make a passable back rest. Or at least I thought so until I moved my hand a little further. What was once solid rock suddenly gave in as I moved my hand further up. Something felt leathery and then furry.

"Don't anyone lean back," I cautioned. "The whole wall is covered in bats!'

"Get them away!" Trifania, Shem's middle daughter, screamed as she flailed her arms. Her flailing only disturbed the bats more, and one by one they began to flutter and squeal about the room. This led Prisca, Tamara, and even Sapphira to scream out as well. Soon every female in the family, and even some of the men, were screaming and swatting bats from around their heads.

"Just be calm and still and the bats won't bother you." Shem said.

Just as Shem finished speaking, a tremendous roar from outside filled the space. What had once been a quiet cave interior was now filled with noise unlike anything any of us had ever heard.

The whole world outside sounded like it was being swept away. A dust cloud made its way down the passage from outside and caused all of us to begin coughing. A deafening sound interspersed with the loud cracks of snapping tree trunks and limbs went on for several minutes. Then just as rapidly as the sound had begun, it stopped.

CHAPTER 24

A full day later, Shem and I emerged from the cave, followed by our eldest sons. Our father was still a little unsteady and was helped to the mouth of the cave by Arphaxad and Elam. As we emerged into the daylight we couldn't believe our eyes. I had expected the air to be filled with ash and haze. Instead, in the hours since the roar had stopped, a soft steady rain had begun to fall, clearing the air. We emerged to a cloudy and damp morning after spending a sleepless night in the cave.

The air was clear of ash but the forest was devastated. In many ways the surrounding area looked like the muddy mess that had been left by the flood. Tree trunks, leaves and limbs completely stripped away lay stacked in giant piles of rubble. Ash and mud coated every surface. Nothing looked familiar. I was disoriented and unsure in what direction our homes were for a moment. Everything looked completely different.

"Look," Shem pointed toward the distant peaks, well to the east of the mountain where the ark rested. "Look at the steam rising from that mountain."

"Not only that," Dad added. "That mountain is shaped differently. It is as if the entire side has been blown out of it. Look there...look there...I can see orange fire glowing from within the mountain.

There had been explosions and geysers of water shooting up into the air during the flood as the fountains of the deep opened up, but we had never seen anything like what we witnessed today. A mountain had been nearly leveled.

"Look!" Meshech exclaimed. "The creek looks like porridge."

We all turned toward the stream to see that the boy was not exaggerating. The stream, which only yesterday had been clear and pristine, was now saturated with ash. I walked over numbly and scooped some of the water into my cupped hands.

"The water is tainted," I cautioned. "We will have to find some containers and draw water from within the cave right away."

"There is no way my Dad and brother lived through this, is there?" Cush asked.

No one wanted to answer. Finally Noah said, "We don't know that. The last I saw of your dad he was running toward the mountains in the west. If he was able to climb high enough in time, he may have been protected."

"Perhaps he will meet us back at our houses," Elam said.

At Elam's comment, Shem, Japheth and Noah looked at one another. From the looks of the forest, there would be no houses left.

CHAPTER 25

I bent over and lifted a corner of our large family table which had sheltered my parents. As I tried to lift it to its normal position, I realized that I only had hold of one corner. The rest of the table was scattered for many yards all around me, as were many of the comforts of our lives in the valley.

My home was gone as well as Shem's. The ash and mud had followed the contour of the valley nearby so that amazingly, Ham's house and Dad's tent up on the little knoll were relatively untouched. They were however, completely coated inside and out with powdery ash. Our favorite spot-- the outdoor fireplace-- was buried in two to three feet of ash with only the chimney showing. The benches around it where we so often gathered were either splintered or buried. Our livestock was nowhere to be found. The vineyard was severely damaged, as was the orchard. Our largest barn seemed mostly intact. Some of the sheep and goats were gathered inside.

I looked up and saw my family scattered about the area, walking around slowly as if in a daze. Occasionally somebody would pick up some small piece of furniture or cloth only to toss it back down again, realizing it was ruined. Recent events had transpired that we feared would adversely affect the idyllic life we had enjoyed in this valley. Now, I was beginning to realize that after this disaster, my family's life here was over for good. I was going to start over. If my boat was still intact I would sail her to a new land. My family would not stay here. Not now.

"What do we do first?" I asked my brother Shem.

"I don't know, it is all so overwhelming," he answered. Then he gathered himself. "No, on second thought, it is obvious. We have to think of the basics first: food, water, shelter."

"In this case I think shelter must be first." Dad had walked up and overheard our conversation. "If another explosion occurs we have to be protected. All the provisions in the world won't help us if we are not safe from that."

"So do we move back to that cave or do we trust that the barn will remain standing?"

"The barn barely has any damage. It would seem to be protected by the hill between it and the mountains," I said. "Much of what we need is already in there. We can stock it with food much faster than we can stock the cave. I feel that we could be safe quicker by moving into the barn."

"I agree with Japheth," Shem said. "I say we get everyone secured in the barn with a weeks' worth of food, and then me and some of the boys can go and search for Ham…or at least try to find Ham's body."

"I don't think that will be necessary," Dad was looking past Shem and I and staring into the distance. Both of us turned at the same time to see what he was looking at. Off in the distance we saw puffs of ash rising up from our brother Ham's feet as he shuffled toward us. He looked exhausted, but unhurt.

"Are you okay? Did you find Canaan?"

"I'm not hurt but I am far from okay. Yes, I did find Canaan but I couldn't catch him. There were a few minutes there where I think I would have killed him if I had. He is alive, I am certain of it. The last time I saw him he ducked into a tunnel up on the mountain. I was crouched at the mouth of a tiny cave when the eastern mountain blew. I jumped into the cave high up on the side of that mountain. It mostly protected me from the shock wave and debris. But over the next few minutes the mouth of the tunnel that Canaan dove into was sealed by mud and ash. I think Canaan may be trapped in there."

"I doubt he is trapped," Cush said as he walked up. He walked over to his father and the two shared a hug. "I have been through that tunnel with Canaan before. He hung out in that area all the time. It's very creepy and dark inside but Canaan knew it. He told me he knew how to come out at several different areas around the mountains."

"Well, that will save us sending a search party. Canaan chose this path. He chose to leave the family at a critical time. He is on his own," Dad said. "There is no more time to stand around here talking. Let us direct everyone to get moved into the barn."

Ham looked around the devastated site of our former homes. He then walked closer to his house, saw that it was damaged but not destroyed like the other houses, and turned back toward us. He raised his arms out and let them fall to his sides with a slapping sound.

"What has God done to us?" he blurted out.

Everyone stopped and looked up at Ham.

"Hasn't this family been through enough?" Ham asked again. "First he breaks up my family, then he takes my wife, Canaan is missing, and now this?" He let his arms slap to his sides again.

Ham stretched his arms out wide and turned around in a circle to indicate the destruction all around us. At such a time as this, I didn't say what first came to my mind, which was that God did nothing to cause the first three things Ham mentioned. Those were the result of the sinful actions or terrible choices Canaan made. Ham went on, "I mean, all of you have always said that God designed and controls His creation, right? Well, what happened? We do know that this was some act of creation, right? A mountain blew up! That is something God could have prevented. So why did He let us build our lives here and then not protect us? Why did He let us lose our homes and all that we have worked for and built?"

At first Shem, Dad and I just looked at one another. Ham and the others were staring intently at us, clearly waiting on an answer. I could not speak for Shem and my father, nor did I have an answer. I didn't know why God had allowed this; I only knew that He must have a reason and that just as with the flood, we were all spared once again. I hadn't thought it through beyond that point. It was as we stood there searching for answers, that Ham's daughterRuth spoke up.

"I don't mean to be disrespectful to you, Father," she said. "But did you learn nothing from Mother when she was with us?"

There were tears forming in Ruth's brown eyes, the eyes of her mother, but her voice was strong. All of us couldn't help but picture Adina standing before us.

"If mother were here she would ask us, 'who are we'? All of you adults, are you not the same people that Almighty God put in the ark? Were you not all present on the mountain to hear the voice of the King of the Universe when He made a covenant with you?"

We all stood there stunned. Suddenly this little girl, who had always been under her mother's skirts and had barely raised her voice, was speaking to us with great power and authority. I looked over at Mother and Dad. Dad's mouth was agape, but I saw a slight smile forming at the corners of mother's mouth.

"What? Will we now hang our heads and stare at the ground as if we have no hope?" Ruth didn't realize it but her little hands were forming fists, and her voice grew louder and stronger.

"Are we going to murmur and groan against God now? Two days ago I saw my mother buried; today everything I have ever known is lost. Yet, these are the first trials of my life. For my entire life God has blessed me to live in this valley with never a day of sickness. Almost every day has been a day of joy. I won't doubt Him now. One of the last things I learned from my mother was that He will take care of us. He even takes care of the flowers."

Suddenly I wanted to cheer. I never knew this child had such faith. I never knew any child could have such a heart. My Dad walked over to her with outstretched hands. He grasped her face and kissed the top of her head.

"My God, my God, thank you for the gift of my family to me, your unworthy servant," he said. "I don't deserve this family. What a wonderful truth you have shared with us, Ruth."

"Of course she is right," Shem said. "We are all alive just as this family was after the flood. God is not going to forsake us. There must be some purpose in this."

Dad climbed atop the ash covered fireplace hearth and spoke loudly. "Ruth has the right spirit. Shem you are right as well. God must have some purpose in this. As I stop now and just try to rely on my faith and not my own finite mind, I realize that I cannot understand the groaning of God's creation. I don't know why the mountain exploded with fury. But I do know that it cannot be a coincidence that it happened right here at the place where we have made our home all these years. I also know that while much was lost, much was also saved.

The barn is where we store all the poles and materials for the tents you all dwelled in during that first year after we landed. We are not homeless. We have shelter. There is enough food stored in the barn to sustain us for several weeks. We are alive and unharmed. God did not destroy us or our lives. I do believe that

He is sending us a clear message. Now is the time for us to move beyond this valley."

"Dad," Shem spoke up. "I almost always agree with you but I cannot do so now. All of our work, all that we had built, the home I had provided for my children, is gone in an instant. I don't need to be reminded of what it feels like to lose my home. I have already done that once. I don't want to go through it again. I don't want to move, I don't want to start over."

"I understand your frustration Shem, I truly do. And yes, it is true that God has demanded much from us. But you are wrong. You did not provide your family a home, God did. The ark landed here," Noah pointed at the mountain where the ark rested. "It landed above this, the most fertile valley any of us has ever seen. When we landed, logs were already lying around ready for you to work into lumber. Just as the stored food on the ark began to run out, we were able to find fruits and vegetables in abundance to sustain us. When we planted crops they didn't grow as they had in the world before the flood. They instead exceeded any level of production we had ever known. Shem, rather than look at today as a time when God took from you, look back on the last nearly twenty years as a gift that He gave to you."

Noah continued to admonish his son. "Look at the faces of your beautiful family. They have been born and prospered in this valley all these years with no sickness or sorrows or barely a care until these recent days. You have had the privilege of raising them to their current ages in a world that was not full of toil, strife and sin like the one you grew up in."

Shem looked at the ground and pondered what his father was saying to him.

After a long pause, Noah said, "I believed it a few weeks ago when we camped in the ark. Now I believe it all the more, God told us to fill the earth, not just this valley. I still have not directly heard God's voice on this, but now that this has happened I feel certain that He is speaking to us through His creation, through our circumstances. He is pushing us to spread out. Perhaps the new areas that He wants us to inhabit will provide an even better home in some way that we cannot see right now."

"Spread out, eh?" Ham said with sarcasm. "Populate the earth, just our little family? You see, I knew he would say that. I just sensed that he would go back to that covenant." As Ham spoke he looked around at both his brothers, looking for some level of agreement from them.

Shem and Japheth looked back at Ham with more than a little surprise.

"Actually, Ham," Shem said. "I never really focused on that part of the covenant all that closely until Dad spoke to us about on the mountain. I don't know that I ever fully realized what it meant until then."

Ham stood up, appearing to be hurt by Shem's comment.

Ham only waved a hand at him dismissively. Then he looked back at Noah. "You all can spread out all you want to. I'm not going anywhere," he said. "For now I am in mourning and I have a house to restore." Then he turned and walked back toward the shell of his home.

No one made any attempt to try and stop him. They all just watched him for a few moments before beginning their conversation again.

"My family and I will be leaving right away," Japheth broke the silence.

Tamara looked up, startled. "Japheth, were you going to talk to me about this first?"

"No," Japheth answered in a way that was much more abrupt than anyone could recall hearing from him. "I am sorry, Tamara. I have made this decision for you and the children. That is the way I knew it would have to be."

Tamara placed her hand on her forehead and then seemed to steel herself as she motioned for her daughters to follow her to the barn where she began to pack.

Finally, Japheth said, "Dad, Shem…everyone. Since we began construction on the ark, I have done whatever was asked of me. Over and over again I have set aside my desire to explore the world around me and discover what is beyond the horizon. Instead I have tilled the soil and planted crops, a noble pursuit for some, but not for me. For me it has been a dreaded chore much of the time. Now we are forced to rebuild. And if I am going to have to rebuild then it will be in a place of my own choosing as I follow God. I want to see where He might lead me and my family instead of always deferring to what He has said to you."

"I think that following God's influence on Dad has served you and your family pretty well, Japheth." Shem protested.

"No, no Shem," Noah stepped over and placed a hand firmly on his eldest son's shoulder. "No, Japheth is right. He has sacrificed for a very long time. His time to seek his own land has come. His time to explore the horizons has come. He has more than earned that."

Then Noah turned to address Japheth. "This has been your heart for a long time, hasn't it son?" he asked, smiling.

"Yes, Dad, it has. Please don't feel that I have not had many joyous times here with all of you," Japheth said as he looked around at the group. "I do realize that God provided just what we needed to start our family and to raise our sons. Yet, despite my efforts to remain satisfied here, I have had a burning desire to see more of the world."

"Look at everything. Our homes are destroyed, our orchards and crops are ruined. What we have in the barn now and what we can hunt will have to get us through winter. There will be very little harvesting to do now. You won't be depending on my sons and me for labor. We are going to have to start from scratch no matter what we do. If that is the way it must be then I would prefer to start over in a new land."

Noah looked at the ground. He was saddened but he knew it was time. Japheth was a good son. Noah knew that if forced, he would stay, but he would also resent it. Japheth needed to do this. He had wanted to for years. Finally, Tamara stepped outside the barn and sat down, exhausted, before breaking the silence. She was clearly being cautious after Japheth's earlier response to her.

"Where will we go?" she asked timidly. Tamara wasn't angry, merely surprised. She knew her husband would not have spoken so abruptly if he had not felt very strongly about leaving - and thought it through very carefully. Japheth came and knelt beside her and placed a hand on her shoulders.

"I promise you that I have thought this through for years. I believe you and the children are going to be just as safe on this voyage as you were when we were on the ark."

CHAPTER 26

"On what voyage?" Tamara, Gomer and Javan all exclaimed at once.

"Japheth, is your boat that far along?" Shem asked.

"Except for putting the sail on she is ready. I plan on using some of my part of the tent fabric for a sail."

"What do you mean?" Tamara asked. "What is a sail?"

"You will see soon enough. I will need your help to make it. But when we finish it I plan to sail along the length of the great lake. Once on the other side, we can find a suitable place to build a new home. Until our houses are ready, we will sleep in the boat"

The discussion went on for a while but there was too much work for the others to do to discuss for very long. The first priority was to determine what cookware and other essentials could be salvaged. There was ample food for several months in the barn and all the containers were intact. Everyone decided to stay together there for a few nights to escape the ash. The shutters and doors on the barn, combined with its location between two small hills, had done a good job of protecting its contents.

That evening the boys shoveled out the fireplace and even excavated the first row of benches. Gomer got a fire going and the family cooked a large kettle of soup. When everyone had hot food in their bellies they began to think more clearly. Then conversations about the future began again.

"Dad," Shem asked. "What do you think about the risk of staying near this mountain? Couldn't it explode again?"

"Certainly it could," Noah answered. "It happened once after all."

"Dad, you should plan on staying with me. You and Mother don't need to be alone if that happens again," Shem said.

"We will stay with you, my son. Sapphira and I are too old to have children and to populate some part of the world anyway. But I fear that if that mountain explodes again no one but God will be able to protect us. It will not matter if I am with you or not."

"That is probably true," Shem said. "Still, I would feel much safer if we moved thirty or more miles upstream. None of us has ever been that far in that direction."

"I remember when we walked for two days in that direction soon after we landed," Japheth said. "It is a beautiful country."

No one spoke much as we spent the hours just before dark sorting through supplies in the barn and making pallets to sleep on. Soon, the entire family, except for Ham, was back around the outdoor fireplace. One lonely candle was visible from Ham's window. His silhouette could be seen occasionally as he stepped in front of it to dump another bucket of ash outside. Noah felt sorry for him but knew he would not change Ham's mind. For now he focused on his other two sons and the rest of the family.

Noah stirred some coals with a stick and thought of many more concerns that could have been raised about what was to come, but he chose to keep them to himself. This family had been through enough in the last few days. He searched each person's face as they were illuminated by the firelight. They were exhausted and emotionally spent. But there was a quiet strength present in each one. They would make it, Noah knew. They would make it as they always had before.

CHAPTER 27

Ham lay on his back on his bed frame staring at the ceiling, completely alone. He lay there on a crude pallet, his bedding having been tossed in a garbage heap because of all the ash covering it. It reminded him very much of twenty-one years prior when he had lain on a pallet in the storage room of the ark. Only then, Adina had been by his side. As he had back then, Ham had once again distanced himself from the rest of the family. Everyone else was together in the barn. Even in the midst of all this tragedy, he overheard occasional soft laughter from them as candles were extinguished and sleep approached.

The moon was high, its beams crashing through the cracks between closed shutters, but Ham still hadn't slept. At this moment he wished that he would fall asleep and never wake up. Ham didn't toss and turn. Instead he lay there with one image after another of Adina playing across his mind's eye. He simply couldn't grasp the fact that she was gone. He couldn't even begin to forgive himself for all the times, especially on the ark, that he had treated her poorly.

Somewhere, as he was lost in those images, sleep finally overtook him and he began to dream vividly.

Ham was walking along the stream bank on a pristine morning. In the distance he heard laughing, a soothing lilting laugh. He was drawn to it and began to walk rapidly toward it. He was approaching a small waterfall hidden from site by tall reeds. Ham parted the reeds and as he looked through, he saw lush green grass on the banks and large rocks in the stream. The rocks were covered by a carpet of moss that was dampened by the cascading water of a water fall. On the far side of the stream, Adina lay on a quilt. She was propped up on one elbow. Upon the quilt was spread a bounty of fruits and cakes that she often made to please him.

Adina looked up and saw him. She smiled her radiant, welcoming smile and then beckoned him to come to her. Ham knew instinctively that she wanted him to spend the afternoon there with her. He knew that just a few feet away was an opportunity for some of the happiest hours of his life. But just as he was about to step into the stream and feel the cool water, another voice called to him.

Ham turned to see another woman on his side of the stream. Her back was to him but she looked seductively over one shoulder, as if asking him to follow. Ham couldn't quite see her face as it was hidden from view as her black hair spilled across her shoulders. As she stepped through the reeds and disappeared, Ham looked back at Adina. His wife had a hand outstretched toward him. She was calling to him but her voice was inaudible. Ham read her lips and sensed that she was warning him, pleading with him to stay with her.

Ham looked back toward the reeds again, and then one last time at Adina. He saw tears running down her cheeks. "Why must she always stand between me and what I want?" Ham thought. With that he shook his head as if to clear it, rose to his feet, and ran headlong into the reeds. Just before he emerged on the other side he heard Adina's voice for the first time cry out, "No!"

Ham came out of the reeds at a dead run. The raven haired woman was off in the distance walking slowly away, moving seductively. In her hand she now held a scepter. Without turning to face him, she held it out as if to offer it to him. Ham ran toward her, desiring this woman and what she was offering him.

As he approached her, he reached one arm out to grasp her around the waist. With the other hand, he grasped the scepter and attempted to rip if from her grip. For a brief moment Ham was shocked to discover that she was stronger than him. He could not take the scepter from her. Then she wheeled upon him. The long shiny hair surrounded the face of a skeleton, red eyes bulging from the eye sockets. The creature held the scepter out away from him, and with the other bony hand grasped Ham by the throat. Ham felt air being trapped in his chest. He couldn't breathe, couldn't exhale.

On the thumb of that hand protruded a long black claw. The creature held him in place easily and dug the claw slowly into his jugular, piercing it until Ham felt his lifeblood running down his neck.

CHAPTER 28

Ham woke in a sweat, disoriented. He was back in his house, only now, instead of looking into the face of the creature, he was looking into the face of his own son, Canaan. Canaan sat upon his chest holding a large dagger to his father's throat. Ham realized that he hadn't seen a weapon like that since before the flood.

"Ahhh," Canaan cooed. "Did I wake you?"

Ham felt a painful stick as Canaan held the dagger firmly against his throat. He felt certain that at any moment the dagger would pierce his skin and enter his jugular. He dared not move or he would surely be killed.

"What is going on?" Canaan asked. Something was different about Canaan, Ham realized. His eyes were wild, his countenance dark.

Ham's anger flared at this assault by his own son. "What do you mean? Get off of me right now, boy!"

Rather than give his father any relief, Canaan pushed the dagger in harder. Ham began to feel warm blood trickling down his neck. Ham knew that he could easily fling Canaan across the room, but with the dagger so close to inflicting a lethal wound, he dare not move.

"I know what you are thinking. Take my word for it. This knife is razor sharp. You should be proud. You described for me the way these things were made in the old world. I spent lots of my time learning how to make them on my own. You didn't really think I was just roaming the countryside all those times when I would disappear, did you? Now I ask you again, what is going on? I was watching from up high today. It looks as if everyone is getting ready to leave."

Ham spoke carefully as he feared the movement of his jaw would cut his own throat. "Everyone's home was destroyed. They are going to leave here. They're going to start over somewhere else."

"You can't let that happen," Canaan spat. "I can't control them unless they stay together. You taught me that, or have you forgotten?"

"What are you talking about?" Ham was shocked. Then a look of recognition came across his face, and guilt began to flood his consciousness.

"You have always wanted to lead this family. You told me that before many a fireside when no one else was around. Now I intend to achieve what you were too incompetent to do." Canaan spat. "You planted that seed."

"Kings don't kill their own mothers," Ham answered, anger now overcoming his fear.

"Even if I had killed her, I was doing you a favor. She made you soft. It was her fault! You were never going to take over as long as she was around."

With the mention of his mother, Canaan began to stare off into space. He loosened the pressure on the dagger a little. Ham saw in that his opportunity. He wrenched his head to the side violently in order to protect his neck. He twisted his hips in the opposite direction to throw Canaan off balance. Then he swung a thick forearm around, knocking the slender boy across the room.

Ham felt the dagger gash his throat and neck, but as he felt with his fingers it was apparent that it was only a flesh wound. He sprang to his feet and tried to find Canaan in the dark.

As he moved around the interior of the house he stumbled on one obstacle after another. Due to all the clean-up he had done that day, nothing was in its usual place.

"Where are you?" Ham called out furiously. He lashed out wildly at every shadow. He went to a window and threw the shutters open to let in some moonlight. As he turned back toward his bed, he was stopped short by a glimmer along a curved blade. This time the blade was much longer and Canaan was holding it pointed at Ham's heart.

"This is another of my little creations," Canaan said. "I have enough weapons stockpiled in those mountains to kill everyone here a dozen times over. Did you notice how easily I escaped from you the other day Daddy? I know those caves up there like the back of my hand. Just try and come for me. And know this; you may have lost your guts and your desire to lead but I have not. It is my destiny to control this new world and I will do it with or without you."

The blade whipped the air and Ham moved backwards instinctively. As he did so he tripped over a chair and fell with a thud. As he regained his senses he heard Canaan hop to the ground from the window. By the time Ham grabbed a stick of firewood and ran outside, Canaan had disappeared.

Ham paced back and forth for a while before finally dropping the firewood. What had just happened? Had he just heard his own son utter the words he thought he had? Ham sat down on the ground and let his back slide along the outer wall of his house. He buried his face in both hands and looked toward the horizon, still covering his nose and mouth.

Adina had warned him so many times. She had warned him about how he coddled Canaan and put up with his outbursts. She warned him about his refusal to punish Canaan's bad, sometimes violent behavior. She warned Ham over and over about aggrandizing the world of sin they had left behind as he sat and talked to his children. Now, for the first time Ham realized that it was worse than even Adina had thought. Ham was responsible for raising a monster.

CHAPTER 29

Everyone was gathered on the banks beside our boat. They were very gracious, ooh-ing and ahh-ing over the workmanship. No one had ever seen anything like her. Though I had dreamed of this day for many years, today I had nearly turned back. I nearly agreed to go along with Shem, Ham and my father as they headed up stream toward what we had named the plains of Shinar. From the exploring we had done in earlier years, it had seemed to be nearly as beautiful as our valley.

We all milled around for what must have been over an hour procrastinating. Even though Shem and my Dad had accepted that this was God's will for my family, their faces betrayed their reluctance. Ham stood far apart from the rest of us, as it seemed he always had, and looked frequently toward the surrounding hills. He stared in that direction frequently nowadays, as if he was expecting a storm or some other trouble. But it was hard to tell with Ham. He had so recently lost Adina that no one bothered him or tried to force him to be near us.

"Well sons, I think it is time," I called out. "Gomer, you and Madal and Tubal be ready on those ropes to hoist the sail when I tell you. Javan you may help too."

I wanted to give them each a task to take their minds off their sadness. There were tears in every eye. Tamara clung to Prisca. It was clear to me that she was still in shock from all that had occurred. In my mind that made this as good a time as there would ever be for her to start afresh. Gomer went down the line and hugged each family member tightly before he slung a compliant Rowdy over his shoulders and climbed aboard. Madal and Tubal were next, followed bravely by Javan and my middle daughters. Meshech and Mareyea were a different story entirely.

Mareyea especially clung to my mother for a long while before she would let Tamara take her aboard. And then it was my turn. I couldn't allow myself to think about what I was doing or I would never go through with it. Still, everything in me told me this was right.

I too hugged each family member saving my brothers and parents for last. I walked over to Ham first. He looked stricken. I couldn't tell if he was that sorry to see me go or if he was still reeling from the loss of Adina. I was quite shocked when he grabbed me and pulled me to him. He clasped a strong hand behind my head and held me so tight that I couldn't breathe. He had never hugged me this way in our lives.

"Japheth, take them far from here my brother. Don't turn back. I love you." With that Ham pushed me away, turned, and ran toward the distant mountains. I stood there dumbfounded.

"Let him go," Shem said. "We will keep an eye on him. He'll be okay. He needs time and much prayer."

I turned to smile at my eldest brother. What this man had meant to me I could not put into words. I just couldn't stay here and be his little brother forever. I had to become my own man. He knew it too.

"I am not sure I am as brave as you, baby brother," Shem said. His voice was failing him as he tried to hold back tears.

"Nonsense," I replied. "You have always been the bravest of Noah's sons. Thank you Shem. Thank you for your leadership. Thank you for the man you have always been."

I hoped Shem could understand me because my voice was muffled as I spoke into his chest. We hugged and kissed one another. The Shem pushed me away and held me at arm's length with tears spilling from his eyes.

"I love you Japheth," he said. Then he stepped over, took Prisca's hand and strode over a nearby hill.

I turned to face perhaps the greatest man and woman of God who had ever lived. My mother and father were beyond tears and were having difficulty speaking. My mother only smothered me in kisses, then held my face in both her hands for a time before kissing my forehead one last time.

We hugged, all three of us. We were crying, then laughing at ourselves, then crying once again. Finally my mother turned abruptly and trotted toward the hill where Shem and Prisca had gone. I turned toward my father.

He held me by both shoulders and tried to smile. "May God enlarge Japheth," he said barely above a whisper. "May God increase Japheth."

I knew he was blessing me once again and I stood in reverent silence.

Dad moved one of his hands and placed it on the side of my face. "Go now," he said. "Go, please go quickly, while my heart can still bear it."

Dad stood his ground. It was my turn now to walk away. I looked at the ground for a long moment, then turned and walked toward the boat that now held my family. I climbed inside and pushed the ladder clear. I looked up to signal Shem but Elam and Cush were already raising the axes to cut the last two ropes holding the boat.

"Everyone, get a firm hold," I warned.

"God Bless Japheth," my father yelled to the top of his lungs as the axes swung down. The boat creaked once and then slid rapidly down the wooden rails. The water seemed to boil as she slid into the water. Her bow sliced through the surface and a huge wake momentarily gushed over the edge. I held my breath as tightly as I grasped the rudder, but in seconds my fears calmed as she tilted left, then veered right and finally came to rest level and steady. She drafted almost exactly as I thought she would with all of us and our provisions aboard.

"Hoist the sail," I called out to my sons with relish. I was nearly giddy. I had waited for this moment for so long. As if on cue, the Lord sent a perfect wind that filled the sail. We all marveled as it popped and stretched taught. We were sailing!

In all the excitement I temporarily forgot my great sadness. I continued to grasp the rudder firmly but then looked over my shoulder. Shem and Prisca had returned to the shoreline and everyone was waving and crying. Mareyea called out, "Goodbye

Grandma, bye Grampa, bye Aunt Prisca and Uncle Shem…"
She went on and on, never missing a name or forgetting a family
member.

All too soon the shore where they stood began to fall below the
horizon. In the last seconds, I locked my focus on Shem and
Dad. The last thing I saw was their hands as they waved them
high over their heads. There was a sense of freedom but no sense
of relief. Only at that moment did the reality hit me that I might
never see my father again.

CHAPTER 30

Ruth was flattered to be allowed to stay behind with some of the older children at the lakeshore. Japheth's family had disappeared from site more than two hours ago. There had been plenty of tears shed before the adults began walking slowly back to the barn. The teenagers begged to stay by the lake for a while and were told they could. Ruth was thrilled to be included at only seven years old.

They had talked about many things and wondered aloud about the future. Ruth had mostly sat and listened. Elam broke the silence.

"I suppose we should go back. It will be getting dark soon," he said.

Cush raised his head up. He was sitting just at the water's edge with his knees pulled up, letting the water lap at his toes. "I wonder where my brother is right now."

The others, sitting well behind Cush, looked at one another sympathy. Finally, Cassandra said, "I'll bet he is safe. He hung around in those mountains a lot. I bet he knows some hiding places."

Cush rested his chin back on his knees. "Yeah, I am sure he has some kind of shelter," he replied.

There was silence again for a moment before Arphaxad asked what everyone was thinking, but was afraid to say aloud.

"Cush, why do you suppose he acts the way he does?"

Everyone stiffened at the question, fearing Cush would get mad. Instead he only shrugged his shoulders and said, "I promise you I am as baffled as you are. You all know we have never been very close. He doesn't talk to me that much. But he did tell me something that made me feel creepy on more than one occasion."

"What was that?" Cassandra asked.

"He said he heard voices sometimes. He claimed to hear voices that sounded like they were coming from the rocks somewhere up on the mountains."

"What kind of voices?" Arphaxad asked.

"I don't really know. That was all he ever said," Cush answered.

"I think they were voices of the darkness Grandpa talked about in the old world. The darkness of evil," Elam said.

"Do you really believe all that darkness and evil stuff Grandpa talks about?" Cassandra said.

"I do," said Arphaxad.

"So do I," said several of the others.

"Well, this kind of talk is giving me the creeps," Elam said as he stood and dusted off his bottom. "Come on all of you. We need to start walking now. Dad told us not to stay too long."

Everyone began to stand up when Cush asked, "I wonder why none of us hear the voices?"

The children looked at one another. When no answer came, Elam and Arphaxad shrugged and began to walk back toward home.

Ruth had never moved. She had not stood up nor had she chimed in on the latest conversation. She just sat there staring at the lake water gently lapping the shore. Her eyes were focused intently and to anyone who bothered to notice, it was clear that she was in deep thought.

Elam, who was now a good one hundred yards up the hill, called back over his shoulder.

"Ruth, come on. Don't sit there by yourself or you'll get left behind."

For yet another moment Ruth didn't look up. She whispered under her breath, "We do hear the voices, Cush." Taking a quick look toward the distant mountains she added, "The difference is…Canaan obeys them."

Then she stood up, threw a rock with all her might into the water, and ran to catch up.

PART II

CHAPTER 31

The young boy ran through the forest as cedar boughs whipped his face and arms. He gave their stings no heed, but instead pressed onward with great urgency. His breathing was deep but even and controlled. He had already run three miles and felt certain he could run three more if necessary. He wore a leather knife belt around his waist, a hunting knife large enough for a grown man was in the attached sheath which in turn was tied to the middle of this thigh. In his hand he carried his bow. Across his back was a quiver containing six arrows.

The instructions of his father Cush and the other men had been clear. He was to stay with the women and other children. At the age of twelve years, he was not old enough to hunt the large animals that the men would be stalking on this trip. A cape buffalo or a large stag would feed the families of the men for weeks. In this age, families had largely stopped raising livestock for food, preferring to use their time and energy in mining, building, and trade of finished goods. Hunting wild game had become the favorite method for attaining food for the people.

The man that could provide the most abundant game for his family was a man indeed.

"Son, I know you want to go along. I know you are more interested than any of the other boys in hunting. But the last thing we need on this trip is a child getting hurt or scaring the game away at a crucial moment."

The boy's succeeding protests had fallen on deaf ears. Finally, not having been swayed, the boy had grown angry and glared at the men as he spoke.

"I can do anything any one of you can do and more. I *will* go on this hunt and I *will* prove it to you."

With that he had stepped forward to walk around the men and onto the trail. Before he could take another step, he found his face in the dirt, his father having cuffed him so hard alongside the head that he was sent flying. Eventually the boy had been locked in a shed despite his cries and screams of frustration at being left. It was for his own protection his mother had tried to assure him.

The shed had not held him for long. By now the boy reckoned that his mother and the others were coming to let him out, a loaf of sweet bread and a cup of milk likely in hand as a peace offering. By the time they thought to send a party to look for him, he would have a three mile head start. He grinned self-assuredly at the thought.

He would be in big trouble after this but he would also be a legend amongst the other boys. As it was now all the boys his age feared him. Young men as much as five years his senior resented him. They resented how he repeatedly defeated them in every endeavor from foot races to wrestling matches. His arms and legs were already starting to show more muscle than even the older boys and he seemed devoid of fear. He wrestled as if the match were a life and death struggle as opposed to sport. He ran as if there were a prize of great treasure awaiting the victor instead of a trinket.

He ran with that same intensity now. His bare chest glistened with sweat but his breathing remained steady. That is until he caught a glimpse of the hunting party ahead in the distance. He pulled up abruptly, dove and rolled behind a hedge managing to protect his quiver and bow in the process. He held his breath momentarily. He hadn't expected to catch up so soon. He had crowded the men and feared that any second he would hear his angry father bellow his name. But after several seconds no call came. Had he managed to hide before they could see him?

He raised himself up on his elbows and peered through the hedge. The men's full attention seemed to be in front of them. No one was looking back in his direction. When he saw how focused they all were at whatever they were watching the boy quickly decided what he would do. He would show them how well he could hunt and stalk. He would stalk *them*. He would sneak up behind them and give them such a fright that they would surely acknowledge that he deserved to be included in the hunt.

With his breathing slowed, the boy began to belly crawl forward. The ground scraped and scratched his chest but he hoped the discomfort would soon be worth it. When the surrounding forest cover would allow it and the men ahead looked busy talking to one another, the boy would allow himself to rise to all fours and crawl rapidly. In this way he covered twenty to thirty yards at a time in bursts.

During one of the times when he was lying there, he saw a bright red ladybug climbing valiantly toward the top of a blade of grass, readying itself for flight. The boy reached out a hand and the ladybug climbed upon the back of it without ever breaking stride. He turned his hand over and over and watched the ladybug climb. He loved nature. He loved to observe creatures of all types, he loved the outdoors. He was at home outside.

Finally, he turned his fingertips toward the sky. Instinctively sensing which direction was up, the ladybug climbed to the tip of his index finger and took flight. After the boy's eyes followed her flight his focus returned to the men. He had gotten lost in the moment as he sometimes did in nature. Now it was time to return to the business at hand.

As he drew closer, he could see that they were looking down at a large hole or pit in front of them. He began to move closer still when he was stopped by an almost guttural shriek. There was something in that ravine that was very angry.

The boy, easing back down to his belly, inched closer. Now, in addition to making sure he did not draw the attention of the men, the boy also focused on whatever creature was creating a whirlwind of fury within the pit. Apparently his best efforts were only partially successful, for every time he moved, the creature flew into renewed rage. The boy's breathing began to increase, as though he had been running. Beads of sweat broke out upon his forehead and stung his eyes. He was not afraid. Instead, he was beginning to shake with excitement and anticipation. It was not until the boy had drawn within ten feet or so of the men, and approximately fifteen feet from the creature that he saw what the men were watching.

A huge wild boar had fallen into the pit. The steep sides prevented him from using his short but powerful legs to climb out and escape. Dust and dirt flew as the boar reared and clawed desperately at the sides of the pit with his front hooves. The furious creature used everything at his disposal, even digging his gleaming tusks into the top edge of the pit wall and using his bulging neck muscles to try and lift himself. At this attempt the men reeled backwards, falling atop one another in a heap. The boy smiled at this, sitting his bow and quiver silently off to one side and reaching around to grip the bone handle of his hunting knife.

"We had better watch it," Cush said. "If we spear him and don't kill him outright, he will surely make it out of there and attack us all."

"We need to come up with another strategy," Magog, the son of Shem spoke up. Magog had learned his love of hunting from his father, going so far as to make his living by selling game and furs to the others in the valley of Shinar. He continued, "We can use our bows and all shoot an arrow into him at the same time."

"I have an even better suggestion," Magog's brother Arphaxad, or X as he was called, said. "Let's leave this brute alone and go and find a nice stag to bring down or some other source of meat that doesn't fight back."

"Are you kidding?" Cush exclaimed. "This boar can feed all of our families for a couple of weeks, not to mention the hide we will take home. No, we will take him while he is vulnerable."

At that the boar made yet another furious attempt to either escape or reach the men. It was impossible to tell which one he wanted to do more. Despite themselves, all three men startled visibly and threw their arms up in front of their faces.

"He doesn't look that vulnerable to me," X said, now breathless.

"One thing is for sure," a voice spoke behind them. Before they could turn around to see who was there, the boy flew by them in a blur as he ran toward the pit. As he passed he continued, "you all talk too much.'

"Nimrod!" Cush screamed as he watched his son run full speed toward the boar. He reached his hand out in a futile attempt to stop his youngest son. Nimrod dove into the pit head first, simultaneously placing his large hunting knife between his teeth. In an instant he disappeared into the pit. Everything exploded before the men's eyes. The earlier fury of the boar paled in comparison to what now ensued.

Cush wanted to rush to Nimrod's aid but fear held him paralyzed in place. He didn't want to see his son ripped to shreds before his very eyes. The melee continued for what seemed like minutes. The boar screeched and screamed, then blood splattered up out of the pit, making it so far as to spray the face of Magog. After another moment, the boar fell silent. The gruesome sounds of gurgling breaths could now be heard from the pit.

X and Magog turned their backs and immediately began to feel nauseous at the desperate sounds of their dying cousin. Cush only rolled over onto his back, clutching his hair in his hands and gritting his teeth.

"Why," he cried out. "Why would he try such a foolish thing?"

"Are you all going to lay there or are you going to help me pull this beast out of the pit?"

It couldn't be. The voice belonged to Nimrod. Magog and X wheeled around as Cush came rapidly to his feet. The men's mouths hung agape. Nimrod boosted himself up out of the pit and stood before them, his bloody knife held loosely, casually now in one hand. His blood covered chest was heaving and blood ran down his legs and onto his knee high moccasins.

"What did you want me to do," the boy asked. "Lay back there and wait for you ladies to finish wringing your hands about what to do next?" At this he smiled broadly, clearly proud of himself, though not surprised.

"Whaaa," Cush tried to question his son but couldn't form the words. He was dumbstruck. "How did you..." his voice trailed off once again. He tried to get angry but anger could not overcome the shock. No man Cush had ever known was capable of such a feat, much less a twelve year old boy.

Though the men in the hunting party were full grown, they eased toward the pit on watery legs. They looked down upon the boar that lay on his side dead, his throat cut cleanly and deeply from one ear to the other. Still in shock, they looked back toward Nimrod, who had now pulled a rough cloth from one of their packs and begun to clean his knife and hands.

"I killed him for you. Now you three can clean him. I am going to head back up the trail towards home. I saw some deer tracks. If I can take a stag I will leave him beside the trail for you. For now, I am going down to the stream to clean up a bit."

The men just stood there, their jaws still slack from what they had just witnessed. As they watched Nimrod fade into the forest it never occurred to one of them to do anything other than what they had been told.

CHAPTER 32

Canaan walked along the stony path high up on the mountainside. He had taken to living in the highlands right before the volcanic eruptions that had occurred all those years ago. Earthquakes and volcanoes had greatly changed the landscape while terrorizing the people. Despite this the population had thrived. Noah and Sapphira still lived, as did all their son's. Adina, Canaan's own mother, had been dead now some 70 years. The last Canaan had heard, Shem and Prisca lived within a half day's walk of Noah. Japheth still lived many miles from these mountains where he had settled on the far side of a great lake with Tamara and their children. They had sailed back a few times so that Japheth and Tamara could choose spouses for their sons and daughters. But that had been several years ago now. Canaan couldn't remember how long.

None of them came up here to see Canaan and the wife he had chosen named Helga. His own daughters had long since moved to the valley, to live amongst the Shemites and the Hamites, descendants of his own father and uncle. Canaan spat black coca juice vehemently into the dust as he thought once again about the curse he still lived under. He felt he had defied the curse. He had three sons still living with him and they frequently followed him on raids into the valley. The raids were rarely violent. Canaan didn't need violence so much anymore. What his former reputation wouldn't do for him, his ability to manipulate others did. He could usually con the villagers out of most of what he wanted or needed.

The solitude he lived with most of the time didn't even seem like a part of the curse at all, since he hated each and every person he encountered, outside of Helga and his sons. He snorted then, thinking that he really didn't even like Helga, but she did come in handy on the occasional cold night.

For now Canaan had no particular place to go or task to accomplish. He was doing what he did most days. He was wandering. He would steal what meager food he needed to sustain him until the next raid, plus just enough extra to keep Helga energetic enough to work.

He despised seeing his extended family. They always talked to him about working for them for a time before he would finally convince them to just give him what he needed. His silly daughters and a few of his sons had accepted this approach toward life and they now worked six days each week for the Shemites. The other Hamites largely fended for themselves and were nearly as prosperous as Shem's line was. His children assured him that they were well treated and fairly compensated for their work, but that just wasn't good enough for Canaan.

Canaan stopped at a place along the trail where he could see for miles down into the valley. Not too far from the base of the mountain he saw the tiny image of someone emerging from the forest and starting onto the trail that lead though the large meadow which stood between the forest and the village. As Canaan squinted he began to make out a boy walking alone. The corner of Canaan's mouth curled up in a sneer and he looked well ahead of the boy for a place to descend the mountain. Canaan had no intention of standing idle when such an opportunity presented itself.

CHAPTER 33

Nimrod kicked little puffs of dust into the air as he walked, covering the top of his moccasin in chalky soil. He had done exactly what he told the men he would do. He had stalked a nice stag, harvested it with his bow and added a doe that he saw later for good measure. He had worked up a good sweat even in the crisp afternoon air as he made two trips to drag them both toward the trail. The men would come home with plenty of meat, all provided by a boy who was too young to be allowed to hunt. Nimrod laughed to himself at that thought.

He supposed he would still be punished in some way for breaking free from the shed but that didn't worry him. His father's spankings didn't hurt him much. And besides, he had the advantage of having been right. He had told them all that he would prove to them he could hunt alongside any man in the village.

Though he was lost in thought, a glimmer of movement off to his left brought him to full alert. Then, with the addition of rustling sounds from the brush, Nimrod leapt to a hiding spot behind some boulders alongside the trail. With lightening quickness he pulled one of his four remaining arrows from the quiver on his back. One of the original six arrows had been broken when the stag ran a short distance with it protruding from his hip after he had been shot by one.

From his hiding place, Nimrod watched the area of brush on the opposite side of the trail where he had heard the sound and seen the motion. The first two fingers of his right hand pulled lightly on the bow string, one on each side of the arrow knock a half inch from the feather fletching. He would be able to draw his bow smoothly and evenly when a shot presented itself, even though none of the other boys could come close to drawing it. Nimrod's bow had nearly as much pull as his father's or any of the other men's. It was another fact that made Nimrod feel proud of himself.

It only took a moment for Nimrod to go from being the hunted to the hunter, for he saw pale white skin and a shock of white hair moving clumsily among the undergrowth. It was his Uncle Canaan. Nimrod rolled his eyes with a mixture of boredom and contempt. He had hoped he was being stalked by a bear or large cat, something that would cause real excitement. Instead, he would be faced with another attempt by his uncle to intimidate or frighten him.

Canaan had been successful in doing this with most of the residents of the valley. In fact he had been so successful that stories and legends abounded around the campfires about some supposed magical powers that Canaan possessed and about how he drank blood and cast spells. It was all poppycock as far as Nimrod was concerned. It was with that thought that he decided he would teach his uncle a lesson. If he could handle an enraged boar, this would be no challenge at all.

Nimrod knelt and set his bow and arrow down silently. He didn't even bother to remove the quiver from his back. There was not much danger of him frightening this particular quarry. He rose to a crouch and stepped smoothly across the trail and into the brush where his uncle now waited.

Canaan didn't know what was taking the boy so long. He had crept into a perfect ambush position at great personal cost. Brambles and briars had scratched his face and arms. It would be a small price to pay to scare the excrement out of one of these Shemite punks. Canaan didn't even know which one was heading this way. "No matter," he thought maliciously. "I like playing with them all."

Once he had the child petrified with fear, he would make him do things for his entertainment. Then before he could make their way back to the village for help, he would disappear into the mountains. He had never gone this far before. In the past he had only scared them a little. Maybe pushed them around. This time, he decided to go further, a great deal further.

"Where is the little dweeb," Canaan thought. Finally, tired of waiting, Canaan rose slowly to his feet to look around. Apparently something had distracted the simple minded little waif along the trail. Canaan reached out and parted some brush slowly so as not to draw attention. As he looked out toward the trail, his line of sight was blocked by a rapidly approaching club.

Before he could even begin to feel what would be an excruciating pain in the bridge of his nose, Canaan looked up through blurred vision to see his nephew Nimrod standing astride him.

"Oh Uncle," the boy said with mock surprise. "It's you! I am so sorry. I heard rustling and thought you were a wild beast come to attack me. I only reacted to defend myself. I hope you aren't hurt."

"Of course I am hurt, you idiot." Canaan gasped as his own warm blood ran from his nose and down the back of his throat. He rolled over onto his side, still trying to gather his wits and clutching his nose gingerly. "I think you have broken my nose!"

"You shouldn't sneak around in the bush like that Uncle," Nimrod said, trying to suppress a laugh. "There could be snakes there. You might get hurt."

"I AM hurt!" Canaan was nearly screaming now.

"Are you cross with me, Uncle? I told you I was merely trying to fend off an attack. If only you hadn't been sneaking about."

"I was not sneaking. I was merely looking for something I lost," Canaan lied, his voice growing steadily louder.

"How did you lose something in the brush if you weren't first sneaking about in the brush?" Nimrod asked.

"Why don't you go home and leave me alone. I was expecting a Shemite, not you. You have done enough damage."

"Perhaps I should stay and help you stop that bleeding," Nimrod protested half-heartedly.

"I don't want or need any help from you. You've done enough; now go."

Nimrod knew his uncle was lying. The only thing he detested more than a liar was a bad liar. He started to call Canaan on it. He almost told him exactly what he thought of him. But his uncle was right. He had done enough for one day. The boy jogged over to the boulders, collected his things and headed back down the trail toward home.

"My father and cousins will be along soon with some fresh meat. Perhaps they can give you a steak to place on that swelling," Nimrod winked and smiled his most charming smile. "I certainly wouldn't sneak around them. Your luck is not so good with that today."

"I wasn't sneaking!" Canaan screamed with frustration at the boys departing back.

Nimrod just kept walking towards home and smiling. As he walked he couldn't stop thinking about how much fun it would be to turn back and continue Canaan's lesson.

CHAPTER 34

Twenty five years later…

Nimrod's horse Milchama pawed at the crystal clear water in the stream bed with relish, splashing not only his own chest but Nimrod's leather boots and his bare knees as well.

"Oh no you don't," Nimrod spoke to his steed as he gently squeezed his heels into the horse's sides in order to get him moving. "I don't care if you are a little hot; you're not rolling in this stream bed with me on your back again." Nimrod smiled as he watched the horse turn his head fully back to look at his master with one large brown eye. "Innocent as you can be, aren't you?" Nimrod was chuckling now. "Come on, let's get across and then I'll strip your saddle and let you cool off.

As they finished crossing the stream, a cacophony of splashing hooves could be heard, for Nimrod was traveling with a train of ten pack animals. Each horse was now heavily laden with salted meat, hides and fresh meat. Nimrod had enjoyed yet another successful hunting trip. Many would feast upon this bounty.

During this ten day excursion, Nimrod had harvested more wild game than any twenty men in the village could have obtained. Hunting was still Nimrod's greatest passion, but now, in his thirties, he was discovering many other more creative outlets as well.

As the pack animals followed dutifully up the far bank, Nimrod stopped them under the shade of a large tree. The trunk of the tree spanned at least twenty-five feet and the huge canopy shaded all the horses with room to spare. As promised, Nimrod stripped the saddle from his horse, who then lowered his large head so that Nimrod could take the bridle off as well. As soon as the bit left the horse's mouth he reared up, spun on his rear hooves and thundered into the stream with a tremendous splash.

"Easy there fellow," Nimrod said as he swiped flecks of moist soil that the hooves had kicked up from his huge forearms. "You nearly took my head off in your rush to swim." He wasn't angry with the horse, and he began to chuckle again as he watched the horse roll in the stream bed, then rise to run through the water and kick up his heels.

At the sight of his horse enjoying a cool bath, the pack horses began to grow restless under their loads. "No, no," Nimrod scolded mildly. "Don't get any ideas. There is no way I am stripping everything off all of you and then re-saddling you." He then reached into a haversack tied to his own saddle, which was now lying on the ground beside him, and pulled out a fist full of sugar cane. He had cut the cane into small chunks prior to his trip for special occasions just like this one. He went down the line, feeding each pack animal a treat to appease them while promising to let them have their time to bathe once they got home.

Nimrod left all the horses tied lightly to a fallen branch. He had every confidence that the well trained animals would stay there. Just as he knew that his own horse would come and find him once he got the frolic out of his system. He had raised each of them from young colts and trained them to his satisfaction, which meant they were the best handling horses in the entire realm.

Nimrod now strolled out of the shade of the tree, one hand resting on the hilt of the sword that seemed to be perpetually at his side, and headed for higher ground. He knew that at their current elevation, all he needed to do was top the rise and he would be able to see for miles into the valley below. As he crested the hill, he pulled a tall stalk of grass from the ground, snapped off the ends, and placed one end in his mouth. He stopped then, rested one boot on the trunk of a fallen tree, and took in a breathtaking view of the valley of Shinar.

To the East he could just make out the moderate buildings of Calneh, the village where he had grown up and which his plans had helped turn into a small city. Just west of Calneh was Accad, slightly larger and several years newer than his home town. At the far eastern edge of the valley was Erech, which was larger than Calneh, but not as large nor as developed as Accad. He couldn't see Erech from here. Finally, near the center of the valley and currently still under construction, sat Babel. Babel would be the largest and most grand city, not only in Shinar, but in the history of the entire world. It was Babel where Nimrod's men now labored and where he currently resided.

Babel would be his crown jewel and the greatest accomplishment of his highly accomplished life.

Suddenly, Nimrod lunged forward in the direction of the city and nearly lost his balance. He had been nudged hard in the center of his back. His horse had walked up behind him and nudged him playfully with his soft nose. Unfortunately, a playful nudge from a horse that stood seventeen hands was enough to nearly send Nimrod head over heels.

Nimrod turned back toward the horse and grabbed him affectionately around his muscular neck. The two began to tussle but then suddenly, just as quickly as they had begun, they stopped. The horse pricked up his ears and listened intently back in the direction of the stream. He was focused well downstream from where the pack horses still stood. A brief moment later Nimrod heard it too. He was certain that he heard the sound of giggling.

***

They held hands so tightly that their fingertips turned white. They squeezed themselves firmly against the embankment. For some inexplicable reason, everything had just become extremely funny. Perhaps it was nervous laughter at the thought of being discovered. In any case, both Elizabeth and Jerah had a severe case of the giggles. They had met early that morning as they did every week, at the point where this same stream dumped its cold clear water into the larger and murkier river. The two had begun to walk and talk and had lost all track of time. They had walked up stream, greatly enjoying their time together and completely lost in the moment, and had wandered very far from home. As they sat side by side on a large boulder in the stream, dangling their bare feet in the water, they heard the sound of horses enter the stream just up from where they were sitting.

The young couple didn't know who had stumbled upon their little hideaway. They only knew that someone was nearby and that if they were caught, they would both be in big trouble. The whole thing was just so terribly exciting and adventurous.

Elizabeth, a Shemite, was forbidden by her father from having anything to do with a Hamite boy. And though young Jerah was of the line of Cush, the one all valley dwellers considered the most preferable of all the Hamite descendants, Elizabeth was still not allowed to associate with him.

Elizabeth's grandfather was Gomer, the eldest son of Shem himself. As such, her parents had plans for her. They would find a suitable husband of their own choosing. And the most important trait they would seek in that young man was a heart for God. So few people these days truly worshipped God, or even took that much time to think about Him, that Elizabeth's parents would choose very carefully. But one thing was certain. The young man would be Semitic.

Elizabeth trusted Jerah. Very few boys would have spent an entire afternoon with her, so far out in the wilderness, and yet remained a perfect young gentleman. Other than splashing her and nearly making her fall into the stream, Jerah had not tried anything the least bit boorish. In fact, just the opposite was true. Jerah had spent the majority of their time together alternately being silly and making her laugh or sharing his wonder for God's creation.

He had shown her many things about the natural world that, being a girl in her culture, she had never been shown before. The entire afternoon had been quite delightful. Even now, snuggling close together under the roots of a large cottonwood that grew at the bank of the stream, and hiding from this unidentified person on horseback, Elizabeth was thoroughly enjoying herself, even though she was a tiny bit scared.

"I don't hear anything," Jerah said in a barely audible whisper. His breath smelled of the mint leaves he had been chewing, and Elizabeth thought that too was quite pleasant about him. "I think they may have gone," he continued

Elizabeth didn't answer and instead only nodded her agreement, her eyes wide and bright with the excitement of their success.

"What do you two think you are doing all the way out here?"

The voice was deep and booming. Both Elizabeth and Jerah wheeled around, now truly afraid. Jerah's eyes widened as he instinctively put one arm in front of Elizabeth, as if he could possibly protect her. It was him. It was really Nimrod.

"Oh no," Elizabeth thought. "Of all the people in the entire valley of Shinar to find us, it simply couldn't be any worse." Already she was beginning to have images of her father Shechem ranting throughout the small cottage where they lived. Once he was told he would be in a horrible rage. She started to say something in their defense, but words wouldn't form. This was the closest she had ever actually been to Nimrod. He had once passed by her at a distance, and then she could see why all the women found him fascinating and handsome. Now, up this close, and with him towering over them as he stood atop the bank, she was much more intimidated than she was intrigued.

"Sir, I beg your pardon," Jerah suddenly found his voice. "We... uhh, I mean I...umm, meant no harm. We have only been on a nature walk and we drifted further than we meant to from home."

Jerah's explanation was interrupted at that moment by a bellowing laugh from Nimrod. "Yes, I am sure you have been on a nature walk," Nimrod said. For a brief moment he eyed Elizabeth in such a way that she felt uncomfortable. Then he quickly looked away, and began talking to Jerah again. Elizabeth thought for a second that she sensed an expression of remorse in Nimrod's eyes, as if he regretted what he had said.

"Boy, do you expect me to believe you drug this young lady all the way up here by accident? Why, you are sitting in a spot that is a good four miles from the nearest farm or cottage."

"Yes sir," Jerah went on. His voice was still shaky and he was clearly afraid, but he seemed to be gaining his footing and Elizabeth was proud of him for that. "That is the farm that Elizabeth is from. I didn't mean to walk with her this far, but we lost track of time."

"Well whether you meant to or not," Nimrod said, "You will be quite lucky to have her home before dark even if you start at a fast pace right now. What do you suppose her father would say if you came dragging his daughter home in the dark of night, hum? Since I doubt very seriously that you even had his blessing, I would say you have committed an offense worthy of stoning."

"No!" Elizabeth cried out suddenly, surprising even herself with her passion. "Please, sir, he was the perfect gentleman. He didn't do one thing untoward. Please don't…"

Nimrod stopped her by holding up his massive palm. "Not to worry little one. I am not going to turn you in this time. In fact, you may both consider yourselves lucky that I am the one who found you. Because what I am going to do is offer you both a ride back to the settlement on one of my pack animals. That's the only way you will make it home before they start searching for you. As for you young man, you had better be much more careful about the time and how far you go in the future."

CHAPTER 35

Noah sat cross legged in the midst of the moist soil. He was digging potatoes from the hilled dirt. He loved his garden. He had always been a farmer at heart. Sapphira rounded the corner of their well-built but humble home and started toward him. They were both very old now but healthy and enjoying their twilight years. Sapphira stopped suddenly and placed a hand on her forehead to shade her eyes.

"Well, would you look who's coming there," she said as she dropped the basket, lifted her skirt, and began to run. She ran awkwardly, as one might expect a woman her age to, but she ran nonetheless.

Noah looked up to see what she was talking about and got to his feet as rapidly as his old knees would let him. He recognized his eldest son's walk even from this distance. He hadn't seen Shem in almost three months now.

"Don't you two run all the way out here, I'll come to you," Shem called to his parents as he smiled broadly and began to run himself.

The trio embraced and then with Shem in the middle, walked arm in arm toward the house, Noah helping with Shem's rucksack. As Sapphira struggled to pull the door open on its leather hinges Shem thought, it hardly seemed fitting that the patriarch of all mankind was reduced to a tiny house, and a small garden.

They went inside the house and sat down to enjoy a cool cup of well water as Shem caught them up on the latest family news. Prisca and all Shem's children were well, though scattered throughout the valley. Only Arphaxad remained close to home, having built a home for his family within sight of Shem's. Finally, Noah got to the question that was heavy on his mind.

"You found him?" Noah said.

"I found him." Shem answered. "And he is well...mostly."

Noah turned stiffly, his neck sore these days from arthritis, and stared at his son, waiting for further explanation.

"Well," Shem went on. "Physically, Ham seems alright. He has put much of his weight back on from the days when he got so thin and pale. And in some ways it seems that his spirit has returned. He has finally stopped pursuing Canaan. He has finally accepted that they will never be reconciled. He spoke of missing Cush and Ruth and his other children, but he refuses to come down from the hills to see them, or any of us. He says that we are all better off without him. He busies himself by coming up with all sorts of inventions to make his life easier. That's good I suppose, it keeps his mind fresh. Still, it seems that he spends way too much time inside that stuffy hut that he lives in, tinkering."

Noah showed his teeth briefly as he grimaced involuntarily. "I had so hoped that by now he would have turned back to God. I had hoped he would be living life once again, perhaps thinking of marrying."

"I know you did Dad, and I would have liked to find him much happier too, but I…" Shem's words trailed off as he looked out the open window. Then he said, "Well, speaking of someone who lives his life, here comes Nimrod."

CHAPTER 36

Though Shem stood and smiled in anticipation of seeing his great nephew, there also seemed to be an air of caution in his demeanor.

Sapphira said, "Isn't this a fine day for visitors? First we get a visit from Shem, and now here comes our great-grandson."

Noah followed Sapphira's eyes. Off in the distance, topping a faraway hill, was a fine white horse with a large rider. The horse was followed closely by a train of ten pack animals, each well loaded down.

"Nimrod seems to have a lot to carry." Shem said.

"Yes," Noah answered. "I had heard he was off on one of his hunting trips. I've lost track of how long he has been gone. That will be him alright, who else would be coming with that much bounty?" The old man shook his head, a look of admiration on his face.

"Good grief," Shem said. "The pack animals are still coming over the crest of the hill. It would have taken me and ten men an entire month to bag that much game. And I am a pretty fair hunter in my own right."

"Well, I say he should be ashamed of himself," Sapphira chimed in. "The world was a better place when we were all satisfied with just eating vegetable stew. Even if one feels that they must have meat, no one person needs that much game. It's absolutely sinful for one man to kill that much."

"Now, Grandma," Noah said. "You know that he is always very generous with it. He shares with so many. Many are fed because of his success. No hide or morsel goes to waste."

"I have to agree with Dad on this Mother," Shem said. "What is the difference if one man harvests all this game and furs or if a hundred men do it for a hundred families? The same number of people are fed either way."

"It just doesn't seem right, that's all." Sapphira let her voice trail off as Nimrod pulled up his horse at the edge of the yard. He was smiling broadly and called out a jovial greeting. Then he saw a perturbed look on his great-grandmother's face and his smile faded a bit.

"What's the matter Grandma? I can tell by your expression you are displeased. What is on your mind?" Nimrod called out as he approached the table where they were all gathered. "Is Grandpa being mean to you again?"

Noah and Shem both looked away from Sapphira and tried to suppress a laugh. Nimrod was cocky, that much was certain, but they both couldn't help but get a kick out of his feisty way with

Sapphira. Only Japheth had ever had the confidence to tease her, and even he had never gone half so far as Nimrod.

"Just don't you worry about what is on my mind boy, you don't want to know what is on my mind." Sapphira replied sharply. She had never been one to back down. "It looks to me as if you have plenty to worry about with getting all this game ready before it spoils." Sapphira stood looking at the table, then turned on her heel and walked abruptly inside.

Nimrod, now with one foot resting on the bench opposite the other two men, only smiled a charming smile in her direction. "Think she will come back out before I leave?"

"Most likely, I would say half her frustration is that you haven't come out to see her often enough." Shem smiled as he spoke, rose, and grasped Nimrod's hand in a firm handshake. Shem had always been a strong strapping man, but compared to Nimrod, he felt like a little boy. The younger man's hand nearly engulfed his own as they shook.

"Grandpa, how are you feeling these days," Nimrod asked as he reached to hug the old man. Noah looked reluctant, and then Nimrod said. "Not to worry, I'll be gentle this time."

Noah laughed and wrapped his arms around the broad shoulders of Nimrod. "I may be old and brittle, but I think I still have a hug or two in me for one of my favorite great-grandsons." They both chuckled at that, then Shem and Noah sat back down.

"I've brought some game for you. I think I can leave enough to take care of the two of you for quite a while. I wasn't expecting to see you, Uncle Shem, but I can give you something to take back for your family as well."

"That's generous of you Nimrod, but I have enough in my smokehouse now to last through the winter even if I don't go hunting again this year." Shem said. "I have to congratulate you though; looks like you have had quite a haul this time."

"Ehh, I've had better hunts, but there is enough here to reward my men and their families."

At Nimrod's mention of his men, Shem squinted briefly. Noah looked at Shem, a subtle look of worry in his eyes. For his part, Nimrod clearly noticed Shem's look of concern. No one said anything for a moment. Then Noah changed the subject.

"Nimrod, God has blessed you with many skills and hunting is certainly one of your greatest. I never cease to be amazed by your success."

"Well, Grandpa," Nimrod said, watching Shem out of the corner of his eye. "God gives us blessings and gifts but it is up to us what we do with those gifts. Other men might have been too lazy to develop the ones that I was given and instead let them languish. I on the other hand have worked very hard to develop my skills, to develop my gift. Now I am not afraid to say that I am the greatest hunter who has ever lived. Hundreds are fed because of my efforts and dedication."

"You certainly have worked at it, Nimrod," Shem said. "I have to give you credit for that. But your work would only be an exercise in frustration if you weren't gifted."

"And my gift would be wasted if I didn't work hard at it."

"I think we are beginning to talk in circles here," Noah remarked with an uneasy smile.

Shem seemed not to hear his father and continued. "Likewise, no matter how skilled you are, and no matter how much you work to develop the gifts God has given you, that would all be for naught if God didn't provide you with game to hunt."

Shem's tone was more forceful now. Both Noah and Nimrod knew that Shem was working towards a larger point. Nimrod decided to go ahead and get it over with.

"Great Uncle Shem, I respect you as all young men should. And I mean no disrespect now. We only see one another once a year or so, and I wonder if there will ever be a time when the two of us can meet and not have to have this conversation? I saw your expression when I spoke of the men I have working for me. You have already made it perfectly clear how you feel about my life's work…my calling. And I have made it clear to you that I simply don't agree."

Noah slapped a palm lightly against his forehead. "You two used to get along so well. For the last few years you cannot be around one another without arguing."

"The reason for that is quite simple, Dad," Shem said, growing irritated. "It was only in the last few years that Nimrod insisted on going full speed ahead in building these cities. We all saw what the city in the old world led to. Or have we already forgotten that?" Shem raised an eyebrow at Noah.

"You are going to throw this in my lap now?" Noah asked, incredulous. "Of course I haven't forgotten what happened." Noah brought the fingertips and thumb of his right hand together and shook the hand up and down at the wrist as he continued, "I preached all around that city, begging people to turn from their sin and join us on the ark. No one in this family suffered the derision and the beatings that I suffered in that town. And you're asking me if *I* remember. This is different. Nimrod is building cities to help people. He wants to improve their lives."

At that Noah waved his palms once towards Shem and turned away. "You tell him Nimrod, he won't listen to me."

Shem turned toward Nimrod, his very expression issuing a challenge to the younger, larger man.

"Uncle Shem, I am certain we have been through this before. There is a symbiosis that takes place when people are encouraged to live amongst one another."

"You think I don't know that," Shem replied. "We all started in this world and survived much difficulty precisely because we lived near one another. We all need community, yet, in those days, we each were responsible for our own families. Each person worked first to provide for their immediate family. No one in my family expected my brother's families to provide anything for us."

"Again, with all due respect Uncle, you are thinking too small. I don't mean when just families live close to one another somewhere out in the middle of the wilderness or on adjoining farms. I mean when hundreds or even thousands of people live together, help one another, and provide for one another."

"God is our provider, He always has been. We don't need to depend on other men," Shem said sharply.

"Shem, my son," Noah said. "You are reading too much into it. The people in the city can love God just as strongly as we do, they…"

"You mean like the love they had for God in the city before the flood?" Shem shot back. His expression surprised Noah. There was intensity in his son's eyes that he had rarely seen directed toward him. Noah dropped his head and stared at the ground for a moment. Shem, regretting the edge in his tone, softened, "Father, I fear you are not reading *enough* into it. It doesn't concern me much *that* they live in a city, it concerns me *how* they live there."

Nimrod broke in, "From each according to his gifts, to each according to his need. That is the philosophy I have encouraged in the cities. What can possibly be wrong with that? If left to themselves the people do not see the grand scheme. They need leaders to step back and see that for them. They need a leader or an organization of leaders to plan for them with a view towards what is best for all. Someone to coordinate....to...to centralize."

"Therein lies the problem, Nimrod," Shem said, raising his voice once again. "You trust yourself to make those decisions for thousands of others. I trust no man that far. The people in the city don't need to be looking to you to plan their lives. They need to look within their heart, a heart that is dedicated to God. God will show them the 'grand scheme' as you call it."

"You assume I intend this role for myself, Uncle. I never said that was the case. As the cities are completed and the currency becomes standardized, the people can appoint leaders as they see fit."

"Oh, come now Nimrod," Shem said. "Who is going to dare challenge you? And if others are appointed, are they going to ever dare disagree with you? I can tell you one thing, my family and I will not be living under any such system of yours, and I think I can speak for Japheth as well."

"Enough!" Noah shouted louder than Shem had heard him in years. The old man's hands shook in midair in frustration as he pushed between Nimrod and Shem and walked into his home.

"Well, Uncle, I am certainly glad you were here to make my visit a pleasant one," Nimrod said, a touch of bitterness in his voice. Then he turned and walked back towards his horse.

"Nimrod," Shem spoke with authority. The younger man stopped with his back still towards his grandfather's brother. Shem continued, his voice husky with passion, "It is not God's will for you to build those cities, to keep his people corralled up there. And whatever you perceive as your dreams or your destiny cannot change that."

Nimrod turned on his heel, anger flashing in his eyes. For all his size and power, Shem had never seen Nimrod angry, or even unhappy for that matter. For a brief moment, Shem felt something he had never experienced before - fear of another man.

"So then, Uncle," began Nimrod, his tone suddenly bordering on disdain. "You alone have the power to determine God's will for everyone? You think you are better than me…better than the people in the city?" Nimrod's arm swept toward the horizon. He took a step closer to Shem until the two were nearly touching. Nimrod's deeply muscled chest was nearly higher than Shem's head. Now it was he who spoke with authority. "The construction of the cities will continue. Someday you will come to realize that I was right and this was best for the people. But if it bothers you that deeply, then perhaps it would be best if you never come near the cities again."

Shem didn't like feeling intimidated. Nimrod would be a fearsome opponent if things ever became physical, so Shem had no intention of letting it get to that point. Nimrod walked to the nearest pack horse, cut the large shoulder of an elk loose, and walked back over to the table with it.

"That's for Grandpa Noah," he said plopping the shoulder down on the table. Without another word, he walked back to his horse. As Nimrod mounted, he reined the animal hard to the left. Then he stopped, placed a hand on the horse's rump and looked back over his shoulder to face Shem once more. "I suppose you think God has appointed *you* to tell us all how we must live our lives Uncle, is that right?" he said. Then he spurred his horse, galloped to the front of his pack train and headed them in the direction of Babel.

Shem looked after his nephew for a moment and thought about his parting words. He looked toward his father's house. His father was tired, and aging rapidly now. After another moment Shem said aloud, "Yes Nimrod, considering the path you are leading others down, I am afraid he has. And God help me in that daunting task."

CHAPTER 37

Nimrod let the reins hang loose on Milchama's neck, for the animal knew on his own exactly what streets they would take and what stops they would make. As they closed in on the outskirts of Babel, Nimrod admired the skeletal framework of what would soon be the tallest spires in the world. Three more buildings that had been near completion when he left had now been completed by his army of workers.

By the time the hooves of his horses began to click on the outermost stone street of the city, the people were already rushing to meet him. Women and even older children sat down their baskets of clay and sand, the ingredients in mortar, in order to hurry to greet Nimrod. From the framework of the spires, men called out and waved. Some of the younger women ran up and patted Milchama, who had long ago grown used to this kind of reception and seemed to revel in it. Pretending it was an accident, some of the women patted Nimrod's legs while staring at him with a look that could only be described as adoration bordering on obsession.

"He's home!" a man with a high pitched voice cried out.

"Nimrod has returned!" the voice of another woman called loudly.

Workers from all around the city began to drop what they were doing in order to run and greet Nimrod. Without being told what to do, many of the younger men and boys began unpacking the game. The choicest selections would be taken to Nimrod's own home, but there would be plenty for everyone.

"Not so fast everyone," Nimrod called out good naturedly. As he spoke, everyone stopped immediately to listen, "Keep out two large bucks and three of the buffalo, for tomorrow night we shall celebrate!"

A roar went up from the large crowd pressing in on all sides of Nimrod and his pack train. A feast would be prepared and the workers and their families would get a break from their labors.

CHAPTER 38

Later that evening, Nimrod arose from the first meal he had eaten in his own house in weeks. As he stood, a servant walked hurriedly toward him with a warm, wet, towel. He held out his hands and allowed her to wipe his hands and face. He had gorged on a cut of the fresh game for his supper but, of course, a man of his size required a great deal of calories. There was barely any fat on his entire frame. Suddenly, he held up a hand.

"Something's wrong," he abruptly announced.

"Sir, I don't hear anything."

"No, you wouldn't. But I sense it," Nimrod said. "Fetch my belt and weapons and have your brother saddle a fresh horse," he said absent mindedly, "Quickly now. There is trouble afoot."

CHAPTER 39

Canaan lurked in the shadows alongside the city street. His sons had been told what to do. There was no need for him to get involved personally, and no need to endanger himself.

"I am begging you. This was intended for me and my family," a man in the street was saying. "It...it is like an addition to my wages. I have worked very hard for it," his voice shaking as he tried to raise it to a shout. He tried to feign anger but was clearly terrified. The man sat astride a shabby donkey and was surrounded on three sides by Canaan's sons, each of whom was mounted on horseback. The man decided to try and feign bravery, "If you want meat, go and ask Nimrod for it. He will most likely give it to you, but I won't let you have my portion."

"And what I am telling you," Sidon, Canaan's eldest son, said, "is that we don't need to ask Nimrod, and we are not *asking* you. We are taking what you have. You can go ask Nimrod for an extra portion and see how *you* fare with him."

With that, Sidon drew a sword. The blade was of polished flint and heavy at the spine. The man had never seen a weapon like it up close and he was paralyzed with fear. He began to wonder if he was going to die tonight.

Sidon, like his father, had almost white hair, and like all of the Canaanites, his eyes were nearly black. There was no compassion in them. Unlike Canaan, Sidon's hair was not thin and wispy but was thick and fell down to the middle of his back. He was also much larger than his father, who had gone from a skinny youth to an emaciated man.

"No," the man with the food said, nearly in tears now. "My children have not had meat in over two months. I won't let you take it."

"You won't *let* us?" Sidon began to laugh a bitter, sardonic laugh. "And what will you do to stop us?"

In what had been a relatively isolated part of the city, a crowd was now beginning to gather. There were more than enough citizens watching to overtake Sidon and his two brothers, but no one lifted a hand to help the man.

"I will fight you," the man said, attempting defiance.

Awkwardly, he reached beneath his cloak with a trembling hand. When he pulled it out again, he held a crude flint hunting knife, his hand shaking violently as he held it out.

There was silence for a moment. Canaan eased forward from the near-by shadows in order to watch more closely what was about to unfold. A smile creased the corners of his mouth and he felt excitement beginning to build. He loved to watch one of the weapons he had created in action. His excitement was short lived, for at that moment, the methodical sound of horse's hooves plodding closer could be heard by everyone except Sidon.

"You insolent little insect," Sidon said. "I will cut out your liver tonight, take it to your house and feed *that* to your louse infested children."

"Zia, do these men have a problem with you?" a voice said.

"Yes, Master Nimrod." The relief in the man's voice was palpable. "They are trying to steal the meat portion that you generously gave to me."

Sidon wheeled around. At first he didn't believe the man, didn't believe that it was Nimrod. As such, there was furor in his eyes. When he turned in his saddle and saw Nimrod sitting upon his own horse, that furor rapidly turned to terror.

"Well, it sounds like you have a problem with me then, Sidon," Nimrod said.

Within an instant, Nimrod produced one of his own swords from a sheath at the front of his saddle, twirled it with precision, and caught it in the air. He then let the hilt rest on his thigh as he looked towards his opponent.

At the very sound of Nimrod's horse, Canaan shrank further back into the shadows, leaned against the trunk of a tree, and pulled the hood of his cloak over his head.

"We...we...were told that you weren't to be in the city tonight. We would never defy your law."

"You are a liar, Sidon. My law states that no citizen of Babel is to ever be harassed or threatened. So whether I was here or not, you had every intention of violating my law. Now the only question is…what should I do about it?"

Nimrod squeezed his heels in a bit and his horse eased forward. He rode close alongside each of the sons of Canaan. He could hear their rapid breathing and their hearts racing.

"I am preparing myself for a big festival tomorrow. Therefore, I feel very festive tonight, very charitable," Nimrod said with a shrug of his shoulders. "I am not going to kill you tonight. We are, after all, family. Instead, you will leave for three days on an expedition of your own. You will come back with enough game to feed this man and his family for a year. You will deliver it to him salted and ready for storage. Is that acceptable to you, Zia?"

The man on the donkey was astonished. He only nodded his agreement, his eyes wide.

Canaan's other son, Heth, spoke up. "But Master Nimrod, with all due respect, the game near here has been so often hunted that only you can harvest it. We will have to ride for days and days to find game that we can…"

"Shut up, you fool!" Sidon reached across his saddle and grabbed his younger brother by the throat, choking him to keep him from completing his plea. "We will begin preparing to leave immediately, Nimrod."

Nimrod smiled thinly at his cousin before speaking loudly. "Oh, Uncle Canaan, take a look at this workmanship." With lightning speed, Nimrod reached behind his head and drew a two edged dagger from a scabbard between his shoulder blades. He hurled the dagger into the midst of the brush, barely missing Canaan and instead piercing the hood of his cloak and pinning it to the tree he was leaning against.

"My men are now making weapons even better than yours. You may keep that and hopefully it will remind you of this night."

No one in the crowd had had any idea that Canaan was nearby. Canaan reached up gingerly to grasp the dagger's handle. It took all of the strength in his bony arm to free it from the tree. He didn't speak. Instead he stepped dejectedly from the shadows, walked up to his youngest son's horse and, struggling with the effort, mounted behind the saddle. He looked like a petulant child as he glared at Nimrod from behind his son's shoulder.

"You gentlemen had better ride before I forget what a good mood I am in," he said. "And Uncle..."

The three sons had begun to ride away but they stopped now so Nimrod could finish, though none of the men turned to face him.

"You tried to spring on me once from the bushes and you still have that crooked nose to prove it. Never hide from me again."

Nimrod sat on his horse for a few moments, his jaw muscles flexing until the sound of the departing horses' hooves died out. Then, as he continued to stare in the direction they had gone, he said, "Go home, Zia, and if I ever hear of you carrying a knife as a weapon again, I will deal with you myself. You should have known you could come to me if they had taken your provision."

"Yes, Master Nimrod, I am sorry sir," Zia said. Then his donkey made quick steps as he rode away. The crowd dispersed, and Nimrod sat alone in the gathering darkness.

CHAPTER 40

Nimrod awoke groggy the next morning. His trip had been long and taxing and he was not yet caught up on his rest. The door to Nimrod's palatial home was bolted closed and he had posted a guard. He needed no man's protection, but he knew that the people loved him and only wanted to be with him. He had been on a long journey and was not yet ready to deal with them. He intended to spend the day lounging before he prepared for what he hoped would be a big evening for him and his people. After rising, he took the inside stairs to the roof. He wanted to start his day with his favorite view.

After climbing several flights of sandstone steps, Nimrod exited through a wooden door onto his roof. As he turned to pull the door closed, he suddenly realized how much this door resembled the front door on Noah's humble abode. As he looked back, he saw in his mind's eye the door to that tiny, humble house slamming closed, a frustrated Noah on the other side. It was only at that moment that Nimrod fully realized how far he had ascended even above the patriarch.

A slight twinge of guilt tugged at him with that thought. It passed quickly though, for it was in that moment that Nimrod heard the murmur of the crowd gathered below. He walked slowly and triumphantly toward the wall that surrounded his roof and looked over. What had started as a murmur from the crowd rapidly grew into a roar. The better part of the city had already begun to gather. He rarely gave them time off and they apparently planned to make the most of it. As he reached the edge of the roof, every citizen passionately cheered for him.

They couldn't understand. They had no idea, really. Even considering the appreciation they were now showing him, the people couldn't comprehend how much better their lives would be once all of his plans were in place. He had known from a very early age that he was gifted. He had known from boyhood that the people needed his gifts and were thus drawn to him and his guidance. No one else in the world could do what he was capable of doing. It was his responsibility to fulfill his destiny.

He looked out at the crowd, but focused on individual faces. He paused on each face to make eye contact with several individuals. Many of the younger women had rushed from home adorned in their best robes. They would be coiffed and perfumed to the best of their ability for the celebratory meal, each hoping to be noticed by him. He could have any one he wanted for a wife. He could even choose several. No one would dare lift a finger to oppose him. Still, he had no interest in women or marriage. His aspirations were much higher and they needed all his focus and energy for a time.

As he thought of those aspirations he allowed his vision to leave the faces and scan out past the crowd. He took a step back as he took in the entire skyline of the emerging city. Babel would be his mistress for now, and soon he would adorn her as his bride. Nimrod scanned the horizon and breathed in deeply. The other cities, Calneh, Accad, and Erich, were complete. Babel would be finished within two months. Then the real work would begin. The foundation was already laid. The center of the city of Babel had been left bare in order to accommodate the crowning achievement of Nimrod's life. It was there that he would honor Babel with the Tower.

CHAPTER 41

Jerah crawled on his belly through the brush. He was almost close enough. He only needed a few more feet. He was pulling himself along on his elbows, when he stopped short. He needed to be stealthy and quiet but there, not more than four inches from his face, was a porcupine nestled down in the dead leaves beneath the bushes. Jerah sucked in a breath but forced himself not to cry out. He pushed himself up just as the little porcupine raised his tail threateningly. As Jerah jerked back, he hit his head on a limb of the bush.

In a reflex he threw himself back down, nearly landing on the porcupine again. Without thinking he crab--crawled his way over the porcupine as rapidly as possible, narrowly escaping a prickly face. Just as he realized that he had been flushed from his hiding place and into the clearing, he heard laughter. It was an unmistakable laugh, throaty, and deep for a young girl, and utterly charming.

He turned to see Elizabeth covering her mouth, her brown eyes twinkling with delight at his misfortune. Jerah, on the other hand, was quite serious about the situation he found himself in, and he jumped behind a nearby tree.

"Stop laughing at me! Your father will be out here any second if he hears that."

"He..." She laughed some more and Jerah couldn't help but smile. He loved to hear her laugh, even when it was at his expense, which was often the case.. "Don't worry, he's nowhere near. He has gone to the forest for timber. By the way, you have a shrub sticking out of your hair."

She reached out a hand and plucked a small leafy twig from Jerah's dark hair. He liked being this close to her. He reveled in the smell of the lavender wafting from her hair.

"You told me he would be working nearby," he said. At first he was a bit angry, but as he watched Elizabeth's face break into another glowing smile, he soon forgot what he was upset about. "That is why I was crawling about in the bushes like some... snake or something. I was going to try to crawl close enough to get your attention so you would come out and talk without him catching us."

"Yes, I know," she said, still smiling brightly. "I've been hiding around the corner, watching you for twenty minutes. You really don't make a very good snake. You should stick to walking upright." She laughed heartily again, enchanting him all the more.

Jerah feigned anger but he, too, was starting to chuckle.

"Come with me," Elizabeth said. "I'll show you something wonderful." As she spoke, she reached up and took Jerah's forearm and then let her hand slide gently towards his wrist as she took a step towards a nearby field. The movement was so natural, so second nature, that for a brief moment neither of them realized their fingers had intertwined. Just like their brief moment on the river bank, they were again holding hands.

A moment later both of them looked down at their hands, and their eyes widened. They both felt their faces grow hot. They were nearly old enough to marry according to the local culture, but they were also both innocent and shy. Neither had dared to instigate anything approaching physical contact.

Jerah fell asleep each night dreaming of taking Elizabeth into his arms and kissing her lips. In real life, in broad daylight, he was more frightened to try such a thing than he would have been to wrestle a large bear. She was far too beautiful for him, he was certain of that. What if she rebuffed him? He wouldn't be able to stand it. What if she actually didn't find him that attractive, but only thought of him as a friend? That rejection would be awful to endure. Better to just enjoy spending time with her. In that way he would never have to know for certain.

Jerah's fears were misplaced. Elizabeth found him cute...even handsome. What Jerah wasn't mature enough to understand was that Elizabeth looked deeper. She could already see the kind, chivalrous, and loving man that Jerah would someday be. And for now, far from repelling her, his boyish awkwardness only endeared him to her all the more. It made her feel more comfortable with her own concerns about herself. If only the two had just articulated those things to one another...

Now the pair stood there, both surprised to see they were holding hands, but not wanting the other to know that they had looked, and certainly not wanting to look even a tiny bit surprised, or excited, or happy, they each loosened their grip and let their hands fall to their sides. Elizabeth looked down at her sandals and kicked at a pebble. Jerah felt his heart sink. He hadn't wanted to let go and he was mentally kicking himself for having done so. There was an awkward silence.

"Well, if we are going to have time for me to show you…"

"Oh, yes," Jerah joined in. "We should probably go before your father comes walking up the path."

"You know, you don't have to be that concerned about him. Although he is gruff and strict, he is a good man," Elizabeth said.

"Oh, I am sure of that. My own father has mentioned him as a person that he respects. I think they have had some dealings with each other," Jerah replied. "I just think it would be better to be cautious, that's all."

"So, is your family going into the city for the celebration that Nimrod has called for?" Jerah asked.

"Oh, yes," Elizabeth answered. "My parents are excited."

"Then you will be near *my* home. Maybe I can show you some of my favorite places."

"I wonder what the celebration is all about?" Elizabeth said. "We haven't had anything like this in so long that it must be something important."

"I keep hearing rumors that Nimrod is going to finally tell us all what that massive foundation is for in the center of the city."

Unlike the other day on their grand hike, Elizabeth took the lead this time. The pair had been pleasantly surprised a few days before to arrive home and realize that neither of their parents had yet begun to worry, nor had they inquired as to their whereabouts that night. They both had Nimrod to thank for that. Now, as they made their way down the trail, Elizabeth regretted that Jerah hadn't kept hold of her hand.

The two walked without talking until they were well into the forest. Then, as the trail crossed a dry stream bed, Elizabeth stepped off the main trail.

"I first found the special place that I am taking you to by following this stream. I was barely nine years old. I was a little lost at the time. I had wandered much farther from home than I was allowed. But at that point, I was too young to know I should be frightened and the whole thing just seemed like an adventure."

Elizabeth was talking in a low voice as she walked, ducking under limbs and low hanging branches as she went. Jerah was impressed by her sure-footedness on the rocks. It was clear that she had come here many times and knew each step to take. After what seemed like a long walk on the large flat rocks in the streambed, they came to a wall of vegetation. Prickly bushes grew all around them, creating what appeared to be an impenetrable wall.

"Time to try out your crawling skills again," Elizabeth said.

"You mean we are going to try to get through there?" Jerah asked.

"If you get down low, you will see there is a clear tunnel through the bushes. I've always supposed some animal made it. It's quite open really, though I have to confess it was much easier to pass through when I was nine."

Both of them crouched down, and Jerah could see that there was indeed an open tunnel. They didn't have to belly crawl but instead were able to pass through on their hands and knees. Jerah looked down to find a hand hold and when he looked back up, Elizabeth had disappeared from sight. Jerah froze. Then, just as he was about to cry out her name, Elizabeth's face popped up about twenty feet in front of him.

"When you get right here you will have to climb down a bit. Come on, you're almost there."

Jerah scrambled to catch up, and as he drew even to where Elizabeth's face had appeared, he saw a steep drop off.

"You climbed down all this as a nine year old little girl?" he asked.

"I know, it still surprises me too. I guess I was too little to know the risk I was taking. It's an easy climb now, though."

Jerah turned around in the tunnel and climbed down backwards. It was not until he had done so that he realized he could hear water falling. Then he felt a damp mist. A moment later he dropped to his feet and stood beside Elizabeth.

"Welcome to my garden," Elizabeth said. "Other than my dog, I have never brought anyone here. Ever since God showed it to me, I have just kind of kept it to myself. It is sort of my place to talk to Him or just sit and be quiet."

Jerah looked around and couldn't help but gasp at the absolute beauty of the tiny valley they were in. They truly seemed to be standing in a secret hideaway. The thick hedges they had crawled through to get here now surrounded an area just slightly bigger than one of the large buildings in the city. Spilling out from what had seemed to be a dry stream bed was a small waterfall. There must have been a subterranean flow of water beneath where they had crawled, for the water emerged from high up on the rock wall they had climbed down.

The waterfall spilled into a small, clear pool. Elizabeth was already shucking her sandals and sticking her feet in as she sat on a large stone near the edge of the water. Large rocks surrounded the pool, each of them almost completely covered in lush green moss, ferns, and flowers. Vines covered in various colored blooms cascaded down from the hedges above, some nearly touching the pool on the far side. As Jerah sat beside Elizabeth and felt the coolness of the water on his feet, a small turtle slid off a nearby log and into the water, startling Jerah.

"My gosh!" Jerah exclaimed. "You really have chosen a special place." He could feel Elizabeth smiling at him though he wasn't looking at her. "The whole thing looks like some expert gardener designed it just so people could come and rest here."

"I think a master gardener did design it, as a matter of fact," Elizabeth replied as she plucked a tiny violet flower and placed it in her hair.

"You mean like…God?"

"Yes, silly, of course like God. What other master gardener could there be?" Elizabeth answered.

"Maybe there is no need for a gardener. Maybe all this stuff just grew here on its own. The water ran across the ground, and wherever there was softer ground, the water eroded the soil away and over time formed this stream and waterfall."

"Then where did the water come from? And where did the flowers come from?" Elizabeth asked.

"The water comes from the river, I guess, and the flower seeds could have gotten carried here by a bird or animal."

"No," Elizabeth giggled. "I don't mean where did they come from to get in this garden. I mean, where did they first come from? How did the first flower get here? Did it just pop up out of midair?" Elizabeth lifted her palms toward the sky and shrugged her shoulders.

Jerah was about to ask her how she was so sure if she had never seen God, but words failed him, because at that moment, Elizabeth turned to face him with a smile. In the soft light, with the flower highlighting tiny flecks in her eyes, Jerah thought Elizabeth looked more beautiful than he had ever seen her. This vision of her, the way she looked in this moment, would imprint itself in his mind. He didn't realize it then, but he would never forget it in his lifetime, and in the future it would both sustain and haunt him.

The moment was even more powerful than Jerah's shyness, more powerful than all his self-doubt. In that moment he did the only thing that seemed appropriate. He reached out and took her hand in his, and their fingers intertwined. This time, he didn't let go.

CHAPTER 42

The greatest honor a citizen of Erich could receive was to be invited to sit at Nimrod's table. This grand table seated fifty people and even the farthest seat was coveted. The table was covered by a tent awning and was surrounded by other smaller tables filled with those privileged to be favored by Nimrod. Still farther out, the people were gathered on blankets or around makeshift tables fashioned from left over building materials. These were the workers and their families. All were overjoyed to be included in the celebration.

The tent, Nimrod's table, and the surrounding dignitaries were all elevated on a stone and mortar platform approximately twenty-five feet high. The top of the platform was finished smoothly with mortar. The dimensions were two hundred and fifty meters wide by two hundred and fifty meters long, making it the largest foundation ever built in the history of man. When Nimrod was a very young man, he had taught the people how to make brick. Nothing had been the same since. It seemed that no matter how ambitious the project, they could build anything Nimrod envisioned, just as they had built this foundation.

No one, with the exception of Nimrod, knew what the foundation was for. The workers had only followed his exact instructions. All wondered and speculated what he would build upon it. The foundation was perfectly centered on twenty five acres of land, which was itself at the exact center of Babel. Years before, it had been a flat meadow in the valley and much of it was still covered with lush grass, with the exception of the areas where workers had hauled in brick or mixed mortar.

Tonight everyone was laughing and talking raucously. The air of celebration was palpable. Later in the evening, Nimrod would be giving a speech. The mood was particularly lighthearted at his table, until a lone figure entered the far end of the tent awning. Suddenly, the celebration was interrupted and the conversations died down to a low murmur. Even Nimrod himself was momentarily disarmed by the site of this single man. The man stood still for a time, as if he were deciding whether or not he would proceed. Then he walked deliberately toward the head of the table where Nimrod sat.

Nimrod, having stopped his conversation with a man sitting in the corner seat, now sat his golden goblet down on the table. Then, dabbing the corners of his mouth with his napkin and placing it on the table, he stood.

"Cush, so nice to see you," began the man at the corner seat.

"I hear you have been back since last evening," Cush interrupted, ignoring the other man and speaking directly to Nimrod. "You might have at least come by and paid your respects to your mother. She had to hear of your arrival through the gossip of the women."

"Well, the important thing is that he is here now." The man at the corner spoke again. Neither Nimrod nor Cush even looked at him.

"Father, I am glad to see you," Nimrod said stiffly. Then he added, "Reuben, it would be most kind of you to relinquish your seat to my father."

"But Nimrod, I have donated much to the building of this city and this is the first time I have gotten to sit with you…"

"Yes, Reuben, and your generosity is appreciated. I will be even more grateful to you for agreeing to extend that generosity further," Nimrod replied firmly.

Reuben grew more indignant. "Nimrod, I've only just received my meal. Surely you don't…"

"Then I'm sure you won't mind enjoying it somewhere on the nearby grounds." Nimrod's voice was startling in its rigidity.

Finally sensing the seriousness of the request, the man took up his plate and left without another word.

"It seems you have grown quite accustomed to having men follow your orders, son," Cush said, an air of sarcasm in his voice.

A clean plate was set before him by the daughter of one of Nimrod's hired men. The young woman wore gold bracelets on her upper arms and heavy make-up around her eyes.

"I don't intend to stay for dinner," Cush said.

"I insist," Nimrod replied sharply.

Nimrod's tone remained as abrupt with his father as it had been with the man he had just cast away from his table. Though Cush despised this, he was becoming used to it. For years now he had felt intimidated by his own son.

It wasn't just his son's size, strength or expertise as a warrior and hunter. Those traits, though apparent, were not primary in Cush's mind. This was his son, after all. Cush had survived a volcano, and he himself had hunted ever since he moved to this valley, well before Nimrod was born. He had never been known as a fearful man. No, Cush's discomfort stemmed not from Nimrod's physical prowess, but from his certitude. Nimrod was always so self-assured, always so certain of the rightness of his personal course in life. Cush had never known quite how to deal with that trait in his son.

"I...I assure you I am not hungry," he said thinly.

Nimrod didn't answer. Instead, he nodded again at the girl, who didn't seem at all nervous around Nimrod. She was too busy admiring him. With a big smile for Nimrod, the girl served his father a large helping of meat onto his plate.

"I don't want...that's not necessary," Cush stammered. "Please, I really didn't come here to eat, I..." Then suddenly he slapped his palms down on the table. "I don't want your food, son!"

When Cush shouted, the surrounding crowd went from subdued to dead silent. Quiet quickly spread to the outskirts of the crowd until it seemed the entire city was frozen in stillness.

Nimrod eyed his father coolly. Cush thought he saw a flash of anger, but if it was there, Nimrod quickly brought it under control.

"Very well, Father," Nimrod said quietly. "You don't have to eat with me."

Cush began to whisper. "Don't make this worse than it already is, and don't try to act hurt," Cush said. "If anyone is allowed to be hurt in this family it is your mother and I. Why, you barely acknowledge that we exist, much less invite us to this grand celebration. What exactly is it you are celebrating son, yourself?"

"I am simply allowing my people, especially all my workers, to have an evening to relax. They rarely get meat, and with me sharing my game with them they will feel reinvigorated. I am thinking of them, not myself. But then we have had this discussion before, far too many times. Did it ever occur to you that I may not visit you and mother because I don't want to hear about how self-centered I am, when all I am trying to do is help others?"

"Son, I know it must seem that we are always lecturing you, but that is only because you never heed our advice. We are concerned for you. We worry that you are losing yourself in trying to keep up with all the responsibilities of building cities and feeding the masses." Cush was still whispering, though at a greater volume.

"Please get outside yourself for a time. Come back to the country with me. You have too much going on here. There are too many people adoring you. It is not good for you *or* them. Did you ever stop to think what would happen to these people if, heaven forbid, something happened to you. The younger generation doesn't even know how to hunt, gather or plant. All any of them know is building what you tell them to build and eating what you feed them."

Nimrod held up a hand. His eyes narrowed and a fire began to blaze behind his eyes. "You are my parents. That doesn't mean you are experts in all things. Neither of you know anything about leading the people."

"Leading the people?" Cush's voice raised now. "You are not a king. You have not been appointed a ruler. This is crazy talk." Cush squinted in disbelief. "I understand that, though you have had no time to come and see your mother in the past two years, you stopped and visited with your great grandpa, Noah. Would you let him give you any advice on leading people? Would you listen to *him*? Well, I have talked to him, only a few weeks ago, and I can assure you he does not comprehend all that you are undertaking here. He believes everything you have told him. Son, your mother and I have some idea of your plans here, and it scares us. We are frightened for you. This is all going to your head."

"Father," Nimrod said, "you should go now." As he spoke, Nimrod grasped his father's forearm. His hand was so large that it wrapped around Cush's arm as if it were a twig. Nimrod began to squeeze and the veins bulged in Cush's hand until he thought they would burst. Cush refused to cry out though the pain was becoming intense. The two locked eyes for a moment, then Nimrod released his grip.

Cush felt something falter within himself. He searched in vain for the right thing to say, for some way of leaving with his dignity intact, but he could think of nothing. Everything he could say or do should have been done long ago. Cush knew in that moment that it was too late now. Instead of speaking further, he dropped his face to the ground. He hoped the people nearby could not see the shame and hurt in his expression. Then, turning on his heel, he slowly exited the tent. Cush could feel all the people gathered around the table staring at him with disdain.

An attractive middle aged woman had been watching the drama unfold. She walked quickly now and stood in Cush's path. As he walked by she reached out and grabbed his upper arm.

"That is not good enough," she said firmly. "He has to be brought in check."

"I've done all I can. He won't listen to me anymore," Cush said dejectedly. "Perhaps he never did. He is going to do what seems right to him." Cush didn't look up as he was speaking, and the woman hurt for him.

"You're his father, Cush. If you don't bring him under control…"

"Why don't you do it, little sister?" Cush shot back. He was angry now. He had found an anger that had failed him only moments before. "You know, Ruth, you always seem to have all the answers, so why don't you go and talk to your nephew. I am sure you can persuade him with your infinite wisdom." With that he tore his arm from her grip and disappeared into the crowd.

Ruth, the daughter of Adina and the equal of her mother in beauty, turned back to face Nimrod's tent. She looked through the crowd to catch glimpses of her nephew, who had quickly turned his attention back to the celebration. She didn't say anything more, nor did she try to catch Cush. Instead she set her jaw, folded her arms and stared with determination toward the tent.

CHAPTER 43

Jerah was unaware of all the commotion that had just taken place at Nimrod's table. He was much too busy trying to get Elizabeth's attention. She was sitting on the ground eating with her brothers and her parents, but it looked as if their meal was nearly done. Jerah had gobbled down his food and the second his mother had gone for a walk, he took off to find the girl who had enthralled him so.

Surely in the midst of this crowd I can steal a few minutes alone with her, Jerah thought. The last thing he wanted to do was endanger her for his own selfish reasons. As much as he wanted a few moments of her time, he would forfeit that before he would risk her falling under the wrath of her father, Shechem. For that matter, he had not breathed a word about Elizabeth to his own parents. He had no idea what to expect from them if they found out.

Jerah thought he saw Elizabeth's father looking his way, so he quickly ducked behind a group of men who were standing around talking.

"I am telling you, it will be some kind of sports arena," one of the men said.

"No…no," said a second man. "That is a ridiculous notion. What time does a man like Nimrod have for sport? It would seem he is a little busy feeding the entire populace with his hunting skills or from his fields and protecting us from Canaanite raids."

"Why, until last night, there had not been a Canaanite raid in over two years. I don't think that threat would stop him from engaging in a little sport," the first man replied.

Now a man who had been eavesdropping spoke, "Yes, and the very reason there haven't been more raids is because Nimrod put a stop to them. But it won't be a sports arena in any case. It will be a massive storehouse for food." The man swept his arm in an arc to indicate the huge crowd and lavish meal, and then laughed heartily.

"That is where you are wrong," the first man spoke again. "A man like Nimrod lives for competition, whether that competition comes through hunting or battle. He is going to build a huge arena where he will entertain us by challenging any and all men in the valley to matches."

"What kind of matches? Nimrod could kill any man without even perspiring."

"He won't be allowed to maim or kill. There will be rules, of course. And probably a governing body."

Now the eavesdropper burst into laughter. "And just who will make up this governing body that will give orders to Nimrod? Will you be the chairman?"

The man raised his voice. "I nominate this man chairman of the group who will give Nimrod rules to fight by." He laughed heartily for a moment as both the other men tried to shush him. They seemed concerned that Nimrod might hear, though he was much too far away and the area much too crowded.

Suddenly, a man who had been listening all along but had yet to speak stepped forward. "It won't be an arena and it won't be a storehouse. It will be an altar."

Now all of the other men began to chuckle, one spraying a mouthful of cider onto the other two.

"An altar? And you said my idea was ridiculous! An altar for what?"

"Why, for worship, of course."

"Worship of who? Of God? Who worships God anymore? You sound like Great Grampa Noah. We haven't heard from that old dried up bag of bones in years, but the last time I did, that was all he talked about. My father said that is all he has ever talked about. Worship of a supposed God is all well and good for fanatics like Noah. But I think we have advanced a little beyond building some giant altar to a mythical God."

"That's just it. That is exactly why I say it will be an altar," the quiet man said. "Nimrod is going to accomplish what Noah was never able to accomplish. He will help us overcome some of the judgmental things that Noah and Shem used to try to teach. He is going to put an end to the intolerant parts of religion that many of us find so unpalatable and show us a way to worship that we can all agree on. Don't you see? Nimrod is all about bringing people together, just as he has tonight. It is a perfect role for him."

"Well," the first man said as he wiped cider from his chin, "if anyone could do that, Nimrod could…but I still say it is going to be a sports arena."

Jerah didn't hear anymore. He moved past the men and looked toward Elizabeth's family again. Everyone was sitting there except Elizabeth. Jerah felt a little knot form in the pit of his stomach. Had he tarried too long? Had she headed for home?

Just as he was becoming disappointed, he felt a soft hand touch his forearm. He turned to look into Elizabeth's glowing smile. Initially, he tried to maintain his cool, but that was an exercise in futility. Instead, he smiled broadly and his voice rose an octave or two as he began to speak.

"I was afraid you'd eaten," he said.

"I have eaten, silly. This was a dinner, you know."

"Oh, I know, I just meant, I was afraid you had finished eating…" Oh no, Jerah thought. Why does she always throw me off so bad when I first see her? She smiles at me and I can't think straight.

Elizabeth decided to help him a bit. "I knew what you meant," she said. "I was only joking. No, I am still here."

Jerah felt the now familiar flush of his face subside and began to gather himself. "Would you like to walk with me?" he asked as he looked nervously toward her father, who was now gathering things to head for home. Any moment now he would begin looking for Elizabeth and his wife.

"I suppose we have a few minutes," Elizabeth said.

Jerah knew this was a risky time for them to be alone together. But his own father had much work for him in the coming weeks. He didn't know when he would get to see Elizabeth again. Once again he took her hand and they headed through the now thinning crowd in the direction away from Shechem.

It seemed like an eternity before they escaped the large open area and were finally able to duck behind a nearly completed building. The entire time they had been walking, Jerah felt as if fire was shooting from Shechem's eyes and boring holes into his back.

"You showed me your secret place, now let me show you one of mine," Jerah said, ducking into a gaping opening that would soon be a grand doorway into yet another new building. "You live on the outskirts of the city, but I spend most of my time right here among these buildings. There is always another one to build. We finish one and my father pushes us to start the next. So sometimes, when the workday is complete, I come back here. I pretend that I am a great man like Nimrod and that I will do great things."

In the sharply angled rays of the fading late afternoon sun, the large unfinished room took on an ethereal quality.

"I bet you will," Elizabeth said suddenly. "I bet you will do greater things even than Nimrod."

Jerah blushed again. He was thrilled that Elizabeth would say such a thing, but he wondered if she really believed that. He certainly didn't believe it himself. He hadn't planned what they would do when they got here. He had only hoped they would have some time together.

He took a step toward what would soon be stairs descending to a large open floor. It was the largest single room in the city, at least that Jerah was aware of. He braced himself with his arms and lowered his legs down the 4 foot drop to the main floor.

"I don't know what Nimrod has planned for this building, but sometimes I pretend I am a leader like him. Sometimes, now don't laugh, I pretend to make speeches here, perhaps when this entire room is filled with people anxious to hear what I will say."

Elizabeth didn't laugh. Instead she joined in, picking up where Jerah left off. She ran from one end of the landing to the other, as if on a stage.

"Yes, I can see it as well," she said enthusiastically. "You would enter here through the front door. The people would all be assembled, just waiting for you."

Jerah was more intrigued now by what Elizabeth might come up with than by anything from his own imagination.

"What would I speak about?"

"You would say….well….you might start out with something like…." Elizabeth feigned a deep and commanding voice and tucked her chin to her chest in an exaggerated manner.

"ALL OF YOU PEOPLE….UMM…STANDING AROUND HERE…."

Jerah, unable to help himself, burst into laughter.

"What," Elizabeth said placing her hands on her hips and stamping a foot. "You made me promise not to laugh at *you*." She tried to act mad but her face broke into a brilliant smile, and now she was beginning to laugh as well.

Jerah laughed harder and harder. "What kind of an opening line was that? I'm sorry to laugh, Elizabeth, but…" Now Jerah imitated Elizabeth's commanding voice, "All of you people standing around here…"

Soon they were both laughing so hard their sides hurt. Elizabeth bent over and covered her face with both hands while she laughed, and accidentally took a step off the edge of the landing.

"I'll help you," Jerah rushed to her. He stepped forward and without thinking grasped her firmly around the waist. As she fell, muscles Jerah had developed from three years of construction work enabled him to lift her weight easily, so that instead of completing her fall, she ended up suspended in front of him in midair.

Jerah knew he should sit her down, only he didn't. Instead, he found himself pulling her close to him. For a moment Elizabeth started to protest, but then realized that she didn't want to. She placed her hands on Jerah's shoulders and then wrapped them around his neck. He pulled her closer still. Jerah's heart was beating so hard that she could feel it as if it were her own. She looked down, closed her eyes, and pursed her lips. She felt his breath on her face.

"What are you two doing in here?"

Without thinking about it, Elizabeth pushed Jerah hard to separate the two of them. Then she looked fully into the eyes of her father, Shechem.

CHAPTER 44

Minutes passed like hours as everyone stood in silence, waiting for the decision of the two fathers. There had been discussion that degraded into argument. Who was at fault? Who tempted whom to come here and be alone inappropriately?

"I found this boy alone with my daughter?" Shechem continued to glare at Jerah, who could only stare at the ground. "A young man, being found alone with a young woman when they are not betrothed, is a disgrace." Shechem's voice was growing louder.

Jerah's face was burning hot once again. He wished he could control his embarrassment, and he hoped that Elizabeth didn't notice. He hoped Nimrod's speech would begin any minute and, since none of the adults would want to miss it, he and Elizabeth might be saved further embarrassment.

In their culture, Jerah had not only slighted Elizabeth, he had disrespected Shechem and his wife Hannah, Elizabeth's mother. Elizabeth wondered which one of those things angered her father the most.

"Before you hurl accusations, I ask you, how much resistance was your daughter putting up? Perhaps it is not my son who has lured *her* here," Jerah's father replied. "My son would mean a secure life for your girl. She may have drawn *him* in here to trap him."

Shechem balled a fist and took a step toward Jerah's father. Then he thought better of it. He was in the city, and if there was any sign of a confrontation, Nimrod would be over here in no time. He would not tolerate fisticuffs, especially on the night of his speech.

Jerah did not want to see his father and Shechem come to blows. That would be disastrous for everyone. Still, his focus at that moment was on Elizabeth, who he was watching from the corner of his eye. She was staring at him, her arms folded across her chest. Jerah stole a glance in her direction. There was expectation in her eyes, but Jerah wasn't sure what to make of this.

Jerah's dad held up a hand "No, let's not jump to conclusions. He is a good young man. Do him the courtesy of asking him. Jerah, have you only just met Elizabeth tonight?"

Jerah hesitated. This could not be any worse or any more embarrassing. He had always known that he might one day be caught seeing Elizabeth, but he always just assumed he would get a stern lecture from his parents, or at worst be beaten by Shechem. In his wildest dreams, he never imagined some "council" being assembled like this where he would have to talk about the way he felt about Elizabeth in front of both families. In this moment he could not see beyond that. He was not thinking any further than finding a way to get relief from his embarrassment. He couldn't stand the thought of it. He was terrified before about the prospect of telling Elizabeth how he felt when it was just the two of them. He was mortified now.

"Your silence is your answer," Shechem said. "So it seems we have a true problem before us."

"We are only friends, nothing more!" Jerah blurted. "We were only pretending…that's all. Pretending that we were going to make a speech like Nimrod."

From the corner of his eye, Jerah saw Elizabeth's shoulders sag. He looked at her once again and saw something beyond hurt in her expression. Only then did he realize what her expectation of him had been. This was his chance to be chivalrous. This had been a chance to take a stand for her and he had lost that chance. Jerah felt he had been punched in the stomach.

Shechem looked from Elizabeth to Jerah. Then he looked at his wife who returned his gaze with a knowing look of her own. Suddenly, Shechem didn't care much about saving face. Elizabeth and this boy were in love. He knew it to be true from the pain now in his daughter's countenance. He decided then to drop the issue. He needed to get Elizabeth out of here. He would take her home and let her mother talk to her, even if he had to miss Nimrod's speech. At least, that was his priority until Jerah's father spoke up.

"You think a bit too highly of the daughter of a dirt farmer." Jerah's father said. "You flatter yourself if you think I would let my son pay dowry to the likes of you. All of you people who resist coming into the city to pitch in for the greater good like the rest of us disgust me. You who insist on going your own way and living for yourselves are nothing but selfish."

Shechem's face grew red. "I don't want anything from you. And farming is an honorable profession. I'll thank you to remember that Noah is a farmer, and as for contributing…Nimrod already takes sixty percent of every crop I raise. Where do you think the bread you eat comes from? You wouldn't have the strength to work for Nimrod every day of your life if it were not for the grain that he *takes* from me."

"All of you who refuse to participate fully in Nimrod's plans, more of which I believe he will reveal tonight, deserve whatever comes to you. Someday your crops will fail and you will come begging for some of Nimrod's stored grain. Then you will see that his ways are best for all of us."

"What are you talking about?" Shechem asked. "It was my grain in the first place!"

"I am sorry, Elizabeth," Jerah's father spoke directly to her. "But unless you are all willing to move into the city and start a new vocation, I don't think it would be fair to Jerah for you two to be married," Jerah's father said. "And if you are not to be married then it is not appropriate for a young man and young woman to keep sneaking off together." Then he turned to Jerah.

"Married?" Jerah practically shouted. "I just told all of you we were only friends." Jerah couldn't stop himself now. He just wanted to appease the parents and get them away from here. Maybe he could steal a second with Elizabeth to mend things. Then he would tell her his true feelings. Yet when he looked over at her, he saw tears welling in her eyes. Then she turned her face away from him.

"And Jerah, you have a chance for a good life here in Babel. You are already working for Nimrod. As long as you remain in that job you have freedom that Elizabeth doesn't have. You are free from worries about what you will eat or whether or not the locusts will wipe out a whole year's worth of income. The best thing for you to do is to stay away from this girl."

"Elizabeth," Shechem said. "What he is talking about is not freedom. All Jerah will end up being is a spoke in whatever big wheel Nimrod chooses to build. A life like ours allows everyone to be equal in our right to pursue a better life. What he is talking about," Shechem waved a hand dismissively to indicate Jerah's father, "is each man being equally in the service of Nimrod."

"I don't mean any of this as an insult," Jerah's father replied. "But you don't know what you are talking about. And I would say that after the speech tonight dozens of other families like yours are going to flock to this city for a better life. You are going to regret your stubbornness."

"I doubt that very seriously," Shechem said as he turned in a huff. "I am finished talking about this. A few years ago a boy who had done this would have been stoned. You are lucky I don't bring him before Nimrod." Then Shechem motioned to Elizabeth's older brothers who had been standing off to the side. "Help her get home safely. We will be right behind you. I may listen to a bit of Nimrod's speech, and if it is as you say, I don't care if we ever come back to this city again."

Elizabeth was helped gently up to the landing but she only shoved her brothers away. There, standing on the landing that had been the source of so much laughter only moments before, Elizabeth looked back at Jerah, the tears now running down her cheeks and her chin quivering. Then, in an instant, she turned and was gone.

Jerah felt sick to his stomach. How could this night have gone so wrong? How could it be that Elizabeth was walking away from him perhaps without ever knowing how he felt about her? Shouldn't his father or one of the other adults say something? Wasn't someone going to put a stop to this? No one did.

Shechem, unsure now of what all had transpired between Jerah and his daughter, was sure of one thing. This was not the family he wanted her to marry into. He pointed first at Jerah's father and then at Jerah. His anger was growing, not only at the words of Jerah's father, but at the hurt that Elizabeth had suffered as well. He seemed to be searching for words when he finally just said, "Never again." With that, he was gone.

One by one the others left. Jerah's father clapped him on the back in sympathy as he left the building. Then Jerah was standing all alone. This room would never be a hideaway for him again. In the flickering light of the rapidly fading torch, Jerah stared at the now empty doorway as if Elizabeth would suddenly step back in and he could undo the previous disastrous minutes. But he couldn't have them back. He stood, and though it was too late, he said what he should have earlier - "Elizabeth, you are not just my friend. I love you, please don't go." And then, his own tears began to flow.

***

As Shechem hustled his family back to the square to await the speech, he turned on his wife. "I blame you partly for this," he said in anger. "Always letting her wander off. Always letting her spend idle hours in that so called 'secret place' of hers."

"Shechem, she is still a young girl. She works hard for us. She needs time to be alone with her thoughts and dreams. She needs time to be quiet."

"Well, apparently she is not spending much time alone!" Shechem said. "She could be meeting *him* there. All I know is the next time you see her heading for that place, you had better let me know. I know of another way in to that waterfall. I am going to watch and find out what she is really doing there."

"Don't you dare spy on her."

"I don't consider it spying. I consider it protecting her from someone she does not understand."

Elizabeth's mother pursed her lips. "I don't think either one of you two fathers understand half as much as you think you do," she said.

CHAPTER 45

This wasn't how it was supposed to be. This was to be a night of great triumph for Nimrod and the people of Babel. Now, since the visit from Cush, the enthusiasm had been dampened. Nimrod rolled his shoulders and rotated his head as he let the stress drain from his muscles. He would not allow this night to be ruined. He had planned too long for it. This night was too important for the citizens to let anything deter him.

He stood and walked purposefully past his guests and out the end of the tent. Still on the huge platform, he signaled to two men who quickly brought a lectern and sat it before him. Within seconds, those who had been eating along the perimeter of the stone platform began to stand, as if they were soldiers at attention. Nimrod made no immediate announcement. Instead, he waited while the people relayed his introduction throughout the city's center.

"Nimrod is going to speak," said one man. "Quiet, I want to hear."

"Everyone, listen!" called out a woman in the crowd. "This is what we have been waiting for. Perhaps Nimrod is finally going to tell us of his plans. I can hardly wait to hear."

These shouts of encouragement spread rapidly through the crowd until finally, all pressed in close and looked up attentively. Far back in the crowd, Ruth watched skeptically, more interested in watching the reactions of the people than in listening to her nephew. Something prompted her to look to her left, where she saw Cush sitting dejectedly on the stump of a nearby tree which had long ago been cleared to make the way for yet another building project.

On the opposite side of the plaza, unaware of the drama surrounding Ruth or Cush, stood Jerah. Like Ruth, he was only marginally interested in what Nimrod was about to say. Rather, he was still busy searching the crowd, hoping for some sight of Elizabeth. He was still hoping for a chance to repair the damage. Some appeared a bit annoyed as he tried to make his way through the ever tightening lines of people. Finally, Nimrod began to speak in a booming voice that reached the outer edges of the crowd.

"I am so proud as I look upon your faces today," he began, "that you have decided to live alongside me in this wonderful new city we have created together. I am honored that you have entrusted me in a leadership position." Nimrod was immediately interrupted by cheers. He waited for the applause to die down so he could continue. Just as it was starting to subside, a man called out from the crowd loudly.

"You *are* our leader!" With that, the crowd erupted again. Nimrod smiled and then looked toward his feet. He seemed almost embarrassed by the adoration. In a moment he looked up again, still smiling shyly as he held up a hand to quiet the crowd and continued.

"I appreciate your support and love, but I do not stand before you today to talk about me or what my role should be. Instead I come to talk about all of you. I come to talk about the citizens of this grand city, people whom I have grown up with and love." The crowd cheered passionately.

"Several years ago, I shared a vision with some of you that I had for the valley of Shinar. Many of those whom I shared my vision of a series of cities with are sitting here at my table this evening. I envisioned cities where families could live in peace, where they could help one another, where they could share their labor and the fruits of that labor. We began small, and we built Calneh. Some of the fine citizens of my old hometown of Calneh are here with us tonight." Nimrod gestured to one particular section of the crowd, which in turn was given a warm reception by the other listeners.

"Then we built a slightly larger city in Accad." Without prompting from Nimrod, everyone turned to face an area among the crowd where visiting residents of Accad had gathered. Nimrod smiled.

"Yes, yes, these friends deserve your affection as well," he said as he waited once again for the applause. "Then came Erech." Again there was applause.

"Finally now, we have nearly completed this," Nimrod swept his arms and turned slowly in a circle to indicate the surrounding buildings of Babel. Some buildings were completed and occupied, and some were nearly complete with their roofs and walls in place. As Nimrod began to turn, the crowd applauded again. As he continued his turn, the applause grew into a roar until finally, when he faced the lectern once again, the noise was deafening. Now Nimrod smiled broadly and pumped his fists in the air. Everyone was thrilled with their achievements. Many who were present had worked diligently for years to develop Babel to this point.

Nimrod allowed them their celebration for several moments. Then he held up his palms to quiet the crowd before continuing.

"This is our greatest achievement to date. This great city has been a testament to the creativity of men united in a common cause. You have a right to be proud and you deserved this celebration tonight. But please notice, I said that Babel was our greatest achievement," Nimrod held up an index finger, "yet."

***

As Nimrod was speaking, he could not see the men gathered at the outskirts of the city. The men were frightened, awaiting their orders with angst and consternation. Meanwhile, the one they waited for, Canaan, melted into the back of the crowd. As he often did on trips into any of the cities, he wore the large hood of his cloak over his head, shielding his face. More than anyone else within the reach of Nimrod's voice, Canaan longed to hear what Nimrod had to say.

CHAPTER 46

"You see, tonight is not only a celebration of past achievements, it is also a celebration of the larger vision we will soon realize together. I know all of you have speculated for many months as to what this platform I am standing on is intended for."

Men in the crowd, including the one's standing near Jerah, began to shout out their favorite theories.

"It is an arena for sport," one said.

"It is a theater," came the voice of a woman.

Nimrod held up his hands again, "No, no, friends. I am afraid that even with all the speculation I have heard in all these weeks, none of you have come close to guessing, and I don't think you are likely to do so now. My dear fellow citizens, since the time I was a young boy, what have you known to be the focus of my very life?"

No one answered, but most thought that the answer would be hunting or showing everyone that he was the best athlete or hunter in all the world. That was not the answer Nimrod had in mind. He continued, impatient that no answer had been shouted from the crowd.

"It has been to help assure the safety of those I care about the most. As a boy, I destroyed a vicious boar to protect my father and his friends. I have battled many beasts since that day that would do harm to you or your families, and I have never asked for repayment, nor have I experienced anything approaching defeat.

"And speaking of beasts, I have all but eliminated the threat from the Canaanites."

This time the crowd erupted even more loudly with howls of laughter, followed by cheers.

Canaan didn't cheer. Instead, he emerged from the dark corner of an alley where he had been listening, and moved stealthily through the crowd until he was standing within a hundred yards of the platform. Once there, he removed his hood and stood silently.

The applause was fading and Nimrod was about to begin another phrase, when something caught his attention. There, in the distance, was an unmistakable shock of white hair. Nimrod recognized his uncle immediately. His eyes narrowed as he looked determinedly at Canaan's face. He hesitated briefly in his speech. As he began again he continued to look directly at Canaan, as if the next phrase was intended only for him.

"The Canaanites have not been a serious threat in months. Now, they are more of a nuisance. Soon, that too will stop." Nimrod allowed himself a long pause and then looked toward another area of the crowd.

"This should help you to realize that I have dedicated my life to your safety and provision. No one standing here has ever gone without. Even in difficult farming years, I have provided game, which I have shared without repayment. My point is that those who live in my cities have always been taken care of. I have provided for you. So I ask you, why do some of you still insist on praying to an entity you call God?"

For the first time, it appeared that some in the crowd were not so captivated by Nimrod's speech. Their smiles faded and expressions of joy turned slowly to confusion. Some began to murmur.

Nimrod continued, "It's harmless, I suppose, if some of you want to believe in an imaginary friend you call 'God'." Nimrod laughed at his own joke. A few in the crowd joined him, but looked around nervously as they did so. No one had ever stated such a thing this boldly and publicly before.

"I understand that your faith in an imaginary god is an opiate for many of you, but I ask you, have any of you ever seen this God of yours? Does He talk to you, or perhaps come by for a visit?" Nimrod laughed louder, and more of the crowd joined him as he continued.

"A few years ago when we had that drought, I didn't see him come down here and feed anyone or bring food to the city. No, I was the one who did that. When the Canaanites raided and terrorized, I did not see any god come down and stop them. No, in fact, it would still be occurring if not for me and my actions. Citizens, what I am saying is that you can believe in God if you want, I suppose, but your belief is in a fantasy. We don't need God. We have one another and you all have me. We have and will continue to take care of ourselves and our own needs.

Rather than having some of you waste time and energy, thinking about some myth, I want to encourage you to explore the good that is present within your own mind. I want you to believe in yourselves like I believe in myself. Look what I have accomplished, and I have yet to scratch the surface of my potential. And that is what this structure is all about." Nimrod dramatically swept a hand to the right and then to the left to indicate the foundation he was standing on.

"Why does God have to be this singular entity that legend from my own great-grandfather Noah has taught us about? I love nature. When I see the busy insects, the lovely flowers or the beautiful trees, I don't feel the need to call it God; I see it as more of an energy or force for good that all things possess.

So upon this foundation we will build a testament to those ideas. To those who insist on belief in some mythical God and speak of heaven, I say that with the goodness in our own hearts, the wonder of our own intellect and the observance of the beauty and energy contained in nature, we can reach heaven from right here on earth!"

Though the applause had died down earlier, it returned with a vengeance now. Most didn't really comprehend all that Nimrod was talking about, but his passion and his sincerity was infectious. He was so charismatic that one could not help but be swept up in his plans.

"On this platform we will build a tower," he continued. "It will be a tower like the world has never seen or imagined. It will reach higher into the sky than any mountain, and will be visible from miles and miles away. It will be a testament to our belief in the goodness of man and the power of intellect. It will be our intellect and our reason that will defy nature and will make the seemingly impossible, possible. And the stark visual of this tower from the distance will be a monument to that.

"Not only will it be visibly magnificent, The Tower will also be a center for the celebration of reason, an outpost for the observation of nature, and it will be surrounded by gardens that will solicit the adoration of that nature. Men from all around the world will come here to admire and participate in what we, the citizens of Babel, will accomplish here!"

Nimrod's voice bellowed with his final phrase.

"For far too long, my fellow citizens, we have forgotten the strength of our own intellect. Most of you have spent so much of your time and your lives scratching for survival, that we have had little opportunity to develop our minds. Now, under my system of planning and organization, where each person contributes an amount of work, and I and my men dole out an equal amount of food and provision, there is going to be time to pursue reason.

"There need be no return to the haphazard systems of the past, where everyone competed at producing as much as his abilities would allow him, and where only a few excelled at the expense of the common good. Therefore, this tower will also be a testament to our coming together under an organized plan for production and distribution of food, clothing and shelter in a way that benefits every citizen the same. This tower will be a monument to the end of individualism. Rather, individualism will give way to a greater good for our entire city."

Once again the crowd erupted. Nimrod walked purposefully off the stage and left the area. Cheers continued for many minutes. Some weren't completely sure what they had just heard, they only knew that they had experienced emotions more powerful than any they could recall. There was something very special about Nimrod.

Jerah could barely distinguish the voices around him, but he did manage to recognize one of the men who had been debating earlier say, "You see - no one can bring people together like Nimrod. I told you, we are headed for the best times that man has ever known."

There were similar sentiments from others who passed by Jerah as the crowd began to disperse.

Nimrod's speech was not received well by at least two who were present. Ruth shook her head in disbelief. There was something terribly wrong with what Nimrod said. Her nephew was coming across as magnanimous. She didn't believe he would use so much of his power, influence, and labor force simply for the good of others-- he was too egotistical for that. Ruth was also most taken aback by the response from the crowd. Most seemed so enamored with Nimrod that it wouldn't have mattered what he said. For them, it was more important the *way* in which he said it.

She turned to her husband, Abdon, who was shaking his head and smirking.

"What are you thinking?" she asked.

"Oh," Abdon said, "I was just thinking that this is only a first step. From this point forward, slowly at first, and then more rapidly, I feel that all of our lives are about to change in a tragic way.

CHAPTER 47

Canaan looked around at the smiling, satisfied faces and shook his head slowly, only his disgust was from a much different source than Abdon and Ruth's had been. Suddenly, he jerked his hood back over his head and melted into the crowd. He began to walk back toward his waiting sons and tribesmen. They would turn into marauders with but a word from him. That is, if he could convince them that Nimrod wouldn't catch them.

In his current mood, Canaan didn't feel like a small raid. Stealing food or taking a few coins from some townspeople wasn't going to be enough. No, Canaan had just heard Nimrod declare that he and his tribe were neutralized, no longer a threat. Today, he would leave a calling card that Nimrod would remember. He would create a memory that every citizen in all four cities would not soon erase. He would show them all just what a threat he and his sons were. All he needed was a couple of assistants to help him make the point. That is when he saw Elizabeth.

CHAPTER 48

Jerah was far from giving up. Though the crowd was breaking up and people were heading for home, though he had searched before, during and after the speech, Jerah was determined not to stop looking for Elizabeth. He had to undo whatever hurt he had caused her.

He stopped for a few moments to rest, discouragement coming over him like a wave. Then, though the plaza was still quite crowded and many people were still milling about, he looked up and saw her. She was talking with another girl her age. He was over a hundred yards away from the two, yet he almost had the impression that they were talking about him. "No, don't be stupid," he thought. "You're being vain." Still, Elizabeth was talking and gesturing in a very animated fashion, as though angry or exasperated. Then the girl put her hand on Elizabeth's shoulder as if to comfort her.

Jerah began moving quickly toward Elizabeth. He wanted to shout out at her but he feared Shechem would be nearby. He kept his eyes focused on her as he weaved his way through the people. His vision of her was blocked momentarily as two stocky men passed between them. When he could see again, the spot where Elizabeth had been standing was empty. She was gone.

Jerah broke into a run. She had to be nearby. Suddenly, he heard a faint scream. He looked in the direction of the sound just in time to see her disappear behind the far corner of a building. A person that he could not quite see had her by the forearms, and as she struggled to keep from being dragged away, a hand thrust out and punched her in the side of the head. Elizabeth collapsed and fell out of sight.

Jerah felt nausea wash over him. He couldn't believe what he was seeing. He ran as fast as he could, but when he arrived at the back of the building, there was no one there. In the dust of the alley he saw marks that appeared as if someone had been dragged. He followed the marks at a run until he arrived at the edge of the city. There, he saw a man pulling Elizabeth across the front of his saddle. She appeared to be dazed. Another man was pushing her onto the saddle from the ground. In his struggle to get Elizabeth on the horse, the man's hood slipped back. Jerah had never seen Canaan before but he knew from the legends that it had to be him. Jerah's blood ran cold at the sight. Though terrified himself, he cried out, "Stop, leave her…"

He didn't complete his sentence. His mind was racing out of control. He was desperate to get to Elizabeth. Canaan turned at the sound and smiled coldly. He pulled back his long cloak and drew a glossy black dagger from his belt. He took a step toward Jerah, grinning. Jerah had never seen such a weapon and he hesitated, but only briefly. He looked around for something, anything, to use in his defense. There in a pile of construction debris was a partially broken post. The end was jagged enough to stab with.

As Jerah lunged for the post, Elizabeth began to regain her wits. She looked up in time to see Canaan beginning to trot toward a crouching Jerah, the dagger raised over his head. Then she saw one of the other horsemen, Canaan's youngest son, whip his horse across the neck. The horse ran towards Jerah as his rider raised a javelin.

"Don't trouble yourself, Father," he said as Jerah regained his feet.

"Jerah, look out!" Elizabeth screamed in warning.

Jerah ran towards Canaan with the post. He was totally focused on the man he had seen strike Elizabeth. He didn't see Canaan's son riding in hard from his left, who at the last second swung the javelin around, catching Jerah in the chest with the blunt end, knocking him from his feet and flipping him over. Jerah had never felt such pain. He had had the wind knocked out of him before but this was much worse. He couldn't catch his breath. He felt paralyzed. He looked up helplessly at Canaan, who now knelt down over him. Canaan raised the dagger, and before Jerah could react, he plunged it deeply into the the boy's thigh. Jerah cried out.

Canaan put his face close to Jerah's. For some surreal reason, Jerah focused on Canaan's eye lids. He was horrified by the fact that they were nearly transparent over the coal black eyes. Canaan's breath reeked as he hissed into Jerah's face.

"There, that should slow you down, boy. Tell the people that this is what happens when you cross the Canaanites. Make sure you tell everyone," he said. Then he stood, raised up an arm, and as his youngest son rode by, was swooped up and into the saddle.

"Jerah!" Elizabeth screamed as she stretched her arm out towards him. She was still across the front of the saddle on her belly. She was reaching out not only for her own rescue, but because she wanted to help Jerah as well. Jerah now noticed for the first time that the men had her friend Camellia too. But he could only watch helplessly as the riders disappeared into a dust cloud. Jerah clawed the ground trying to get to his feet.

***

Nimrod stood on his roof watching the crowd break up. Though the evening had started poorly, he was most pleased with how it had turned out. Yes, he was angry that Canaan had shown the audacity to return so quickly, but that would be…

What was that commotion off in the distance? He had only just arrived on his roof after bathing. By then Canaan and his sons were mounted and riding away from Jerah. Nimrod quickly processed what he was seeing. He saw Jerah, obviously hurt, trying to get to his feet. He saw that the Canaanites had taken prisoners and for the first time in years, he felt a black anger rising up from within. Nimrod didn't like anger. It interfered with clear thinking. It led to rash movements and mistakes. He swallowed hard and suppressed the feelings for now. His instinct was to ride after them immediately.

But he would never catch them. They had too great a head start. Instead, he would take an alternate route. He was certain that he knew where they were going. When they arrived, he would be waiting.

CHAPTER 49

Elizabeth was so terrified that it didn't seem that any of this was real. This must surely be a nightmare that she would awaken from any moment. Her ribcage cried out in pain as the horse bounded over the rocky ground. Sidon, Canaan's oldest son, was showing her no mercy on this brutal ride. He would soon show her even less, she was certain of that. The fear of that, the fear of what would happen to her when the horse stopped, was more powerful than any physical pain.

Elizabeth prayed now with great fervor. She prayed for herself and for Camellia. She knew there was no way for them to be saved, so she prayed that she would fall off the horse and perhaps hit her head. She prayed to die before the horses stopped.

***

Nimrod shuffled his closed hand back and forth, absent mindedly rattling the small pebbles he was holding. He didn't even look up when he began to hear the distant drumbeat of horse's hooves. He had known they would come to this spot eventually, so he had waited patiently.

The horses of Sidon and Heth, Canaan's two oldest sons, barreled around two large boulders and entered the small box canyon. The rock walls on three sides would make it more difficult for the sounds of screams to carry. This was the spot they had been riding toward. They had used it before. Sidon reined his horse in hard, nearly sending the animal head over heels as it tossed its head to the side to escape the pain of the bit. The abrupt stop caused even more pain to shoot through Elizabeth's side.

The two youngest of Canaan's sons and some said the most brutal, dismounted before their horses were fully stopped. One pulled Camellia off the front of his saddle by her hair. She screamed out in pain as he dragged her toward some logs that had been used as campfire seats in the past.

"Tie them up," Sidon said. "We will let Father decide…"

"No one is going to be tied up today," Nimrod said calmly as he hopped down from his perch at the top of the boulders. In their haste, and due to the height of the stacked boulders, the brothers had ridden right past him a moment before without seeing him.

Elizabeth pushed herself up on her elbows and looked past Sidon in the direction of Nimrod's voice. She was as shocked as the others to see him here. As she strained to see if it was really him, she couldn't help but notice that urine was suddenly running down Sidon's bare thigh where it emerged from beneath his tunic.

"We….Father ordered us…"

At that exact moment, Canaan, who had fallen behind, arrived. He grimaced, first at the site of Nimrod, and then at the words he had just heard from his son.

"Don't speak, Sidon," Nimrod said. "I have no interest in anything you have to say. You will give these girls your horses." No one moved for a few seconds until Nimrod looked intently at Sidon and said, "Right now."

As soon as Nimrod's order registered in Sidon's brain, he dismounted. The thought of disobeying Nimrod, or even momentarily protesting, never occurred to Sidon. He had only once seen Nimrod angry, and he hoped to never see that again. He suppressed his nearly overwhelming desire to beg Nimrod for mercy, for he had been told not to speak.

For his part, Canaan wasn't sure what to do. He had expected Nimrod to be caught up in the celebration. He had anticipated that he could get away with doing something to humiliate this mighty man, and then run to hide in the cliffs that had been so familiar to him since childhood. He had not expected Nimrod to notice their crime and pursue them so soon, and he didn't have a plan.

Sidon lifted Elizabeth up and helped her right herself on the saddle, but she was in no shape to ride. She looked as if she might pass out, but then something in the nearby rocks caught her eye and she opened her mouth a little. Nimrod, his back to everyone except Canaan, cocked an ear, and then smiled.

"You're a brave boy, Jerah. Come out now," Nimrod called loudly. A few moments later, from the direction in which Nimrod had originally come, Jerah appeared. He came sheepishly into the canyon, mounted on a burro that belonged to Nimrod. A crude, blood soaked bandage was wrapped tightly around his leg.

"I...I couldn't ask your permission to borrow this burro, Sir," he said to Nimrod. "I couldn't find you and I had to..."

"I know," Nimrod said with an understanding tone. "You wanted to help your friend. You're alright, don't fear Jerah. Hop down off the burro. He will find his way home on his own. You can ride with your friend and lead the other girl on her horse. Take them both home now and see that they are cared for. You're a brave lad. I will reward you when I get back."

Jerah, too shocked by this unexpected benevolence to move at first, stared at Nimrod briefly, who only smiled in return. As he turned and looked from Sidon to Canaan, his smile disappeared.

"Go on, now. These young ladies need to be attended to," Nimrod said with a calm and reassuring smile.

Jerah came to himself then. He slid a leg over the front of the burro and eased down onto his healthy leg. He trotted as best he could toward Elizabeth who now sat unsteadily on the horse. Jerah patted her hand as she rested it on the horse's neck, before stepping over and grasping the reins of the horse Camellia now rode. He pulled himself gingerly up in the saddle behind Elizabeth, put his arms around her to grasp the reins, and rode carefully out of the canyon without another word.

"Nimrod, I had a right to..." Canaan began to say.

Nimrod shot him a hard look and pointed a stern finger at his uncle. "Do you really want to have this talk with me in front of your sons?" Nimrod asked with a touch of sarcasm.

"You boys start walking. Your father and I need to talk. If you three can get to a place where I cannot find you by morning, then I may let you live. And tell your brothers and sons that they had better not cross my path, either."

Nimrod didn't turn around to see if his directions were followed. The sound of running footsteps told him what he needed to know.

***

Jerah steadied Elizabeth in the saddle as she sat in front of him. Both his arms were around her as he clutched the reins tightly, for he was not a horseman. Under any other circumstances, the two of them would have been thrilled to be so close. Now, the embrace only meant a small semblance of comfort for them both. Jerah himself was growing faint from blood loss. Elizabeth, though her physical injuries were not as serious, had been struck on the side of the head several times by Sidon and punched in the back when she screamed to be let go. Camellia had not been hurt, but still rode silently behind them, dazed from the trauma of their ordeal.

"I thought you were dead," Elizabeth finally said. Her voice was as timid as the mew of a new kitten. It enraged Jerah anew to hear the usual strength gone from her voice. He didn't answer, but let go of the reins with his left hand and wrapped his arm around her gently, careful not to squeeze too tight. Elizabeth said no more as she turned and nestled her head on Jerah's shoulder. He looked down at her, pulled back her bangs, and tenderly kissed a bruise on her forehead, as his heart broke for her.

CHAPTER 50

"Come, Uncle," Nimrod said. "I want you to take a ride with me." With that he whistled and his horse walked up to him from behind the boulders, reins dangling.

"I heard your speech and it was not what I was expecting. I felt I needed to remind you...," Canaan's words trailed off. There was fear and anger in his voice. Nimrod ignored him and began to ride towards the West. Canaan obediently followed. They rode silently for a time, Canaan trying to read Nimrod's mood, wondering where his nephew was taking him. He considered running, but he had no chance of out riding Nimrod. Canaan reached slowly and carefully inside his cloak and felt his favorite dagger, the one that he was never without, nestled there. Then, he glanced down to the sword on his hip. He would need to strike quickly, unexpectedly.

After a time, they arrived back in the valley of Shinar, but far from Babel. Nimrod pulled up alongside a huge forest. Along the forest edge, timber had been harvested to build the cities. Nimrod turned to speak.

"You dismount and sit there on that stump. There is something I want you to see."

"We had an agreement," Canaan said, fear beginning to overtake his anger. He didn't know what Nimrod was about to do.

"You failed to honor our agreement," Nimrod shot back through clenched teeth, wheeling to face Canaan. Then he forced himself once again to calm down a bit. As he climbed down from his saddle, he took a deep breath and rolled his shoulders before turning to walk into the edge of the forest.

Canaan did not sit down. He had to seize this opportunity while Nimrod's back was turned. He drew his dagger, for it left its sheath more quietly than his sword, and lunged at Nimrod with the dagger raised high. Canaan had killed many men in sneak attacks and had become quite skilled at it. Nimrod, however, sensed something. He effortlessly side stepped Canaan's thrust, wrapped Canaan's skinny arm beneath his and snapped it at the elbow.

Canaan's eyes flew open wide and his mouth gaped as he shrieked in pain. Nimrod jammed his elbow back into the older man's nose, breaking it as he had once years before. He spun, grasped Canaan by the back of the neck, picked him up off the ground, and threw him against the stump like a rag doll. Before Canaan could get over the shock, Nimrod was upon him again. He grabbed a handful of Canaan's cloak, jerked him from the ground and sat him down hard on the stump. Canaan was sobbing now.

"I just told you to sit down on this stump," Nimrod said. He was beginning to let his anger come to the surface. Nimrod, his hands on his knees as he crouched before the much smaller

Canaan, leaned in so that his nose was barely an inch from his Uncle's. He went on.

"I told you to sit here. Just like I told you, you were only allowed to attack the people that I gave you permission to attack, and at the times I told you to attack them. It was bad enough when you ignored my orders and tried to steal from the old man. Now you think you can touch any one of my subjects whenever you want to?"

Canaan threw his one good arm awkwardly over his head as if that would shield him should Nimrod decide to strike a blow. He looked pitiful as his hands trembled violently. He sat crookedly, pain searing through his rib cage from the blow against the edge of the stump.

"Now, as for what I was going to show you," Nimrod said as he turned on a heel.

Canaan, always petulant, never knowing where the barriers were, should have contained himself. He did not.

"They are not your subjects," he screeched towards the back of Nimrod's head. "I am the one who…"

He didn't finish his sentence. Nimrod wheeled, lifted him from the ground by his cloak once again, and backhanded him hard across the face. Then he slapped him, two, three four times. Now Canaan's mouth and nose gushed blood.

"If you speak again today, I will make sure you experience pain that you cannot imagine. Now sit here and learn, old man!" Nimrod said.

Finally, too injured and in shock to protest further, Canaan sat, trembling on the stump. Nimrod walked over into the edge of the forest some hundred yards away, and approached a large tree. The bottom of the tree was hollow. Nimrod reached down and picked up a large limb that had fallen from the tree. He held one end of the limb, which was also hollow, up to his mouth and began to speak. Though he spoke at a normal tone, somehow Canaan could hear him clearly, even from so far away.

It was like...an echo or something...it was like the voices that Canaan sometimes heard in the rocks, like the laughter he heard on that day his mother had her terrible accident. But...no... it was not that either. The voice was clearer, much louder than that. And he heard it with his ears, not his mind.

"Yes, Uncle, you are hearing me. The sound carries through this hollow trunk, you see. I can speak in a normal tone and be heard all across this clearing."

It was Nimrod's voice for certain, but how could it be? Canaan was nearly passing out from pain and blood loss, but he found himself strangely mesmerized.

"You see, Uncle, this is what my tower will be. I will design it like this, only better. From The Tower I will speak to the people, my people."

Suddenly, Nimrod pulled himself free of the tree, stood, and ran very fast toward Canaan, who felt himself practically shrinking from fear.

Nimrod reached him quickly and knelt on one knee very close to Canaan.

"You see, I know how to lead. You do not. The people love me, they admire me, and they fear me. They only fear and hate you. I will build my tower and I will communicate to my people, all the way to the outskirts of the valley. And they will learn to love it. They will look forward to my talks with them. They will soon learn that they cannot rely on themselves and will gain comfort that they can rely completely on me.

I will tell them when to rise, when to go to sleep, when to eat. Instead of supplementing them with meat, I will make them live off of only grain. They will get meat only when I say so, which will keep them more docile and easier to control. They will rely on me for *all* of their food and they will soon love me for it, like a child loves even the most stern parent."

Nimrod leaned in closer now. He placed one massive hand around the back of Canaan's head and pulled his Uncle's ear so close to his mouth that it looked as if he would kiss him. He tightened his grip more and more until Canaan felt as though his head was in a vice, and then Nimrod whispered. "Like a worshiper loves his god," Nimrod said. Then, he pulled Canaan's head back, and with lightning speed pulled his own dagger and held it to Canaan's throat.

Canaan tried to plead, tried to speak, but words would not come. Then, just as quickly as he had grasped him, Nimrod let him go roughly and stood.

"I don't suppose I will kill you after all," he said, beginning to calm. "I think you understand now how this will go. You and your people no longer have any part in this. I don't want to see you or any Canaanite in the valley of Shinar again. You can stay in the hills, as long as I don't have to see any of you."

Canaan spat a long stream of blood. "You think the people will worship you," he mumbled through broken lips. "You think you will just cut me out? I won't take this so easily. I will tell the one person left on earth who you will listen to."

Nimrod had taken a step or two away from Canaan and back towards his horse. He stopped now, his back to Canaan. His eyes rolled back in his head momentarily and his eyelids fluttered.

"Yes, that's right," Canaan went on. "You're not so confident now, are you?" His voice was still trembling but there was a part of him that wouldn't concede. He had terrorized too many for too long. It was all that he had.

Nimrod looked at the ground for a moment and then shook his head as if in disbelief. Finally, he blew out a sarcastic chuckle and said, "You'll tell, will you, Uncle?" he asked. "You see, Uncle, this is why you could never lead. You're clumsy."

In one smooth motion Nimrod spun, drew his sword and swung it in a mighty arc, severing Canaan's head from his shoulders, and sending it skittering across the dusty ground. He then wiped the blade on the cloak that was left on the slouching body before returning his sword to the scabbard. He stepped over and knelt by Canaan's head.

"You were a useful idiot for a time, nothing more. Your service is no longer needed. He stood then, walked over and leapt onto his saddle. He took one last look at his uncle and shook his head again in disdain and unbelief at Canaan's hubris. "The jackals can take care of your stinking carcass," he said. Then he wheeled his horse and rode toward the city. If he had listened closely enough, he might have heard a strange chorus of demented laughter coming from somewhere in the rocks.

CHAPTER 51

By the time Jerah and Elizabeth rode within a quarter mile of her parent's farm, they could already hear a commotion. Sunrise was still a couple of hours away and the fluttering light of torches was visible.

"I am telling you once again, Shechem, there was a great deal of activity. None of us saw anything. If we had, we would have tried to stop it," a man was saying.

"I just cannot believe that this boy could run off with my daughter and get away without anyone in this entire city seeing him!" Shechem's voice sounded frantic.

"You don't know that she was taken," Hannah, Elizabeth's mother said. "You know how she loves the forest. She is there all the time. Maybe she went for a walk and got lost."

"With the trouble she is already in, she would have known better. And besides, she knows the woods too well to get lost. I already looked in her so called 'secret place' and she was not there."

"Maybe she went somewhere else this time. I just cannot bear the thought that Jerah took her. I don't think he is that kind of boy. I won't think about it, that's all."

"Well, you had better think about it because I just know that is what happened."

"This isn't getting us anywhere. We have to start looking," another farmer said.

"But I have no idea where to look," Shechem said as he threw his hands in the air in frustration.

"Daddy," Elizabeth cried.

Shechem and Hannah looked up to see their daughter, her face swollen and bruised, riding in front of Jerah.

"My baby!" her mother exclaimed.

"Oh, dear Lord," Shechem said. "Thank you, God."

Both parents ran toward her. Then, just as quickly as relief had overtaken them, it seemed to be dispelled by anger.

"You see who she is with. Do you see this?" Shechem said, first to his wife, then to the small crowd of searchers.

"I should have known he was involved."

"No Daddy, please…" Elizabeth began to plead.

"Get her in the house. She is injured," Shechem said. "Be careful with her, oh no, she can barely stand!" he cried.

"No, Daddy, I am not hurt that bad. He came to save me. He didn't have anything to do with it."

But Shechem wasn't listening. Instead he turned on Jerah.

"Let all of these men be my witness," he cried out. "I forbid you to come near my daughter again. Do you hear me?" Shechem shook a balled up fist at Jerah, who was nearly too weak to protest.

"Sir, I promise you, I would never hurt your daughter. I tried so hard to help her."

"Well, you did a fine job, dragging her in here bruised and battered. I should pull you off that horse and beat you and see how you like it."

"Shechem," one of the men said. "I know you are angry and frightened, but the boy looks hurt himself. Here, let's bring him into the light. Give him a hearing. He needs help as well."

"No. I tell you this boy has defied me and violated my daughter." He turned to Jerah. "If you are not off my land before I get my sickle I will kill you where you sit. Now get out!"

There was no need in trying to explain himself further. Elizabeth's parents were panicked. They were too upset to listen to him and he was too weak to defend himself. He had to try to make it home. He would come back later and try to help Elizabeth talk to him.

As he rode back into the darkness, trying desperately to maintain consciousness, he heard Shechem call out from the distance.

"If I ever see you here again, I will kill you! Do you hear me? You are forbidden to be near Elizabeth ever again."

CHAPTER 52

Five years later...

Ruth used her wrist to wipe perspiration from her forehead. The heat from the large ovens was nearly overbearing after working near them for over ten hours. She then took a moment, blew out a breath and looked around. She wondered where her husband, Abdon, was and worried over his safety. Several of the men had died in only the past month. They were working too hard, being pushed too much. They were bound to lose their focus and concentration. And with the height being so great and the work so dangerous, disaster was sure to follow.

Ruth looked down at the loaves stacked in rows before her. She used to make much better bread at her home on her own hearth. She couldn't remember the last time she had had the privilege of cooking for her own family. Cooking was a joy then. Now, it was drudgery. How had things gotten to this point? How had she and Abdon and even the children been turned into virtual slaves? And why did she seem to be the only woman in this massive assembly line that minded this turn of events? The rest ran around as if they were numb to it, as if they didn't long for the days when each family made their own way.

"What are you standing around for!" exclaimed Carpus, one of Nimrod's new lackeys.

"I only stopped to take a breath," Ruth shot back. "I have been on my feet without so much as a drink of water for hours, where were you then? And besides, you should have rang the bell over an hour ago. I would like to see my husband before dark."

Carpus, a full foot shorter than Ruth and at least fifty pounds lighter, stepped uncomfortably close.

"I ring the bell when *I* determine you can stop working, not based on any time you set. You have been spoiled because I have let you all off at a regular time every day this week. And how do you repay my kindness? We don't have enough bread to meet our quota for the week. The men don't work effectively if they don't have bread to eat."

He turned and walked away a few steps, then he looked back over his shoulder at Ruth. A sinister grin broke across his face, making her shiver. Carpus turned on his heel and walked back toward Ruth, leaning even closer to her this time, and said, "And by the way, I just bet you would like to see your husband tonight."

With that Carpus reached up and stroked Ruth's arm with the backs of his fingers and leered menacingly.

"Don't you dare touch me, you Cretan," Ruth said as she slapped his hand away.

Carpus only parted his lips in a wide-mouthed smile and walked away, laughing.

"You had better work faster, ladies," he shouted. "No one will return to their homes until we have two hundred more loaves."

Ruth shivered visibly as a chill ran up her spine.

"You don't like him, do you, Mother?"

Ruth looked down at her daughter and wiped patches of flour off her face with the corner of her apron.

"No sweetheart, I must confess I detest the little worm."

"When can we see Daddy, Mama?"

"Soon, dear," Ruth said. "We have close to seventy loaves due to come out any minute. We will be done soon." She handed her daughter a wooden bowl almost too large for her to carry. "Now, be a good girl and fetch Mama more flour. We will get this done and be home before you know it."

She watched her little girl walk away slowly, too tired to run. Her own children forced to work like this, and for what? So that Nimrod could complete his precious tower? It had been over four years now. Nimrod had always pushed his men, even when the first city was being built. But it had never been anything like this. Something had changed. Nimrod had changed. Something seemed to snap in him on the day he rescued that kidnapped girl.

No one knew what happened that day in those mountains, but nothing had been the same since. At first, Nimrod demanded only that the workers from the four cities spend all their time on the Tower. Then he called in all the farmers, and even his fellow hunters. Next he encouraged, and later demanded, that the women prepare food and mend clothes in mass. He had said it would be more efficient that way.

Everyone had agreed to cooperate in stages. At first the demands didn't seem so unreasonable. Then over time, families began to realize that their entire way of life had been changed. Abdon and Ruth had lain awake at night and talked about quitting. So many times they had had that talk. Yet, everyone was pitching in, everyone was participating. The enthusiasm of some for the Tower seemed so strong that the two of them feared there might be repercussions for their family if they refused to work in this way. And then, of course, everyone feared Nimrod more than ever these days.

Ruth hadn't even realized that she had started kneading dough again. She sometimes woke in the night with her hands throbbing from all the dough she had kneaded.

"I think I can trust you." Someone, a woman, had come up behind her and was whispering. Ruth started to turn around. "Don't stop working. You don't want to raise their suspicions, do you?"

Ruth looked ahead, uncertain. "All right," she said. "What do you want?"

"No, first give me your word, you are a daughter of Ham but you are also a daughter of Adina. Can I trust you?"

"As long as you are not about to ask me to do anything against my family or my God, then yes, you can trust me."

"I am Hannah. We were…are…we are farmers."

"I have never been there, but I know of your farm. Was it your daughter who was rescued from the Canaanites a few years ago?"

"Yes," Hannah answered. "If you know of our farm, there is going to be a meeting there tonight after work. We will meet in my house. We are inviting only a select few. We want you and your husband there."

"Why are you inviting me?" Ruth asked.

"Because you fear God."

"Yes, I fear God. So what is your meeting about?"

There was no answer. Finally Ruth couldn't stand it anymore. She turned so she could see Hannah's face, but there was no one there. Ruth looked around through the busy women moving wearily to and fro, but the woman was gone.

CHAPTER 53

Jerah had long ago grown comfortable with heights. He had worked on the roofs with his father on other buildings in the city from the time he was fourteen years old. Despite that, working this high up on the Tower was a new experience. At first the height had taken some getting used to. At some point, he had become comfortable and, if not for the long arduous hours, he might even say he liked working up in the air.

Now, having just pulled up another bucket of fresh mortar for his father, Jerah stopped on the way back down. He tip toed up and looked out the small opening that had been left in this section of the stone wall. The opening would soon accommodate a wooden beam which would be driven into the opening and used as a cross member to support the walls. At the moment, Jerah was more interested in the opening as a passable window when he lined his face up to it just right.

From here he could see all the way to the forest far off in the distance. He thought he could see the corner of one of Shechem's fields, now fallow since he was being forced to work on the

Tower full time. As Jerah looked toward the forest, he strained his eyes to see into it. He wondered if Elizabeth was there right now. He wondered if she was in her secret place. It had been five years since he last saw her, and he wondered if she still thought of him as often as he thought of her. He missed her as much now as he had the morning after he brought her home.

"I am not feeding you so that you can stand around."

Jerah wheeled around with a start. The voice was unmistakable. He had been caught loafing by none other than Nimrod himself.

"Master Nimrod, I am sorry. I only took a minute to rest."

"You are young. You can't fully understand how important this work is. I will let it go this once, but I want you to get back to work."

Nimrod's brow was furrowed with determination. He looked nothing like the jovial man Jerah had perceived that day so long ago when he had giggled with Elizabeth on the riverbank. Nimrod started up the steps toward the top of the Tower where Jerah's father and the others were working.

"Sir, I know you are busy, but if I may…"

Nimrod stopped and turned back to face Jerah. He looked annoyed. Jerah thought for a moment that this section of the Tower certainly was smaller with Nimrod seemingly filling half the space. Jerah swallowed hard.

"I don't mean to take up your time, it is just that…well…I never got to thank you."

"Thank me for what?" Nimrod said.

"Well...for saving me and Elizabeth, of course. Actually, I suppose you have saved us twice now," Jerah chuckled sheepishly.

"What in the devil are you talking about?" Nimrod asked, clearly puzzled.

Now Jerah was the one confused. Was Nimrod trying to be modest? "That day, up in the rocks..."

"Boy, I don't know that I have ever seen you before."

"You saved us that day from the Canaanites. We..."

"I have saved countless citizens from the Canaanites and all other types of hazards. Don't expect me to remember...Oh...oh yes... were you there on the day I took Sidon and his brothers' horses and gave them to those girls?" Nimrod was starting to laugh now.

"Yes, I came to help, too, but you..."

"You came to help? Well, you certainly have a vivid imagination, don't you. I needed your help to stop the Canaanites? Is that what you tell your buddies?"

"No, I mean no disrespect, I only...."

"Get back to work. And don't let me catch you loafing again. What is your name anyway?"

Jerah was stunned. Nimrod had called his name on the day he came to help Elizabeth. He had called Jerah brave, and he had thought Nimrod respected him. Yet, he could tell by the look in the large man's eyes that Nimrod had no idea who he was.

"Jerah, sir, my name is Jerah." He said timidly.

"Well, whoever you are, you had better get some work done. I won't be nearly so lenient when I come back through here."

Jerah watched him for a moment as he disappeared up the steps. He heard his voice bellow out at the other men as he reached the top. Jerah forced himself to move down the steps so that he could continue with his work. As he walked, some very disconcerting thoughts began to come together in his mind. Jerah thought they had become special friends of Nimrod's that day when he found them exploring at the river. He had felt so honored when Nimrod remembered his name and called him brave that day he rode up on the burro to try to rescue Elizabeth. And now, he didn't even know who he was?

Was Nimrod that busy, or was Jerah just not very important to him? Jerah's mind went back to that day in the rocks when Elizabeth had been kidnapped. Nimrod had sensed him there as he sat on the burro hiding amongst the large boulders, and he had called Jerah by name to come on out of hiding. Even in the midst of all the terror of that day, and his own injuries, Jerah had been overwhelmed that Nimrod had known his name…or had he?

As Jerah's mind took him back, he recalled the image of Elizabeth sitting on Sidon's horse. She had been weaving, and Jerah feared she would faint and fall to the ground. Then it hit him. Just before Nimrod called out his name, Elizabeth had brightened. She sat up straighter on the horse because, from that vantage point, she had seen him. And when she saw him, he was almost sure she had mouthed his name!

Jerah had never been important to Nimrod, nor had Elizabeth. Nimrod, with the highly developed hearing of a mighty hunter, had *heard* Elizabeth call his name! Only then had he sensed

Jerah was there. Or perhaps he had even seen him once he had been alerted by Elizabeth. The two of them had just been a convenient excuse for Nimrod to strike against the Canaanites. Suddenly, Jerah was beginning to question lots of things.

CHAPTER 54

Shem looked down the shaft of his arrow. There was no room for error. He had to make this shot. It could be weeks before he would have another opportunity like this one. Perspiration stung his eyes as he strained to hold the bow at full draw a second longer. He had to be sure. Suddenly, the ram stopped eating and raised his head abruptly. There was no more time for precision, for the ram would surely bolt any second. Shem released his bowstring and traced the feather fletching on his arrow as they entered near the heart of the ram. It would be a short tracking job - his shot had flown true.

Arphaxad stood from the spot where he had been crouching behind his father. "Whew Dad, I thought surely you were going to hold that bow back a bit too long. I don't see how you shoot like that, what with all that aiming. I just draw and shoot."

"Well, I am glad that works for you, but I think I will stick with the technique I have used since before you were born," Shem said, slapping X on the back. "But I wonder what made him startle. Neither of us flinched or made a noise."

The two were walking up the knoll where the ram had been standing moments before. From there they would begin the process of tracking. When they arrived on higher ground, they nearly forgot about the ram altogether. For there, off in the distance, they saw what had gotten the ram's attention.

"Do you see what I see?" Shem asked.

"I can't believe it," X said as looked toward the ships sailing in their direction.

The father and son looked at one another. Their expressions of disbelief soon changed to sheer joy. In a moment, both of them began to laugh.

"I'm going to the riverbank to meet them," Arphaxad said.

"No, we have some time. They look closer than they really are. You must realize we are at a pretty high elevation. They won't be near our houses till nightfall. Let's get this ram tracked and quartered. We still have time to pack the meat down and be at the bank to meet them."

The two then began frantically looking on the ground for drops of blood which the ram might have left behind as a trail.

"I can't believe I am going to see my little brother," Shem said jubilantly.

***

"I don't know how things ever got to this point, but I am telling you all something is wrong. I haven't been in my house to do anything other than sleep for a few hours in over three months," complained a man who had once farmed a field adjoining

Shechem's. Three years ago, his farm had been abandoned as he spent more and more of his time building for Nimrod.

"At first, working on the city buildings was a decent way to supplement the food I could raise on my farm. Nimrod always provided a fair portion for every day that I worked. I was able to feed my children better. Then, I found myself spending more time working in the city than I did in my own field. Now, my field is completely neglected and I must rely on the meager allotment that Nimrod's men give me. It is barely enough food for my wife and children, let alone me. Look at me, I am skin and bone!"

"It was inevitable," Shechem whispered loudly. "There was no way Nimrod was going to consistently be able to feed all those workers en masse. Not for any length of time at least. The portion for each was always bound to decrease." Then he said to his wife, "No, Hannah, don't light another candle. We don't want any more light showing through the shutters than absolutely necessary. Nimrod's men are all around."

The group was meeting inside Shechem's small house. There were at least one or two representatives of seven families present. In the case of two families with small children, the whole family had come. All were huddled around a small table at the center of the room. Elizabeth, sitting in the background and comforting the smaller children, had her back to a wall with barely enough room to stretch her legs. As she looked at the faces of the family leaders, she noticed that the one candle on the table gave each face an eerie glow. So far, only her father and the other farmer had mustered the courage to speak up. Each time they did, they looked around first, or rose up and peered out the closed shutters. It was as if they expected Nimrod to burst in the door any second.

Finally, Abdon stood and went to each shutter. Once satisfied that no one could hear them, he stepped to the center of the circle and began to speak.

"There is no doubt, somewhere along the way, things have gotten out of hand. My wife Ruth and I feel as if Nimrod rules our very lives. We are a Godly family. Well, certainly we have not worshipped God in the way Ruth wanted us to when we first married, in the way she was raised to worship Him, but we both do believe in God. And before all this, we answered only to each other, our family and our God. And that was good enough."

Everyone in the room suddenly began to speak at once, "Here, here," said one. "That is how we feel exactly," said another. "Why, we were just saying the other night…" began a third.

"Shh…shh…" Hannah blurted out. "Not everyone at once. They will certainly hear us if we make such a noise."

"I don't want to live like this," Shechem whispered. "This is no kind of life. We work more hours than we ever have and yet we see so much less from our labor."

Everyone nodded and whispered agreement, with the exception of one man. The man's name was Othneil, and it struck Elizabeth as odd that his wife had never looked up from the floor the entire time they had been there. Now the man held up a hand.

"Everyone, please, let's be calm. I think you are all overreacting just a bit. Certainly, the quality of our lives is not what it once was, but Nimrod has told us that this is all only temporary. Soon the Tower will be complete, and not only will life be as good as it once was, it will be better. Nimrod assures us that the Tower will make our lives better than they were before."

"There was nothing wrong with our lives before," Ruth said, "other than letting ourselves get too far away from God." With this, she looked at Abdon, who glanced over at her for a brief second and then looked away. Elizabeth thoughtshe saw his face flush.

"And what exactly do you expect will improve about our lives once this Tower is completed, Othniel?" Shechem asked. "Nimrod has made many promises, but promises are easy and often empty. So how exactly does this Tower affect our lives?"

"Yes," said another, "someone please tell me what it is we are supposed to gain from the Tower. It doesn't appear to be for the purpose of making anything, nor is it a place to raise food. What good is it, other than for Nimrod's ego?" The man's brow was furrowed, and everyone could tell that his anger had overtaken his caution.

"You had better watch your mouth, talking about Nimrod like that," Othneil hissed. "What has Nimrod ever done, other than care for us, protect us, and be gracious to us? If he says this Tower will be of benefit to us, then I think we have to take him at his word. We owe him that much."

"We owe him nothing." Ruth said. This was the second time she had spoken, and what she was doing was frowned upon. No woman had the right to speak when men were meeting. In that day, Ruth and the other women were honored to even be allowed to stay.

"Ruth, please," Abdon said. "The point my wife is trying to make is that we wouldn't need Nimrod's handouts if we were given time to care for ourselves, to work in our own gardens, and to hunt for ourselves, instead of spending every waking hour doing Nimrod's bidding."

"You are missing the larger point," Othneil interrupted. "The work is not going to continue much longer. When the Tower is finished, there will be a few short years dedicated to finishing the rest of Babel, and then we can sit back and reap the benefits of what we have created. We can enjoy the rewards."

"What rewards?" The angry man held his hands out, palms up in front of him as he shrugged his shoulders. "I ask you again, what benefit is there for us?"

"Why, haven't you been listening?" Othneil said. "We will be able to meet there…together…as one. Look around, everyone please, look around this room. Look how small a gathering this is. Now think of how many thousands of people work alongside us each day. They are not here complaining and expressing all these doubts. They believe in their work. They trust Nimrod. They look forward to the days that Nimrod has promised us. Doesn't it give you pause that you are the only ones who are so strongly opposed to something that everyone else sees as good for them? It should, because you refuse to see how gracious Nimrod is being to us."

"He doesn't…" Ruth began. She practically shouted at Othneil before stopping herself and looking pleadingly at Abdon.

"Oh, very well," Abdon said begrudgingly. "Better that she get it out now than I should have to listen to it the second we get home."

Ruth didn't hesitate. She pushed through to the inner circle of men. "What do you mean about him being gracious to you? You don't need Nimrod's grace. He has no right or authority to be either gracious or cruel to you. And by the way, Othneil, I may not remember all that I should about my upbringing, and the things my mother Adina taught me. But I remember that there are no gods and there is no inherent goodness or energy force in a tree or an insect. All goodness flows from God and God alone. And I don't know what kind of worshiping you plan to do with Nimrod, because I have known my nephew since he was a babe, and I have never, I mean never, seen him worship anything, other than, perhaps, his reflection."

"You can't see the greatness in the man because you are too close to him, that's all," Othneil shot back. "And I am going to pretend I didn't hear that last statement because there would surely be a hefty price to pay if Nimrod found out."

"Is that what you are doing here, Othneil?" Shechem asked. "Are you here to spy for Nimrod so that you can go back and tell him all that was said, and who said it?"

The mood was growing tense. Someone had to say something soon to cool emotions, or the entire meeting was going to get out of hand very quickly.

CHAPTER 55

It was completed. The Tower was ready, though no one except Nimrod knew that it was ready. There was still much work to be done on the outside, and there were finishing touches yet to be made on the inside. Regardless, the Tower was ready to function in the way Nimrod had envisioned. He wasn't sure he was going to be able to wait to test it, or that he wanted to wait.

He had been enjoying a couple of hours alone in the upper chamber. It was his first time to take in the view of the darkening city, without the distraction of the beehive of activity surrounding it. He had allowed the workers to go home for a few hours of rest. From here, he could see the ethereal view of distant torches lighting the entryways of houses and buildings. He stood at the top and drank it all in. All that he had envisioned was on the verge of becoming reality.

As he descended to the base of the Tower, he was practically shuddering with anticipation. It was only then that he made his decision. He would not wait another moment. It was time to demonstrate what the Tower was capable of.

***

"I simply can't believe you two are sitting across the table from us," Shem said as he sat with his arm tightly around Prisca. For her part, Prisca was stretching both her arms across the table so that she could hold her sister- in- law Tamara's hands in hers.

"I know, I got so excited as our boat was coming up the river I thought my heart would burst," Tamara said. "I can't wait for tomorrow evening when we can go see Noah and Sapphira as well."

"You won't have to wait quite that long," Shem said, smiling broadly. "As soon as I saw your ships approaching, I sent Arphaxad and his sons to get them. They will likely be back any minute now."

With that, everyone around the table practically squealed with delight. Noah, two of his sons, and their entire families would soon be together again.

CHAPTER 56

The meeting had ended with Shechem and Hannah disappointed. No decisions were made and no plans of what to do about their plight had been formulated. Instead, the meeting had ended on a contentious note. All Shechem was sure of at this point was that there were at least seven couples who were very unhappy with the way things were going in Babel and with their own lives.

Now the gathering had moved quietly outside. A couple of side conversations between some of the men were continuing at a low whisper. Othneil noticed several times that the others were eyeing him with a look of distrust. He started walking up the path toward his home.

"Come," he said abruptly to his wife. "There are no men of reason here. There is no need for us to waste our words trying to talk sense into them."

With that he practically stomped down the path toward the city and his home. His wife stood for a moment and looked back over her shoulder at the rest of the group in Shechem's yard. Elizabeth thought her expression was almost pleading. She looked back toward the path where Othneil had disappeared, apparently unaware that she had not followed. Then she looked back at the crowd again, dropped her head to stare at her hands, and began to walk slowly, reluctantly, down the path.

"It was a mistake to invite him," the angry man said.

"It is my fault," Hannah said. "I noticed that his wife seemed to dislike our work as much as I did. I mentioned the meeting to her."

"Well," Abdon replied. "Let's hope and pray that he keeps his mouth shut. We could all get into deep trouble."

"I say we don't risk it," the angry man said. "We could shut his mouth for him."

"Now, now," Shechem said. He was whispering more loudly now. "We will have none of that kind of talk. Violence is the last thing we need. Besides, there is not much for him to tell. We never even came close to formulating a plan of what to do next."

Abdon clenched and unclenched his jaw muscles before speaking up. "Shechem, first we want to thank you for being brave enough to host this meeting. That alone took great courage. We have something we would like to suggest…"

CHAPTER 57

"Ooh ooh ooh ooh," Noah repeated over and over as he held his arms straight out in front of him, reaching for his youngest son. The old man was nearly sobbing with joy. Sapphira was only a step behind him, and as they reached Japheth, she put one arm around him and the other around Tamara. The all hugged tightly.

"Gomer, Javan, Mashech…" Noah called each of his grandsons and granddaughters by name, each of whom had sailed their own boats with their own families aboard. Soon they were all in a huge embrace with Noah, Sapphira, and several great-grandchildren of all ages, many of whom were seeing Noah for the first time. They were gathered by a large bonfire between Arphaxad's and Shem's houses.

"Dad," Japheth finally said, "There is one name you forgot to call out. I asked her to stay back because I wanted to watch your face when you see her."

Japheth swept his arm toward the darkness at the edge of the firelight. Just then, a beautiful woman with long straight black hair nearly down to her waist stepped forward. Noah and Sapphira looked puzzled for a moment. Finally, recognition and bright smiles broke across their faces.

"Mareyea! What a beautiful woman you have become!" Noah cried out.

Mareyea ran to her grandfather and began introducing him to her own children.

The family reunion continued well into the night. Everyone was too excited to go to sleep. The family laughed and hugged and rejoiced together, each of them completely oblivious to what had transpired in recent months in Babel. They were unaware of the arduous life of the people there. They were not a part of that world. They had deliberately separated themselves from it. Their world was one of independence, and self-sufficiency. As they enjoyed these wonderful moments together, they had no idea how life for the city dwellers had transformed or how intensely their worlds were about to collide.

***

Jerah was far too tired to still be awake. It was late. Normally, after such a strenuous work day, he would have been in deep sleep hours ago. Tonight he was restless. He had slept in fits and starts until finally, his eyes popped open and he was wide awake. These nights still happened to him on occasion, nights where he couldn't stop thinking about Elizabeth. He would be exhausted tomorrow if he couldn't get her off his mind. He kept thinking about defying her father's wishes and going out to see her.

What if he snuck out and went right now? Everyone would be asleep. He could sneak towards the house through the bushes like he had before and try to wake her. If he could manage not to wake her father…how many times was he going to run over such a foolish scheme in his mind before he accepted that it was never going to happen? Elizabeth was out of his life for good, and it was far past the time when he should have been pursuing another young lady.

CHAPTER 58

"What I am trying to say," Abdon stammered, "is that we feel it is time to consult Noah."

Shechem rolled his eyes and waved his hands at Abdon dismissively.

Ruth didn't care for his attitude but she dare not say anything yet. If Shechem felt another man's wife was trying to dictate to him, he would never go along with them. They were going to need his support.

"That is crazy talk," Shechem said. "Having this meeting at my house, just barely outside the city was a big enough risk. There is no way we could ever get away with being gone that far...that long, without Nimrod finding out about it. And besides, what do you think Noah can do to Nimrod at his age?"

"Yes, it is a risk," Abdon said. "That is why we need your help and the help of the others who were on our side at the meeting. We are going to need you all to vouch for us. Tell Nimrod's henchmen that we are sick...or... something. There is a chance that Ruth's supervisor won't talk to my supervisor for at least a day. They won't know that we are both missing from our work at the same time. By the time they figure it out, we will have found Noah. And as for Noah…"

"As for my grandfather," Ruth blurted out. "Don't you underestimate him. You wouldn't be here if it were not for him. None of us would. And there is still a great deal of wisdom in that gray head of his."

"Well, it certainly doesn't look like Noah has had much influence on Nimrod so far."

"Shechem, what else can we do? We have to try something."

"No, no we don't," Shechem said. "This is rash. We have only had our first meeting. We might come up with a consensus. Perhaps we can go to Nimrod as a group and ask for better conditions."

***

Nimrod breathed in deeply, let the breath out, then took in another. He rolled his eyes back in his head and let his head tilt back. He looked through the hollow center of the Tower all the way to the lantern light at the top and his eyelids began to flutter. This would be a seminal moment in a new life for him.

CHAPTER 59

Jerah lay on his back. He still couldn't fall asleep. Likewise, he still had not come up with a way that he could see Elizabeth. He would be satisfied if he could just be near her for a few minutes. He hadn't even *seen* her for so long. He wasn't interested in any of the other girls. He would rather see her and just talk with her for a moment than to be with any other girl for a lifetime. He could still remember the way she looked there by the waterfall. She was so beautiful, so radiant, with that flower in her hair.

"MY DEAR SUBJECTS OF BABEL."

Jerah sat bolt upright in bed. What had he just heard? It was a sound almost like thunder. But no, it wasn't thunder at all. It was a voice. Someone was speaking right outside his house. He jumped up from where he was laying and ran toward a window.

"ENJOY YOUR REST FOR NOW."

Was he dreaming or was he really hearing this? No, he was awake, for he could feel the cool night air on his face as he leaned out the window.

"TOMORROW MORNING THERE WILL BE NO WORK."

The voice was soft, almost melodic, soothing. It sounded like a father speaking to a young child. Then it hit Jerah. The voice he was hearing belonged to Nimrod!

"TOMORROW EVENING, GATHER AROUND THE TOWER. AT THAT TIME I WILL REVEAL TO YOU ALL THAT I HAVE PLANNED FOR YOU. TOMORROW WILL BE THE BEGINNING OF YOUR NEW LIVES."

Ruth backed up, her hand covering her open mouth. Shechem and Abdon, still stunned, stared toward the city. Some of the other couples, who had started down the trail for home shortly after Othneil left, were frozen in their tracks. They were unsure of whether to run back to Shechem's or to run for their homes before it was discovered that they were out past curfew.

"Did you hear that?" Ruth asked.

Shechem looked at her as though she had lost her mind. "Of course we heard it. The entire valley of Shinar likely heard it if they were awake."

"No, I don't mean that. I know you heard the words. Do you understand the magnitude of what he is saying? Who is he to plan anything for our lives? That is God's place and His alone. Abdon, this is wrong. This all feels so very wrong. We cannot wait any longer. We have to try to make it to Grandfather and Shem now."

CHAPTER 60

Shem, Japheth, Noah, all of Noah's grandsons, and his great grandsons, eighty men in all, had spent the morning enjoying a bit of sport. A large pile of straw had been set up as a backdrop and a white spot on an ox hide was the target as every man tried his skill at shooting a bow and arrow or throwing a javelin. Noah, the farmer, ark builder and patriarch was by far the least skilled. It wasn't just his age. He had never had any reason to develop hunting skills in the old world and he had no need or desire to do so in the new. For now he took his struggles in good humor and got more enjoyment out of the loving way in which his family tried to teach him than he would have out of a perfect shot.

"Arphaxad, you come and shoot once again," Noah said, handing one of the bows off to his grandson. "All of you have great skill, but I do believe X's is the greatest."

"Oh I wouldn't say that," Gomer, son of Japheth said. "He barely beat me in the last round and that was only because of a lucky shot."

X cut his eyes over towards his cousin momentarily before rapidly pulling the bow up to a shooting position, drawing the string and launching a perfect shot into the center of the spot.

"What do you know?" X said. "There is another one of those lucky shots."

"Not bad at all," Gomer replied. "But can you do this."

Now he raised his bow, drew it, and aimed at the feather fletching of X's embedded arrow. Suddenly, just as he was about to release his shot, movement far off in the distance caught his eye. Distracted, his shot careened wildly off to the right. Just as the others were about to laugh he called out. "Someone is coming. And they look to be in quite a hurry to get here."

Shem stepped forward and shielded his eyes from the mid-morning sun. Observing the approaching visitor's body language, Shem was struck with a sense of foreboding. "Something terrible has happened," he said.

CHAPTER 61

Nimrod stood as his servants lowered a leather helmet onto his head. Today, he would dress in full battle regalia. Even to the servants, who saw him daily, he looked magnificent. Nimrod stepped back and drew his sword. He held the blade out before himself in a type of salute to his own reflection in the looking glass.

He returned the sword to its sheath, turned on his heel, and headed toward the tower. His chest swelled with every step. He couldn't wait to make this, the most important speech of his life. Before, he spoke more sedately, but today his most authoritative voice would boom from the tower and be heard not just by the citizens of Babel but by every citizen on the outskirts of the city as well.

As Nimrod anticipated his moment of ultimate victory, he was totally unaware of a visitor approaching calmly, methodically, from the east. The visitor had never walked within the city of Babel before but he was most interested in visiting there now.

***

"How could I have been so blind," Noah lamented. "After all I have been through in this life; after all I have seen God do… How could I have missed this and allowed Nimrod to go so far."

He paced back and forth before Ruth and Abdon. Their chests were heaving from their long run to find Noah and explain all that was taking place in Babel.

"This is my fault, my responsibility. I didn't want more trouble. I didn't even try to curb Nimrod's ego. You all mark my words. There is something very sinister at work here. Nimrod is attempting to take the crown that belongs to God and place it on his own head."

"Dad," Shem said. "Laying blame does us no good. The question is what we do about this now."

"We have to go down and try to talk to him; talk some sense into him," Noah replied.

"Dad," Shem replied. "Surely we are long past the point of talking. Nimrod wouldn't listen to me when he was a young boy nor the day he brought his pack train to your house. He certainly is not going to listen now. He is too far into this."

Ruth said, "He wouldn't listen to Cush when he tried to curb his intentions, that much is certain. If anyone tries to stop Nimrod now, I am not sure what he would do."

"Then we won't just go there to talk to him," Shem said. "We will go into Babel as warriors and be prepared to defend ourselves if need be. Every man and boy who is old enough to draw a bow must be prepared to fight. And if Nimrod refuses to listen to us, we may have to go so far as to stop him ourselves."

"You mean we will shed the blood of our own kin?" Noah was incensed. "Things never should have come to this. I have grown old, I was so tired. I refused to stand up to the pride and ego in Nimrod. I refused to even see it when it was right there in front of me. Of all people, I know what the pride of men can do. My ancestor Adam told my grandfather to his face, and my grandfather told me." The old man placed his hands on the side of his face. Then, gradually, something seemed to awaken within him.

Shem, watching his father intently, sensed it as well. The look in Noah's eyes reminded him of days of old and ignited dormant passions within him as well. His eyes were aflame.

"Japheth, do you think your boats can make it upriver all the way to Babel? Is the river deep enough?"

Japheth answered, "One of them has a flat keel. I designed it for shallow waters. I'll bet we can sail *it* there."

Shem said, "Then take your sons. Have your weapons ready. If I signal you with an arrow of flame, you will fire back toward the base of the tower with flaming arrows of your own."

Ruth, realizing what was about to take place, spoke up. "Uncle Shem, please, it has been so long since I have seen you. I want to see you again and visit with you tomorrow. I only came here to encourage you or grandpa Noah to talk to him. I don't want to be a part of you getting hurt. You stand no chance if you go up against Nimrod. It is not just him alone. He has many loyal men now. If you confront them, you will all surely be killed," Ruth pleaded.

"Don't fear, child. We will not be quite so easy to defeat. We will not just walk into the center of the city en masse."

On and on they talked and planned. Shem had no intention of letting the thing which Nimrod had done stand. He knew in his heart that this was not God's will and he was willing to lay down his life and the life of his sons to stop it. What he didn't know was that he, even he, a man of righteousness and so much accomplishment himself, was severely underestimating the warrior that Nimrod had become.

CHAPTER 62

Jerah didn't know what to do with himself. Work had been cancelled for the day so that all could prepare for Nimrod's speech this evening. Most of the city was abuzz with excitement and anticipation. Jerah had once been like them. Until recently he too had revered and trusted Nimrod. But there had been something very wrong the day that he met Nimrod at the top of the tower. Somehow, Jerah sensed that he and Elizabeth had been used.

His concern now was for Elizabeth. Ever since Jerah had heard Nimrod's voice in the night, he had not been able to stop thinking. He kept rolling events over in his mind. Something was very wrong here. There was something wrong about Nimrod and the way most of the people blindly followed him. They had all but abandoned their home lives to slave away for him. And there was something wrong with that tower.

Jerah had made his decision. He knew that Elizabeth's father Shechem was a tough man in his own right. He felt that Shechem had grown suspicious of Nimrod as well. Was it possible that he would have at least a few of his own workers mount horses in readiness to defy Nimrod? Yet, Jerah feared the worst for Shechem. He could not; he would not count on Shechem to protect Elizabeth. Shechem was too prideful. He would try to stand up to Nimrod even if it put Elizabeth at risk...and he would fail. The only way to escape this, the only way to escape a life under Nimrod's iron fist, was to run, so Jerah determined in his heart that is what he and Elizabeth would do.

He was going to find her and take her far away from this place. He didn't know where they would go or how they would live, but for the first time in his life, he prayed to God. He prayed that they would make it somehow.

CHAPTER 63

"So it's decided then?" Shem, Japheth, and Noah stood in a tight circle looking intently into one another's eyes. These had always been peaceful men, spiritual warriors to be sure, but they had never raised a sword in conflict.

"No," Noah said after a long while. "No. it cannot be decided until we ask God for guidance. I don't know His will regarding Nimrod. We have reacted out of desperation and formed plans that we thought were best under the circumstances. After all we have been through; you would think we would automatically seek God's counsel first."

Japheth looked at Shem, each knowing immediately that their father was right. They hung their heads briefly until they each felt a tug on the arm of their cloak. Noah was leading them to a spot nearby where a bolder rested at the base of a large tree. There, with all of the sons and grandsons ready to spring into action, with wives and daughters nervous and a bit frightened over what was to come, Noah and his two sons knelt to pray.

Without being told to, each of the family members dropped to their knees where they stood. They could hear Noah faintly from that distance, yet they joined him in the spirit of his prayer nonetheless. Finally, after a long while, they heard Noah speak a little more loudly as he closed the prayer.

Shem and Japheth looked up at their father as if to ask, "Well?"

Noah shook his head. "He did not speak to me."

"Then what do we do?" Japheth asked. "Do we just wait here and do nothing."

Noah stood slowly and faced toward Babel. "Sometimes, Japheth, the Lord does not clearly instruct us. Instead, He makes it clear that He is not saying, 'No.' Sometimes, when He has given us the information we need, when He has shown us throughout our life the distinct difference between His good and this world's evil, He intends for us to act. He intends for us to protect His children."

"So," Shem said inquisitively, "Should we go?"

Noah turned to face them. In what seemed like divine confirmation, a breeze blew Noah's long white beard to one side and his hair over his shoulder. Gone was the pale cloudiness in his eyes, and his sons were almost startled to once again see the piercing blue that they had seen in their father's younger years.

"We go!" Noah said.

***

"Please, Uncle Shem I beg of you. This is not the way."

"Ruth," Shem said firmly. "You have always been special. You have always had the wonderful heart for God that your mother had. But now is not the time for you to intervene."

Before Ruth could protest further, Tamara gently grasped one of her arms. Prisca grasped the other. They pulled her away gently but firmly. Japheth and Noah came and stood alongside Shem as he stared after his niece for a moment. Shem looked over at Abdon, unwavering. He expected Abdon to protest the way he had just dismissed Ruth. Instead Abdon said, "I will need a weapon."

"You need to eat something. You have just had quite a journey and you ran hard to make it here. Here is bread and cool spring water. Take these and let yourself calm down," Tamara said.

Ruth sat down hard on the bench of an outside table. She clearly didn't like being taken lightly.

"We know, we know," Prisca said. "Sometimes it seems they ignore us, but Shem is right this time. This is a matter for the men. Our husbands have faced greater challenges than this one. They will do what needs to be done."

As Prisca spoke, Tamara watched her closely. She had been separated from her dear sister- in -law for so many years, yet it seemed natural to be sitting here beside her talking this way. It was as if they had never parted. They had been through so much together. They had formed a bond that would never weaken. Tamara only wished Adina was here to talk to her daughter. Adina had always known the right thing to say in any situation. Tamara remembered when Adina had held and comforted her all those years ago on the ark when she was broken and hurting.

"This time is not like other times," Ruth said, tearing a bite of bread from a loaf as if she was angry at it. "I love Uncle Shem and Uncle Japheth. And I couldn't respect grandpa Noah any more than I do. But they were equipped for a work that God called them to. They didn't meet all those challenges in their power alone."

"Of course we know that." Now even Prisca was beginning to get a bit irritated. "We were only saying that…"

"You were saying that you have confidence in your husbands to do the right thing," Ruth interrupted. "That is understandable and admirable. What I am trying to tell you all is you don't know Nimrod the way I do. I have watched this man grow up. I know what he is. I would have known it from the start if I had just listened a little more closely to the warnings that God spoke to my heart."

Ruth stood up suddenly. She reached for her shawl, poured the rest of the water into a goat skin water bag that she had tied to her waist, and stuffed the remainder of the loaf of bread into her mouth.

"What are you doing?" Tamara asked.

"Yes, where are you going?" Prisca added.

"I am not going just to sit here waiting to get word that my husband and both of yours have been slaughtered by Nimrod and his men."

"Well…what are you going to do? You can't protect them."

"I have to try something."

"But try what? What will you do?" Prisca asked.

"There is someone I have to find," Ruth said. Before anyone could stop her, she ran into the nearby woods and was gone.

***

Nimrod was resplendent as he sat upon his horse. He triumphantly rode through the streets toward the tower. It would soon be difficult to move at all anywhere in the city. The crowd that was forming was filling every street and courtyard. Word had spread throughout the plain of Shinar and all citizens of Babel, Erech, Accad and Calneh were anxious to see and hear what Nimrod would say from the tower.

Instead of smiling his charming smile and greeting the people as he rode the way he once had, Nimrod rode stoically. His eyes remained forward and he almost seemed to be in a trance. Some of the young women approached, as they had so many times before, to try and touch Nimrod, if only for a moment. Only this time, Nimrod's horse was surrounded by a circle of his men and they brusquely pushed the girls aside. One poor girl was simply run over by a large guard and was nearly stepped on by the horse's hooves.

"Stand aside, you are not to touch him," one of the men called out loudly.

Instead of protesting, the girls, for reasons they themselves couldn't fully understand, bowed deeply and backed away. This started a trend, for people began to bow to Nimrod as he drew closer and closer to the tower.

CHAPTER 64

Jerah was nearly in a panic. He had to gather enough food to sustain them for at least a few days. He then had to conceal it well enough that Nimrod's spies wouldn't get suspicious. Even more daunting was the fact that he had to accomplish all of this before Nimrod's speech was complete. If he could move among the crowd, he had a much better chance of remaining undetected.

Now it seemed as if every task was taking far too long. The closer it got to the time when Nimrod would speak, the more pressure Jerah felt to get away. He still had to find Elizabeth and convince her of the need to leave with him. Not only did he have to avoid Nimrod and his men, he would have an even more difficult time avoiding Shechem and the men that would be loyal to him. They all knew him after all. Even if they saw him at a distance they might come after him.

Shechem had never believed his and Elizabeth's explanations of what had happened to her that day. All Shechem focused on was that his daughter had been caught twice in a position that could have harmed her and sullied her reputation forever. And on both those occasions, Jerah had been involved. Shechem believed that Jerah had such a hold over his daughter that even her words about their relationship could not be trusted.

Jerah had worked with his father building this city since he was a small boy. Even when he was only seven, he followed his father, a builder, around and helped him scrounge tools or materials. As such he knew every nook and cranny of Babel. He used that knowledge now as he looked for things that he and Elizabeth would need. He didn't like stealing and he couldn't deny that he was stealing from Nimrod. Yet even that seemed perverted. How could a loaf of bread--made from wheat grown by a farmer who never got paid, likewise baked by hands that were never compensated, neither of whom had ever intended to work for Nimrod-- in fact belong to Nimrod? Who was Jerah even stealing from? He felt as if he was stealing that which had already been stolen, twice.

The quadrangle that surrounded the nearly completed tower still had construction debris lying around. Still, the crowd was beginning to press in. This was going to be the largest crowd Jerah had ever seen.

***

The visitor walked freely among the people, none realized who he was. Most had long since forgotten about him and his Father. Some paused briefly as he passed by if only to notice that his clothing was somehow different than any they had ever seen. The fabric of his cloak was finer, the hood that shielded his face from view was larger and more concealing than any worn by others in the crowd.

He walked calmly, his movements seemingly effortless. He projected none of the intense excitement or the pressing for position that the others did. Instead, he flowed easily through the crowd, never so much as bumping into anyone. It appeared to require no effort for him to avoid the bumping and pushing that the rest of the crowd was engaged in. It was as if he knew every step that each person would take before they took it, and he merely stepped where they were not. He seemed to focus on each face as he passed it. Though he was a visitor, he seemed at home with the citizens of the valley.

***

Jerah now felt he had enough food. He had a jug full of water and he would hug the river as they journeyed so they could refill the jug when needed. Now for the most difficult part; he needed a weapon. He had his sheath knife on his belt. A four inch flint blade knife was all that was allowed by Nimrod. Jerah wanted something more than that. He needed to be able to protect Elizabeth.

He was three streets over from the quadrangle now. The crowd was beginning to form even this far away. They had completely filled the quad and now had filled three city blocks in every direction. Suddenly, a tremendous roar went up. It moved like an ocean wave from those closest to the tower and then spread rapidly in all directions. The crowd surged forward as Nimrod climbed the steps that now made up the base of the tower.

Jerah at first was frozen in his tracks by the sheer magnitude of the roar. His ears rang with the cacophony from the excited masses. It was actually physically stunning to him. After a moment, he gathered his wits. There, just up the street, one of

Nimrod's men was leaning on the back of a man in front of him; he seemed completely caught up in trying to get a glimpse of his own toward the tower. Foolishly, he had left a short straight sword leaning against the side of a building. This was Jerah's chance.

Throwing caution to the wind, he jogged toward the sword. He had to grab it and hide it under his cloak before someone turned around and saw him. It was expressly forbidden these days for a common citizen to have a weapon. He made it. He grasped the sword firmly, knowing he mustn't drop it now or the man that it belonged to would surely hear. He began to run with it. As he ran with all his other packs and provisions he found it awkward to get the sword under his cape. He ran around the corner of a building.

There were people in this alley as well so he dashed under an open staircase. There was no view toward the tower here and no one was watching him, but the people, intent on getting to a position where they could see Nimrod, were only a few feet away. He was barely able to stand erect under the stairs and he continued to struggle awkwardly to get the sword hidden.

He would have to untie the water jug and rearrange his food pack. He realized that his hands were shaking as he tried to untie his belt. Then he stopped. He was still looking down at his waist but he knew someone was watching him. He wanted to be brave, in fact he was brave, but he felt his chin begin to quiver. Ever so slowly, he looked up. Would it be the man whose sword he now held? Was he about to have to fight or flee?

Finally, he raised his head completely, grasping the sword in a near death grip. Only then did it occur to him that he didn't know how to use a sword. He swallowed hard. It wasn't

Nimrod's servant. Instead, standing a few yards away was a tall man wearing a fine cape, his face shrouded by a large hood. In that same instant a breeze began to blow in Jerah's face.

"Jerah…"

Jerah was certain that he had heard someone call his name but there had been no audible voice. It was as if the sound of his name was a whisper in the breeze. Jerah felt cool perspiration bead on his forehead. His hands began to grow so clammy that he feared the sword would slip from his grip.

"Jerah, what are you trying to do? The sword you are hiding will not help you. Today, you will suffer loss and there is nothing you can do to prevent it. Things have gone too far."

It wasn't Jerah's imagination; this man was talking to him somehow, talking to him without actually speaking. Jerah felt himself crouch involuntarily as if he could hide there in plain sight. Reluctantly, he looked up at the man. He was more intimidated than he had ever been in his life. Who was this person and how did he know his name? As Jerah looked at him, the breeze shifted and moved the hood of the man's cloak. At the same moment, long flowing hair spilled from beneath the hood. The hair was like the white wool of a lamb.

He didn't know why he did it but Jerah let the sword fall to the cobblestone street He dropped to his knees and fell prostrate on his face before the stranger. He began to tremble violently. He waited for another word on the wind but none came. After another moment, or perhaps two, he mustered the courage to look up toward the visitor once again.

There was no one there. Had he imagined it all? He rose to his knees once again and saw the sword lying on the street. No, he had not imagined it. He had to regain his composure. He began to gather his scattered provisions once again. Then he stopped. Had anyone else heard that voice? Had anyone heard the sword fall? He stood for a moment and peeked around the staircase. No one was even looking in his direction.

"CITIZENS OF BABEL AND ALL PEOPLES OF SHINAR..."

Nimrod's voice reverberated over the roar from the crowd. It was as if Nimrod was shouting right into Jerah's ear. The speech was starting. Jerah looked around. Water had spilled from the water bag and spread across the street. In his confusion he had pulled the cork from its mouth.

What was happening? How could Nimrod project his voice so far and so clearly? Who had this visitor been and how had he known Jerah? How had he known that Jerah had a sword?

"TODAY IS A DAY THAT FUTURE GENERATIONS WILL SPEAK OF. THIS DAY WILL GO DOWN IN HISTORY."

Jerah ran his fingers through his hair and rubbed his face hard. He looked down at the spilled water. He shuffled nervously from one foot to the other like a caged animal. And then he began to run. He left the sword, his pack, and the water. He left everything behind. All he could think of now, was finding Elizabeth. Nothing made sense. He knew she would be afraid as well. He knew where she would go. "Please God," he thought. "Let her be there."

CHAPTER 65

Nimrod spoke from somewhere high up in the tower. He spoke into what looked like a small funnel that was attached to a pipe. Though his voice was just above a conversational tone, the tower broadcast his words for over a mile throughout the valley. He spoke of the people's future. He spoke of how he controlled their destiny and how he would relieve them of responsibility. Rather than each citizen having the burden to provide for themselves and their loved ones, he, Nimrod, would take those cares away from them. He would be their provider, after all, he always had been. All he would require from the citizens of the valley in return was their unending loyalty and devotion. Hadn't he earned at least that?

Since the night before, when Nimrod tested the acoustics of the tower, virtually every citizen of the Valley of Shinar had made their way to Babel. The streets and quadrangle around the tower were now teeming with people. Now as Nimrod spoke, the crowds pressed toward the base of the tower. Many seemed to assume a spirit of worship. Some were glassy eyed as they approached the tower. This exceeded Nimrod's expectations.

He knew that over time, with him controlling all the words that would ring from the tower, that he would eventually win over the entire population of all the cities. He knew that if he controlled the information that the people received, and if he repeated the message he wanted them to hear long enough, then he would control them. Yet he never dreamed that so many would idolize him so soon.

As the people approached, Nimrod ended his speech and began to rapidly descend the curved steps inside the tower walls. He had the people's adoration, now he would ensure their obedience. The tower was very tall, but finally he exited the front door. He stepped back out onto the platform where he had spoken over five years previously, when construction of the tower was just beginning.

At the site of Nimrod, everyone surged forward once again. Some, closest to the platform steps, fell and were nearly trampled by what was becoming a frantic mob. Nimrod shouted out across the tops of the people's heads.

"Can you imagine how wonderful your lives will be now that we are finished with the construction of Babel? Why someday soon you won't even have to worry about where your next meal will come from? All your cares will be provided for by me, your King!" A cheer erupted.

Nimrod had been testing that word, "King". He had wondered how it would be received by the masses. He had been pleasantly surprised by the people's enthusiasm.

"Don't you want that?" he continued. "Don't you want to finally be free?" More cheers went up. "Don't you want to be free from the burden of always striving, always trying to make your own way? Won't it be wonderful for each to have the same things and the same portions?"

The people were nearly hysterical now. There was something special about the magnificence of the tower. The people were overwhelmed that it had all been Nimrod's idea and design. The sheer power of his voice, first as it had resounded from the tower, and now as he whipped the crowed into a frenzy, had stirred something in the people that they themselves did not understand.

"Imagine also a world where you don't have to worship some imaginary God you have never seen, you can worship me who you have seen. I will rule over a world where reason and intellect is first and foremost, not some blind faith in a non-existent God!" Again the crowd cheered lustily.

"Yet, there is an obstacle, my subjects," Nimrod said. "There is an impediment to you having that kind of freedom. That obstacle is comprised of people like these." Nimrod turned toward the tower and called, "Bring out the prisoners!"

From inside the tower came Nimrod's men. They were dragging Othneil and his wife out by their hair. Both were screaming but no one could hear them over the crowd.

"These people, as well as others, who we will soon capture, want to stand in the way of the life you deserve. They want to make their own way, they want to keep all that they earn and then determine on their own how much they will share with you.

These people attended a meeting in a house last night where they explored ways that I could be overthrown."

The crowd booed passionately. Someone threw a stone and hit Othneil's wife in the forehead, driving her to her knees, her head began to bleed profusely.

"I understand your anger my subjects," Nimrod said. I too am angry. That is why, when the others that attended this meeting are found, there…will…be…punishment. There must be punishment for anyone that attempts to show disloyalty to me your ruler and your god! Nimrod was wild eyed now. "It is time now my people. Release your inhibitions, feel free to show all your adoration for me and I will show my benevolence toward you."

"You are not worthy to be worshipped!" A voice cried out from the crowd. The voice was so strong, that it was heard above the din of the crowd.

Nimrod turned toward the voice immediately.

"You are not their King," the voice cried out again. Then, suddenly there was a commotion, the crowd began to part. Noah and Shem had managed to make their way from the river and Japheth's ship, to the bottom step below Nimrod. Noah continued, "You are not the king of this people, and you certainly are not to be worshipped."

Nimrod was incensed. "I am not worthy, grandfather? Then who is? Are you? Was it you that fed them and protected them? Was it…"

Noah interrupted, "I have never sought to rule, even on the ark. Instead I have sought to lead out of love, and though I acknowledge that I let myself be overcome by weariness in recent years, I have always recognized something that you apparently cannot. True leadership can only be attained by a firm reliance on God. Yes, God; the one Abdon tells me you had the audacity to call an "imaginary friend". The Lord God is One. The same God who delivered me, my son's, and their wives from the floodwaters, he alone is God and he alone is worthy to be worshipped.

As Noah was speaking, he noticed that coming up the steps on the far side of the stage was his son Ham. Behind him, and down the steps, Ruth sat astride a horse that was well lathered from a hard run. Ham and his daughter had ridden hard in order to make it here in time. Even at such a vital moment as this, Noah had to resist the urge to run and embrace the son whom he had not seen in all these many years. Instead, he knew he had to stay focused on the situation at hand. He allowed the excitement of seeing Ham embolden his old mind and body all the more.

"How dare you, Nimrod!" Ham said. How dare you question the existence of the One who spoke to me and to your great-grandfather Noah on the day we left the ark. How defy Almighty God."

Japheth now arrived at the steps and stood next to Shem and Noah. He had heard all that had been said. Now he too reminded Nimrod of a truth. "It was God who blessed you with physical strength. It was God who allowed His creation to thrive in such a way as to provide you with game to hunt. You tell people to look to nature to determine what is moral or what is good yet you do not see that God created nature in order to point to His own goodness. You cannot see, or will not see, that He and He alone is the source from which moral law must flow."

Next Shem spoke up. "You talk of intellect and reason, yet your intellect has led you to deny the existence of the One who gave you the ability to reason. Can't you see that God is the source of all that our intellect can comprehend? He gives us intellect and reason so that we might discover more about Him through that which He has created."

Nimrod had worked too long and too hard to allow Noah and his son's to say anymore. He would not have his vision thwarted, not even by Noah. Nimrod drew his sword in one motion, startling in its swiftness. In almost the same instant, he drew a dagger from his belt. Then, with a weapon in each hand, Nimrod hesitated a moment to ponder who he would destroy first.

As this drama was unfolding, the visitor looked on from afar. No one even saw him there at the back of the crowd. Throughout the day, not a single person had noticed him with the exception of Jerah, and even he would spend years wondering who or what he had seen. He had come down quickly. Now it was time to return. He was so proud of his servant. Once again, Noah, faithful Noah, had stepped forward when no one else dared. Shem and Japheth were very brave as well, standing alongside their father, prepared to die for him if need be. Even Ham had returned to stand with his brothers and finally to confess His Father before men. Yet, the visitor knew something that these men did not. They would die if they faced Nimrod in battle. Nimrod was too great a warrior, even for all four of them. This would not be allowed to go farther. Noah, empowered and informed by God, had eloquently said what needed to be said. It was time to end this.

The visitor looked over the crowd one last time. He was saddened for them. There would be heartbreak. Unfortunately, it was unavoidable now. They had allowed themselves to stray too far. What hurt him the most is that they had all known better. If they had just taken time to stop, to pray, to meditate on Him, all of this could have been avoided.

He completed his scan of the crowd and let his eyes rest on Nimrod. Nimrod was a mighty man and a valiant warrior. He would remain so but never again would he stand as mighty as he had been today. He would learn from this. It would humble him.

It was time. As if he were dismissing a misbehaving child, the visitor barely, almost imperceptibly, raised his hand. It was only the most casual flick of his wrist, yet shockwaves passed from that hand and into the sky as if a giant hammer had come down in the atmosphere. Immediately the visitor turned, his cloak billowing behind him as he walked away. In three steps he disappeared.

The earth shook. Then peals of thunder rocked the sky. From out of nowhere, an ominous black cloud began to form. Nimrod's attention was drawn away from Noah and Ham as he looked skyward. A huge east wind began to blow in. Dust stung everyone like needles as debris was swept up into the air. The crowd began to panic and run toward the west, not knowing where to go. Yet, before they could go more than a few yards, a furious lightning bolt struck the ground in front of them. The crowd stopped and as one looked back to the man who, only moments before, had said he would rule them. Time seemed to stop. As lightning filled the cloud that was now poised only feet above the top of the tower, Nimrod, almost involuntarily, dropped to one knee. He was mesmerized by the display of power in the cloud. One lightning strike after another crisscrossed the cloud and illuminated the sky for miles around.

Then, suddenly, one tremendous bolt of lightning came straight down to the center of the tower. Energy coursed through the structure, engulfing it in vivid arcs. Ham, standing on the steps, was knocked from his feet and propelled into the crowd. Noah, having been several yards away, was already prostrate on the ground, bowing, for he knew the source of this power.

Nimrod was suddenly engulfed in blue arcs. Electricity flowed through his body. His head was thrown back as an involuntary scream roared from his very core. The blades of both the dagger and the sword were shattered into tiny pieces that flew in all directions, some fragments piercing Nimrod's skin.

Some in the crowd fell down on their faces like Noah, others, paralyzed with awe by what they were witnessing, stood with mouths agape. In less than an instant, the arcing electricity that had engulfed the tower traveled from one person to another in the crowd. The scene was surreal as those that were not already face down before God, fell down. The tower began to creak and sway near the top. Suddenly with a tremendous CRACK the first floor of the tower collapsed on one side. The entire tower tilted on its now damaged base. Noah and Shem, engulfed in brick dust and debris, thought surely they would be crushed.

Then, as suddenly as it had begun, the lightning stopped and over the next several seconds, the wind blew softly but steadily. The sky cleared, the cloud moved away, and the sun began to shine once again. One by one everyone looked at the tower, a gasp escaped from them in unison. The tower was tilted severely and it looked as if the entire structure would surely collapse. But it did not collapse.

Nimrod, though the lightning struck him, was also incredibly strong. He soon regained consciousness. He opened his eyes and fought to clear his mind. He awoke to a blurred vision of his own hand. He stared at it stupidly for a moment. He was so stunned from the voltage that he actually saw the redness of his palm before he felt the searing pain caused by the red hot handle of the sword. He rolled onto his side and instinctively slung the handle of the sword away. He realized for the first time in his life, that he was undone. He was defeated. It was only then that he blurted out a curse that stunned him and those who were slowly awakening around him back into silence.

CHAPTER 66

Jerah couldn't suck in air fast enough. Ever since he had departed from the stranger, he had run faster and faster until his lungs burned. Now he thought surely they would burst if he didn't stop soon. Yet he couldn't stop. Somehow he sensed it. He was running out of time. He arrived at the tunnel in the brush. He had last been here years ago. It was considerably more overgrown now. Was he in the wrong place? He trusted his instincts and dove into a small opening before him. It had been so long since anyone had visited the garden that he crashed into thistle that had woven itself into a near impenetrable barrier. Still, there were places where the ground looked scrapped clean, as if someone had just passed this way.

He pushed and lashed out desperately at the rough limbs, ignoring the scratches and cuts forming on his forearms. He was taller now than he had been when he last visited, and the brush above him lashed at his back. He could see the opening ahead, he could hear the waterfall running. Then, suddenly, he was through. He *was* in the right place! It was the tunnel. He crawled as fast as he could.

"Please…please be here," he said aloud. But then why should she be here? Her family would have heard the voice of Nimrod bellowing from the tower. Her father had probably closed and bolted the doors and shutters. They were likely huddling, terrified, in their own home. Or perhaps it was worse than that. Perhaps they too had been wooed by Nimrod's words. Perhaps by now they were like the glassy eyed people that Jerah had seen back in Babel.

He could already feel cool mist from the waterfall. Instead of climbing carefully down as he had before, Jerah alternately slid on his stomach and jumped until he was standing on the ground. He thought of turning slowly. He didn't want to look up and realize that Elizabeth hadn't come. Instead he wheeled around, unable to stand the anticipation.

She was standing only a few yards away and she was crying. Jerah, soaking with perspiration and breathless, found it within himself to run a few more steps.

"Elizabeth," he said. "I love you. I am so sorry I never said it before, I don't know what I was waiting for but I don't want another moment to go by without you knowing that." He was still running towards her but she took a step back. She was crying loudly now. Her hands covered her mouth and she was shaking her head in disbelief.

"I know it has been years since you have seen me," Jerah said. "I wanted so desperately to come to you. Not a day, not a moment, went by when I didn't think of you. I love you so much Elizabeth.

I love you and I'm not afraid to say it anymore... Elizabeth, what's wrong."

Her body convulsed now with sobs, Elizabeth kept pressing her fists to her mouth and shaking her head. Then she stopped moving backwards. Instead she took a step towards Jerah, and stretched out her arms timidly, clearly uncertain.

"Sweetheart," Jerah said. His own shyness, his vanity, was the last thing he cared about now. The only thing he wanted in this moment was to pledge his love to this woman. "What is it?" He asked as he reached for both her hands. "Are you frightened by Nimrod? I am too, but we can leave here. We can go and live..."

"Jerah!" Elizabeth blurted out. *"Je ne peux pas te comprendre."* She began to cry again. Jerah stopped, even more confused now than he had been as he fled Babel. At least then he had had the goal of finding Elizabeth. Now that he had found her, he didn't know what was happening.

"Qu'est-ce qu'il y a?" Elizabeth was almost screaming now. *Est-ce que tu a aperçu que la terre tremblait? Jerah, tu ne me comprends non plus, peux-tu?"* She dropped one of his hands and placed her free hand across her stomach as she nearly doubled over with sobs. "How can this be happening," she thought. "Why can't I speak to him so that he can understand? She stepped towards him, taking his hands once again. Her face was flushed with red as her distress grew. *"Je suis désolée, Jerah. Tu m'a sauvé, et mon pére vous a forcé loin. Je sais que tu m'aimerais, Jerah. Je suis désolée."* She seemed to be apologizing, but Jerah couldn't be sure.

"You can't understand me, can you?" Jerah asked. "Elizabeth, oh my love, I can't understand you either." Jerah began to cry himself now. Was he even speaking his normal language or did he just think he was? What on earth was going on? The whole world was upside down.

They stayed like that for several more moments, both trying desperately to communicate, both trying to pledge their love. Elizabeth begged Jerah to speak to her and not give up. As they continued, their attempts grew more and more pitiful. They were both crying hard now. They were not only heartbroken but also incredibly frustrated. Then suddenly, their attention was diverted to the far side of the pool where they had looked, carefree, at their reflections all those years before. From the woods just across that pool, the rumbling in the distance was unmistakable. Horsemen were approaching.

The two of them stopped trying to speak. Elizabeth looked up at Jerah, her eyes wide with dread, and he instinctively pulled her closer. There was no doubt in either of their minds what they were hearing. It would be Shechem and his men coming to take his daughter away. In his own panicked state, he would surely kill Jerah if he found them like this.

Jerah searched Elizabeth's face as she looked back at him, uncertain. Her eyes warned him to flee while her hands clung desperately to his arms, not wanting to let go. It hit Jerah like a wave that now he would never have the chance to say the words to her. This time, in this moment, Jerah didn't hesitate. Instead, he wrapped his arms around Elizabeth and pulled her tightly to his chest.

He let his right hand find the soft skin of her neck beneath her brown hair, he pulled her face to his and he kissed her. He kissed her long and warm and wet and deep and as he did so, he held her evermore tightly. Elizabeth seemed to fall into him, wrapping her arms behind his neck, her knees nearly buckling with the emotion of the moment.

He didn't stop. He kissed and held her like a young man who knew that this was the one and only time he would taste the lips of the love of his life. And then suddenly, he was tackled to the ground by Shechem.

CHAPTER 67

Nimrod did not die from his injuries. Instead he would live many more years and actually accomplish more great things, but never again did he acquire the power or adoration he had engendered in those days. He never forgot the lesson of that day, a harsh lesson about his limitations in God's creation. Yet, he never learned the necessity of humility either, nor did he ever fully escape the dangers of pride.

Jerah never got to kiss Elizabeth after that day. The young lovers were victims of a sin that they did not commit. Two weeks after God confused the languages at the tower, Elizabeth and her family assembled with the Semites; Jerah and his family with the Hamites. All people assembled with those of their language, and then each group, led by a son or in some cases a grandson of Noah, would leave the valley of Shinar to seek new homes and a new life in faraway lands.

What had been common became diverse. From a people who had grown far too malleable in their drone-like sameness, nations would arise of very different cultures. Those nations, though made up of diverse peoples, would forever share a common humanity, for each individual was created in the same image-the image of God.

On the day when the people began their separate journeys out of the valley of Shinar, Noah and his three sons met at the center of Babel, near the base of the tower, to say goodbye. Communication was hard for them. Only Shem and Noah now shared a common language. Sign language and pictures drawn in the dust were all that allowed them to talk.

"I wonder what will happen to this," Shem asked as he looked up towards the top of the tower."

"It will be abandoned," Noah seemed to know this with certainty. "It will never be used again, everyone will be afraid to enter it. Instead it will stand for a few more years as a charred monument to the sinful nature of man before it finally begins to crumble and fall in upon itself."

"I thought we escaped evil on the ark," Shem said. "Now I know I was wrong."

"Son, you should know better by now. The ark was never intended to be a ship to escape in. Instead it was a safe haven in which to survive. It was God's way of showing us a shadow of what would be. When we stepped out of the ark, we were still surrounded by the same darkness that was present before the flood. The darkness never left. It was only momentarily held at bay.

Shem shook his head slowly, "I wonder if we will ever escape the curse of our ancient father, Adam?"

It was a rhetorical question. Shem didn't expect an answer.

"No, we will never escape it," Noah said almost menacingly. Then he leaned in closer and placed a firm hand on Shem's shoulder, "But we will be rescued from it."

Shem looked back down at his father and saw that Noah was looking deeply into his eyes, as if seeing through and even *into* him. It made Shem feel both excited and self-conscious. Before he could inquire further, Noah abruptly changed the subject.

"We must confess what we did. We were very tired, we wanted to be able to see one another. I am not so sure that where we lived was so much the problem as how we began to live," Noah said. "After the volcano, we valued our personal peace above service to God. When we heard of all that Nimrod was building, of the way he was assembling people in three cities, you were the only one who protested."

Noah continued, "I simply was not willing to enter into the fray once again. I felt I had done enough in service to God. I was wrong. I should have joined you in standing up to Nimrod long ago. Then none of this would have ever gotten off the ground. When Nimrod fell in love with the glory of building cities, it wasn't long before the forces of evil seized him at his point of pride. Had all of us," he swept his hand to indicate all his sons, "stood decisively with you back then for God's will, all of this might have been avoided."

Shem pursed his lips. He had no desire to crow about having been right. And he too felt he had been far too passive in his resistance to Nimrod early on.

"We will be far apart from your brothers for many, many years now, I am sad to say. I will shed tears after this parting. But I will not leave here without hope, for I want you to help me communicate to your brothers that we must meet again. We have one more journey that we must take together before I die. It will be a journey for just the four of us."

CHAPTER 68

Many years later...

Noah stepped gingerly across the sandy ground. He had ridden much of the morning in the light cart that two of his sons pulled. He had grown stiff being in that position for so long. He needed to walk, if only for a bit to try to loosen his joints. Japheth had him by one elbow to steady him and Shem and Ham pulled the cart which also held their provisions.

Conversation had been spotty at best since he and Shem felt almost self-conscious about talking when Japheth and Ham couldn't participate. Still, they had done their share of communicating, motioning in as many creative ways as they could muster to Noah's younger sons. They moved along steadily but without speaking for a time. Finally, Shem broke the silence.

"Dad," Shem asked. "Do you suppose anyone who ever lived has had such a life as this family? I mean, what other family could have endured all that we have?"

Noah looked over at his son with a warm smile but just kept plodding along until they finished pulling a slight grade. Then atop a low hill, Noah stopped. He put his arm around Shem's shoulders, placed the other arm around Japheth and then motioned for Ham to come over to them.

They stood like that, Noah and his sons, as they had stood before. They had stood like this, arms around one another, so many years ago as Noah showed them the site where the ark would be erected. At that moment all three of the sons thought their father was having some kind of mental breakdown. Then they had stood this way a few days after departing the ark, atop Mount Ararat as they watched the animals disembark and move away across the valley below. That day there was a feeling of satisfaction and accomplishment mixed with heartbreak for those lost from their old world. Now they stood uncertain, once again, of what the future would hold. All were uncertain, that is, with the exception of Noah.

"Your question is a fair one Shem," Noah said. "And I would dare say we have had perhaps the most eventful history that has ever, or perhaps will ever, occur to one family. We must remember however, that your ancestor Adam walked with Holy God and was cast out of the garden by Him."

"Yes, I suppose that does top all that we have been through," Shem said, kicking at a pebble.

Noah went on, "Yes, we have suffered much, and been blessed much. And every step of the way, God has had His sovereign hand upon each of us. I look back now, and there were so many times that I couldn't understand God. I couldn't fathom what He was doing, or why He was allowing so many tragedies to happen. In these last few years, however, things have begun to fall into place." Noah looked ahead and squinted at the far horizon.

"You mean it all makes sense to you now?" Shem asked. "If it does, please fill us in. I would love to know because…what are you looking at Dad?"

"Oh," Noah said. "I'm just listening to His voice now, and I am looking for reasons."

"What do you mean, I thought you said…"

Noah's intense gaze caused Shem to search the horizon as well. Japheth and Ham's eyes soon followed. They all saw it at nearly the same instant. It was so far off that they couldn't make it out at first through the shimmering heat waves. Then it began to take shape. A lone figure moved across the desert in the distance. The figure appeared to be holding to the halter of a burro that in turn pulled a small cart similar to their own.

Noah nodded in the affirmative to himself and said, "Yes Lord, you arranged it that way didn't you? Yes Lord, your timing is perfect. We did not meet until we were in exactly the right place." Then Noah pulled free of his sons and despite his age and ailments, he began to run.

"Dad, what in the world are you doing? If you fall way out here and get hurt we will really have problems."

"I need to see those people," Noah cried. "I want to see him before I die. I want to hold him."

"Dad, calm down, at least get back in the cart…"

Japheth and Ham looked flustered and concerned as well. All of them were wondering what had their father so worked up.

Eventually, the sons won the argument and convinced Noah to ride in the cart until they met up with the other party.

"Here, here, this is good," Noah said excitedly. "Let me out. Stop the cart."

"Easy, Dad, easy, let us at least help you out," Shem said.

"You all stay here. I want to talk to the boy alone," Noah said as he eased to the ground. He walked unsteadily at first, and then steadied himself as he approached the man.

For the first time, Shem and his brothers looked up and realized that it was not just a lone man they had been chasing. It was a man and his family-- a wife and three little boys. One of the boys, who looked to be no more than a year and a half, rode in a cart next to his mother. Noah approached the man, who looked suspicious and defensive at first. However, after Noah spoke with him briefly, he smiled and nodded, pointing toward the cart. Shem couldn't hear much but could tell that the man spoke the language of Noah.

Noah went to the child and spoke briefly with the mother, who then handed the boy up to him. Noah hugged the boy as though he were his own grandson. He kissed both the boys chubby cheeks and ran his hands through his full head of curly brown hair.

Shem looked to his brothers who returned his puzzled gaze. Shem shrugged, and though he knew his brothers couldn't understand, he said, "I have no idea who they are or why Dad is having such a fit over this boy." Finally, curiosity got the better of him, and he eased toward the man. Meanwhile, Noah carried the boy over to a large stone and sat down with the child, placing him on his lap.

"Greetings," Shem said, "I am Shem, son of Noah."

"It is my great honor, Shem. I know of you for I too am a descendant of yours. I am a Semite. I cannot believe I am finally getting to meet Noah and his sons. I do not deserve this privilege."

"Your words are most kind." Shem said. "I must ask why you are way out here."

The man smiled sheepishly. "For some reason, before my wife conceived, I felt led to travel. We have wondered for some months now, living on our own. Then, three days ago, I felt that God was pressing me to move in this direction. We are seeking the place that he would have us settle."

"I applaud your following God's lead," Shem said, and then he nodded toward Noah.

"I have never seen him take on so over a child since his last grandchild was small. What do you call the boy?'

"He is called, Abram," the man answered.

Noah bounced Abram playfully on one knee as he spoke to him adoringly. "Did you know that God told me to come out here and find you? Yes, he did." Noah said. "And I am so happy to meet you." The old man placed his face next to the boys. Abram was completely comfortable with Noah and was thoroughly enjoying the attention.

"You see," Noah said. "There on that hill," that is the place I was telling you about a moment ago. That is where it will be, the place where your sons will build their home."

Noah's eyes were wide with excitement. This would be a secret that he would share only with this toddler who was too young to understand. The day would come however, when he would be told of this place again, and he *would* understand.

"Look, little Abram. Look there. Won't it be a wonderful site upon which to build?"

The boy who had been giggling and cooing as he play with Noah's beard now seemed for the first time to follow Noah's craggy finger. Now he looked to the far hills. Suddenly, he too was focused. He stretched out his own little arm and pointed toward a certain hill along with Noah, who squeezed the child tightly to him.

"Yes, yes, you can almost see it now can't you…yes…it will be there….the city on a hill…YERUSALEEM!!!"

THE END

Made in the USA
Lexington, KY
20 June 2013